WOLF OF CHOICE

CHOICE

THE SHIFTERS AND SORCERESSES TRILOGY

SHAY LAURENT

First published by Midlothian Press in 2020

ISBN 978-0-6487871-0-5

Editing by Samantha Brennan

www.wordsbysamanthabrennan.com

Cover design by Melony Paradise of Paradise Cover Design

www.paradisecoverdesign.com

This is a work of fiction. Names, characters, businesses, places, events and incidents are either the products of the author's imagination or used in a fictitious manner. Any resemblance to actual persons, living or dead, or actual events is purely coincidental.

NOTE FROM THE AUTHOR: This book features Australian spelling such as colour, realise, practise and mum.

BOOKS BY SHAY LAURENT

Everleigh Cole Novels

Haunted By Legacy

Burned By Fury

The Shifters & Sorceresses Trilogy

Wolf of Choice

For Adeline and Jade, my beautiful daughters.
May you both always follow your dreams and achieve any goal you
set out for yourselves.
I love you both, always.

CONTENTS

CHANGE

MY BREATH WAS EVEN. My body, perfectly still. My eyes locked on the large white wolf stalking toward me. A deep snarl ripped from its mouth.

I didn't move.

My eyes stayed wide, focused on the wolf more than half my height. At each step, I could see muscles tense and release under the coarse fur.

Come on. Just take one more step.

My toes pressed into the ground of the mountain cave, just hard enough to get better traction, but slowly enough to make little noise against the small rocks beneath my feet.

Anticipation pulled my stomach tight. I'd backed myself into a corner, with about three metres on my left and one on my right. Eyes alert, I watched the wolf, looking for any sign that would help me decide which way I should move: a shifting of weight, a flicker of its eyes. But there was nothing.

A game of strategy then. Steady.

The moment its paw landed, I dug my left toes in hard and launched myself to the right. Less space, but also less expected.

1

Too far.

Blood dripped from my arm, emitting a sickly tangy smell that caused me to feel nauseated. Ignoring the sting as well as the unsettled feeling in my stomach, I sped back towards the main cavern. My overestimation had cost me. I could feel the wolf's hot breath on my back as the snap of its teeth sounded in my ears.

Don't look back. Go!

With the cave entrance in sight, I could practically taste victory. The crisp morning air from the mountains embraced me and the white snowfall that sheeted the ground called to me. I just had to get one foot out.

Yes!

No.

My foot was an inch from the ground when I felt the wolf's nose shove my lower back. The jolt pushed me face first into the sleet. My arms managed to save me from hitting the ground hard enough to get a headache, but they weren't quick enough to prevent the mouthful of slush. Snow spluttered from my mouth as I turned to face the beast with a scowl.

The wolf was close enough that I could see the sharp white canines capable of ripping flesh to shreds, and the soft fur that ran underneath its coarse outer coat. Impatience had me tapping my fingers.

The wolf's sharp blue eyes cut into mine a moment before the air around its body began to shimmer; the woodsy colours shivering and colliding through the transformation. Within a few seconds, a man was standing tall in front of me, his clothes rippling in the icy breeze. He bent down and reached his rough, callused hand out to help me to my feet. I took it and felt myself rush from the ground as he yanked me up, the cold air biting straight through my wet clothes.

'Easy, Dad. Wolves aren't meant to fly!'

He gave me a hard stare. A puff of air, white from the cold, escaped from my mouth as I sighed.

Here it comes.

'Elita, you know the caves like the back of your hand. Why did you let yourself get caught in the corner?'

My cheeks heated and I stared at the mountain a little to his right. 'I was distracted.'

Dad sighed. 'By what?' Not waiting for an answer, he walked back towards the cave entrance.

'About going to the Academy! I'm almost sixteen, Dad! I need to go—'

'No. You *want* to—'

Exasperated, I threw my hands into the air. 'No, Dad. I *need* to go. I need to be with other wolves, with a pack. It's like a part of me is missing! I need friends like me, not these *humans*. People that understand me...' Seeing the hurt look flash through his eyes, I quickly added, '...as well as you.'

The guilt on his face made me sick to my stomach. I shuffled my feet slightly and chewed on the inside of my cheek, determined to stop myself from just telling him not to worry about it again.

Minutes ticked by and my anxiety grew with each second. Resigned, I opened my mouth to relent when I noticed him hesitate.

Not wanting to miss the opportunity, I begged. 'Please, Dad! It's almost halfway through the school year already. I need to go. Please!'

Anguish tore across his face. I couldn't understand it. All Shifter kids went to the Academy the year they turned sixteen, when they'd make their first Shift.

My chest constricted as I watched him close his eyes and take a deep breath. When he opened them, I could still see worry plain on his face. He shook his head. 'I'm sorry, kiddo. No. You need to finish off your training session. Let's go.'

Without another word, Dad Shifted back to his wolf form and took off. Disappointment flooded through me and tears pricked my eyes, but I knew that if I didn't get a move on, he'd be out of sight. If I wasn't in view when he turned around at our house, it'd be one hundred sit-ups on top of the run, and my body was already burning from our evasion drill.

Stupid human legs. Hurry up, birthday!

Despite being unable to Shift yet, I still moved faster than a full-blooded human and my senses were heightened too, so even with the tears blurring my vision it wasn't difficult to dodge the trees as I sprinted. I wiped the wetness from my face with my sleeve and kept focus on the giant white wolf in front of me, as I followed his path down the mountainside.

Lungs and legs burning, I finally reached the flat at the base of the mountain. Training with Dad was never easy.

By the time I was close to home, I'd managed to mostly pull myself together. Determined to avoid sit-ups, I forced my tired legs to continue sprinting. The last tree entered my peripheral vision as Dad Shifted and walked up the back steps. A flash of red at the end of our porch caught my eye. It was a woman. I stopped in surprise but when Dad rushed over and started speaking to her, I cautiously continued forward.

One step at a time I crept closer until I could see her more clearly. When her scent hit me, my heartbeat became an excited jitter.

She's a Shifter!

I quickened my pace in case Dad tried to rush her away. Her gaze flickered over to me as I neared.

At the top of the porch steps, I turned expectant eyes briefly to my dad, then looked at the tall, thin woman with the blazing red hair.

Reluctance clear in his voice, he introduced her. 'Elita, this is Genevieve Stone. She's... an old friend.'

'Hi! It's nice to meet you, Genevieve.' I stuck out my hand to shake hers. Her firm but gentle grip was paired with a smile and amused emerald eyes.

'Hello, Elita. It's lovely to see you again. You have your mother's eyes.'

I spun to my Dad and just caught the sharp look he threw at his friend. Ignoring him, I seized my chance.

'You knew my mum?'

She smiled lightly, avoiding my dad's glare. 'I did. Though the last time I saw her was when you were a baby. That was when I first met you.'

Questions buzzed in my brain, one after another, like a swarm of bees. Dad cut my first question off before it started.

'You can ask questions later, Elita. Go and have a wash now and I'll call you when dinner is ready.'

His pointed look let me know I wasn't to argue about the decision. Frustrated, I huffed and scrunched up my nose. Genevieve laughed.

'Don't worry Elita, I'm not leaving, but I do need to go to the stable and feed my horse now that she would have cooled down. She's a—'

'You have a Valido?'

She smiled. 'I see you already know about Shifter horses.'

I grinned back. 'I sure do. I've only ever seen a couple and from a distance, but I've read a lot about them. Can I see it?'

Dad interjected again, this time cutting off his friend. 'Later, kiddo. Off you go. Now.'

My nostrils flared as I heaved another sigh. Taking one last look at Genevieve, I stalked off inside the house, new questions buzzing around by the second.

Standing inside my bedroom door, hair dripping down my back after washing it, I tried my hardest to listen to the conversation going on downstairs. They were being too quiet.

Ugh! I need to know what they're saying.

Years of stealth training front and centre in my mind, I tip-toed onto the landing outside my room, taking care to avoid the creaking floorboards. It was almost painful to move so slow-ly, knowing I was missing out on potentially vital information. Weight balanced on the railing to keep quiet, I inched down the stairs. The second their words were clear, I stopped and lowered myself onto a step to listen.

'—only has three weeks and she won't be able to attend the Academy, Raphael. You know the rules. They don't take kids after they have already started Shifting, except in extenuating circumstances. I know you have those but, in your case, I don't think they'll work in her favour.'

'She's not going, Gen.' He paused, then added, 'It's not safe for her.'

'Nonsense. It is as safe for her as... Fine. Maybe not as safe, but safe enough.'

'And what if something goes wrong with her Shifting? What will happen then?'

What?! Why would something go wrong with my Shifting?

Genevieve's voice became more gentle. 'I'll keep an eye on her. You won't lose her too.'

Is he crying?

'Raph, you can't put this off forever,' Genevieve continued. 'There are things she needs to learn and understand that you aren't able to teach her. Before it's too late. It isn't safe or smart to keep her in the dark any longer.'

More silence, then Dad sighed heavily. 'She doesn't need to know everything, Gen. But... you're right. I know you are. Her mother never would have wanted this either.' He was quiet for a few more moments, then his voice returned. 'Promise me you'll watch over her at the Academy.'

'Of course. You're doing the right thing, Raph. I'll keep you updated on her progress by raven.'

My heart thundered so loudly in excitement, I was sure they'd hear it. Genevieve had achieved what I'd been trying to do for months.

Why didn't she get here sooner?!

The sound of food cooking became clearer in the silence below. I slid forward on the step ready to make a run for it if needed, but I was reluctant to miss more of the conversation. As I was about to move, Dad spoke again. 'Gen, there's one more thing. I... I need you to tell her one of the old stories for me. The Crone Infiltration. I just... couldn't, you understand?'

She answered with a subdued voice. 'I understand. I'll tell her on the way.'

The sound of plates being pulled from the shelves startled me. Using the railing again, I snuck back to my room, ready to be called for dinner. The grin on my face was so wide it hurt.

I'm going to the Academy!

Within minutes Dad's voice drifted up the stairs. 'Elita, dinner!'

Okay. You can do it, just keep a straight face.

Air rushed by as I zoomed downstairs and into the dining room. Seated at the table, I got a look at Dad's face. He was crestfallen. The excitement that had made my blood pound through my body slowed. Instead of dwelling on his glum mood, I focused on the smell of dinner and was surprised to discover that Dad had thoroughly cooked the steak, even though we had company. The fact that I didn't feel sick told me it wasn't done wolf style: placed in the heat and then turned almost immediately.

Bleh!

'Don't worry, Elita. Genevieve is a friend, like I said. She doesn't mind the occasional cooked steak.' He gave me a small forced smile. 'Though you may need to get used to the smell since you'll be leaving for the Academy in the morning.'

'Really?! You're letting me go? Why now? Why'd you change your mind?'

Dad shook his head and looked a little bemused despite his lingering sadness. Genevieve gave a small chuckle then started eating.

'Yes. Genevieve—or Miss Stone to you since she'll be one of your teachers—has managed to convince me that I should let you

9

go. I only agreed because I know she'll be keeping an eye on you. A close eye. I'll let her tell you about the school stuff, but I've kept you up to date with most of the lessons and training. And I imagine you'll be ahead of others in your weapons skills.'

A squeal of delight slipped out.

I can't believe this is happening! I get to go to the Academy and make some Shifter friends! Oh—

'Is there a library?'

'There is,' said Miss Stone. 'It's quite large, and has a lot of books and some comfortable spots to sit by the fire.'

Yes. Yes. Yes!

'What about other Shifter kids? How many are there? Where will I stay?'

Miss Stone laughed outright this time, her emerald eyes twinkling in the light from the gas lamp that rested on the edge of our wooden table. 'There are ten to fifteen students in each year who come from the three Packs, usually a pretty even mix of boys and girls. All students sleep in the dorms, but you'll have your own room.'

Glee filled my insides and I turned to Dad with a grin so wide it hurt my cheeks. 'Thank you, Dad. You're the best! And we're leaving in the morning you said, right?'

Dad shifted in his seat. 'I won't be able to take you, kiddo. I'm sorry. You'll be going with Miss Stone.'

My shoulders drooped at the news. 'Why can't you take me?'

'I've already made arrangements to meet someone from the Trevini Pack. I need to leave tomorrow as well. You were going to stay with old Mrs Rodgers, remember?'

'Oh, yeah. But you'll come and see me soon, right? For my birthday?'

My chest tightened when he refused to meet my gaze and instead kept his focus on the plate in front of him. 'I'll do my best, kiddo, but I'm not sure how long my trip will take.' Suddenly, he looked right into my eyes. 'When it's your time to Shift, if I don't make it back in time, I want you to do it by yourself. Not with friends. If anything is... odd, just wait and tell me, or see Miss Stone. Okay?'

Odd? Why is he being so weird?

'Why would something go wrong when I Shift?'

'I'm sure it'll be fine. I'm probably just being over-protective, like usual.' He gave me a gruff smile that was closer to his usual one.

Relief settled my speeding heart at his reassurance, but the thought continued to niggle at the back of my mind as I ate the last of my dinner.

'All right. You're finished. Go pack your stuff. You can use my suitcase.'

I looked at Miss Stone. 'But—'

'You'll have plenty of time for questions later. You don't have plenty of time to pack. Off you go.'

Disgruntled about not getting to ask anymore questions, but too excited to really let it get me down, I rushed up to my room to pack.

It was official. I was going to the Academy.

Fingers clenched around Dad's suitcase handle, I made my way down our front steps and over to the small wooden carriage in the clearing. Miss Stone was connecting her horse to the front of it.

Wow!

The Valido was huge. Its sleek, midnight-coloured coat shone in the early morning light.

Miss Stone's sudden chuckle made me realise that in the midst of gawking at the beautiful beast, I'd moved much closer.

'Sorry, she's just so beautiful… and still.'

Miss Stone nodded as her hands ran down the horse's soft, wavy mane in rhythmic strokes. 'You can pat her if you like. Her name's Ivy.'

Excited at the prospect, I nodded and placed Dad's suitcase on the ground then stepped closer. Hesitantly, I lifted my own hand and patted the glossy fur in the same way she had.

The movement of Miss Stone's flaming hair caught my attention and I turned to follow her gaze. My Dad was outside and had locked up the door, a small pack resting over his shoulder.

Chest tight, I raced over and gave him a hug. After a moment he stepped back and wiped away the tears I hadn't noticed falling from my face.

'Alright, kiddo. We all need to go,' he said gruffly.

I nodded quickly and stepped away, emotions at war with each other. For months I'd begged Dad to let me go to the Academy, but I'd never thought about having to say goodbye. It'd been just the two of us since Mum had disappeared when I was three. I hoped we'd both be okay. My arms were around him again in no time, needing the reassurance.

Dad squeezed me back, then walked with me to the small carriage and helped me in. He loaded my suitcase into the small compartment on the back and embraced Miss Stone before helping her inside too.

She uttered a clicking noise at her horse, who immediately took off. I stuck my head and hand out of the carriage window so I could wave goodbye. Dad waved back, continuing until he disappeared from my vision. My stomach felt like I'd taken a long tumble down a steep hill.

Once the tears had dried on my cheeks, Miss Stone started talking to me about my life and I got to quiz her about the Academy. I learned lots of things, like that I'd be in her first year class "Sorceress Lore", and that after lunch I would have specialist lessons. I was disappointed when she couldn't tell me what they would be, but she just laughed lightly and told me I would find out soon enough.

When she quizzed me on my Pack history, my stomach tightened in anticipation.

I know where this is going!

'It seems like you know most of the major history points you are expected to, except one. The Crone Infiltration. Would you like me to tell it to you now?'

I nodded. Then sat very still and waited, eyes wide. Hearing about the different Sorceresses and their magic was a rush, though since they were our enemies I tried to pretend I wasn't interested. She smiled at me, seemingly amused, then began.

'Back when the ancient Wolf Lords, Salvatore Niveus, Mikhail Furvus and Demetrius Canus, led the only Shifter pack in existence, the winter storms were deadly. To be trapped in a storm meant certain death, even for the strongest of Shifters. When one of the most horrific storms fell upon them, all of the Pack gathered in the castelet for safety.

'On the first evening of the storm, three women arrived seeking shelter. The sentinels on duty sought the counsel of the Wolf Lords, for the law was to never let a human set foot inside the Academy, lest we be discovered and hunted down. It was said that the Wolf Lords deliberated, and eventually came to a decision—Mikhail, the middle brother, was outvoted by Demetrius and Salvatore—and the women were allowed to stay through the storm.

'A warning was spread through the Academy to remain in human form, and to be particularly careful around the women. As days turned into weeks, tensions began to run high. The storm had them all trapped. Women started bickering over their children, men started fighting over the women, even the children would not play together with the same toys. Meal times had become hostile.

'The Wolf Lords surveyed the Pack, and intervened when they felt it was necessary, separating fights and soothing egos. They prayed to the Wolf Gods for peace and guidance, but none came. What did come, was death.'

Miss Stone paused to look at me, a serious expression on her face, one that questioned if she should go on. I swallowed hard, and felt it burn down into my chest, but I nodded. I wanted to know. I kept my face as clear as I could, and breathed a small sigh of relief when she continued.

'At first there was just one death; a wolf was killed in a fight. The Wolf Lords knew something was not right. They had lived through many winters and, though tensions had run high, no deaths had ever come to pass. They began to watch the women more carefully and had their sentinels do the same. What they discovered was alarming. During meals and throughout the day they saw the women whisper into the ears of the Pack members and then, in no time at all, arguments and fights would begin.

'The Wolf Lords decided to confine meals to rooms in an attempt to keep their Pack from the women, but knew if the unrest continued much longer they would need to banish them to the storm; to their deaths.

'Not one week had passed when the next death came. But this death was of the eldest son of Demetrius: Thrain. Murdered in his sleep by another Shifter. The Academy shook with Demetrius' rage and heartbreak.

'He led the other Wolf Lords and their two best sentinels to banish the women. They decided to do it themselves, because it seemed only those of the original bloodline were unaffected by their guests. What they discovered in the guest lodging was not the three beautiful women, but three wraith-like beings. Their faces were pale and drawn and held eyes as black and hollow as the night sky with no moon or stars to be seen.

'The sentinels immediately Shifted to their wolf forms and attacked, closely followed by the Wolf Lords. Before they could make contact, the Crones whispered words of powerful magic and the sentinels were blasted into the walls. They managed to get back up and join the fight—their role was always to protect the Wolf Lords. The women fought viciously with both magic and weapons, but they began to slow from injuries of tooth and claw.

'When they realised they would not win, they fought harder to gain an advantage. They managed to stab Mikhail in the chest—not through the heart, but close. The sentinels circled as Salvatore and Demetrius dragged their brother away. The women used the opportunity to stand side by side and join hands. The two on either end pointed their palms to the Wolf

Lords and began whispering words of power. As the light began to drain from the room, the sentinels launched themselves at the women. Just before the sentinels reached them, the dark light tore through them. They fell immediately. Dead.

'Salvatore and Demetrius saw that the women began to waver, presumably weakened by their sorcery, and used the opportunity to launch themselves forward. But by mid jump one of the women had thrown a glass vial onto the floor. It shattered and the room went dark once more. When the Wolf Lords landed, the women were gone. As they searched the room in the aftermath, they discovered talismans and potions amongst their abandoned possessions. Some smelled so poisonous they burned the wolves sensitive noses.

'The Wolf Lords told all in the castelet of the Sorceresses—who they later learned to be The Crones of Old—in the hopes that the Pack would understand that their behaviour and emotions had been influenced by dark magic. That they could return to normal. But the damage had been done. By the time the storm passed a week later, there had been countless more fights and deaths.

This was when the Pack was split from one and became three. Salvatore, the eldest, stayed to lead the Imperial Pack. Mikhail, the middle, left to begin the Cladden Pack and Demetrius, the youngest, established the Trevini Pack. Never since that day has a Sorceress of any kind been allowed to step foot into the Academy or onto Pack lands.'

Shocked, I sat in silence and just stared at Miss Stone. Finally I understood the hatred my dad so rarely spoke of but then recalled something else I'd learned from him. The Packs had liaisons who worked with the Sorceresses.

Surely they aren't all horrible.

'What about the Sorceresses that help us with protection from the Crones? There are some good ones, right?'

'Ah, yes. Our liaisons do work with some of the Sorceresses created by The Ladies of Light so we can live in peace and safety, but they are still considered enemies and not trusted to enter our lands. It would take something catastrophic to change that, but that is not a discussion for tonight. You need to get some sleep now. Besides, you'll get to learn more about the different types of Sorceresses in my class.'

'I'm not even tired,' I grumbled as I stifled a yawn. 'But I suppose I can wait.'

I fought against heavy eyelids for as long as I could, but slowly the carriage went dark.

IMPRESSIONS

A GENTLE HAND SHAKING my shoulder roused me from my sleep. I blinked my bleary eyes and turned to see the halo of Miss Stone's red hair glowing from the sunlit carriage window. I sat up straight and realised the carriage had stopped moving.

'We're here?!'

She smiled at me and nodded. 'We're right outside the gates that will lead you up to the Academy. I sent a raven to let them know of your arrival, so you need to walk straight up to the main building and you'll see the Administration Office. Just tell them your name.'

'But... aren't you coming?'

'No. I need to go back into the town we just passed through and get Ivy settled with the stable master. You'll be fine, I promise.'

I nodded, stomach tight with anticipation and anxiety, then hopped out and collected Dad's suitcase. At the front of the carriage, I patted Ivy gently on the neck, then looked towards my new home.

A pair of ancient cast-iron gates stood tall in front of me, with the name "Lupine Academy" crafted in melded metal across the top of them. It looked creepy and I sucked in a deep breath and let it out slowly, trying to ignore the chill that ran down my spine as I walked between the gates.

As I moved along the gravel path, I looked at the washed-out, three-storey grey stone buildings that lined both sides. Dorm buildings, Dad had told me when I'd asked him about the Academy. They looked gloomy compared to our house at the base of the Sovereign Mountains, but it didn't stop me from being excited that I'd be living in one of them soon anyway.

Outside the last dorm before the Academy I spotted a thin, blonde girl who looked about my age standing in the doorway on my left.

'Hurry up, Meena!' she shouted into the dorm. 'We're already late. Just leave your hair as it is!'

I slowed right down as the girl rushed out of the dorm to join her friend, her long dark hair pinned into a perfect high ponytail. Before I could pull myself together enough to go and introduce myself, they'd already shot off in the direction of the Academy.

Once I'd passed the dorms, I moved over towards the tree line beside the gravel path to avoid the sun in my eyes. I passed through another gate and walked over to look at an old fountain. I ran my fingers along the smooth stone then looked up. The Academy was made of uneven charcoal stone slabs and it towered over me like the castelet that it was. The enormous structure had matching turrets on both sides, which framed giant wooden doors in the centre that reached almost as high as the entire first level. Iron edged the door, with large metal bolts holding it in place. Two levels above the doors, right at the top, was a magnificent stained-glass window of a wolf; it was made from all black glass surrounded by shades of grey ranging from the colour of storm clouds to one so light it was almost transparent. The Academy stuck out like a boat in the middle of an empty lake against the vibrant green grass and deep mossy forest that encompassed it.

My heart skipped a few beats when I spotted the two monstrous dark stone wolves sitting on either side of the steps leading up to the doors; ominous sentinels guarding the entrance, just like those that had guarded the Wolf Lords in the story.

I clutched Dad's old suitcase tighter to my side and walked up the stone steps, following the smoothed-out imprints made from thousands of other Shifters before me. My eyes stayed forward to avoid looking at the wolves, but their menacing gazes followed me anyway.

Get a grip, they're just statues.

I pulled hard on a round metal handle to open one of the gigantic doors, my muscles straining from the weight. The musky, canine scent of wolves hit me square in the face; even in human form, I could clearly make out the scent. I let the door go as I stepped through and it slammed shut behind me. All the kids in the entryway turned to stare. The silence was deafening.

Typical. Just keep walking.

Desperate to avoid being stared at, I quickly looked around to get my bearings. To my right, there was a door with a ragged wooden sign that read "Food Den". Someone had drawn a wolf on it, with blood dripping from its mouth. I was willing to bet the food here would be just as bloody as the sign seemed to suggest.

Bleh!

To my left, there were two sets of stone steps, one leading up and the other down. Probably to a basement. I shuddered.

Why do creepy looking buildings always have a basement?

I looked straight ahead and found where I needed to be: "Administration Office". For the first time since my dramatic entry I felt my lips curve up slightly; the name sounded perfectly mundane after the Food Den.

If the entry wasn't so full, I knew my footsteps would have echoed around the large chamber. As it was, I could just hear the faint tap my boots made as I walked across the stone floor. I was so focused on covertly watching all the students, I didn't notice there was a chunk missing from the floor until I felt my foot catch on it. My knee smashed into the ground.

'Ouch! Oh, for the love of Salvatore!'

Knowing everyone would be able to smell the embarrassed sweat that trailed down my spine, I scrambled to gather the contents that had fallen from my suitcase and onto the dusty floor. I paused and looked up when I noticed another set of hands had started to help.

'Don't worry, I tripped on my first day too,' said a cheerful, silvery voice. 'I'm Dominic. Dom for short. What's your name?'

I took in the tall, lightly muscled frame and deep brown hair and eyes of the boy in front of me. His colouring would make him hard to spot in wolf form in the forests around here. At his sudden cough my eyes flew to his to find an amused expression. A hot flush rose to my cheeks.

'I'm Elita. Did you really trip too? Or are you just trying to make me feel better?'

I cringed as he handed back the last piece of clothing that had escaped my suitcase, which was naturally my most unflattering undergarment.

Everything back in its place, he helped me up. 'Nope, I definitely tripped. Embarrassed the crap outta my dad since he's the Beta wolf here.'

The slight tinge of pink in his cheeks when he admitted who his dad was made me relax a little more. 'Thanks for stopping to help me. I just need to go to the Administration Office so I can get my dorm keys and put my bag away.'

He smiled, picked up my suitcase and gestured to the room behind him. 'After you.'

The room was simple. It had an old worn desk, a couple of wooden cabinets and a friendly looking lady who lifted her gaze to us when we entered.

'Hi,' I said quietly. 'I'm here to check in and get my dorm assignment. My name is Elita White.'

At the sound of a barely stifled laugh, I whipped around to face Dom. Amused, I shook my head and rolled my eyes at him. Clearly my white hair and matching last name were just as funny to wolves as they were to humans. At least the clerk managed to keep it together as she handed me my keys and some paper.

'Here you go, Elita. There is your timetable and you'll be in room thirteen. If you go back out the front and down the lane, First Years are in the first building on the right. You share your dorm building with the Second Years. Girls live on the first floor and boys on the second. There are washrooms on each level; you just have to wait your turn to use them. On the ground floor is the co-ed Common Room. Would you like me to take you?'

Dom answered before I could. 'It's no worries, I got it Mrs. R.'

'Alright, Dom.' She smiled indulgently at him. 'But you better hurry up so you can make it back for the end of your last class. Oh, and make sure you take Elita to the Library to meet Axel.'

He winked. 'Sure, sure.'

Dom looked back at me and then pointed to the door we'd come through. I led the way carrying my keys. He still had my suitcase.

Once we'd reached the first dorm building, the one the girls I'd seen earlier had come from, he paused and pointed. 'The dorms on the right all belong to the students. First and Second Years stay in this one. The older you are, the further from the main Academy building you live. The ones on the left are for the staff, and for visitors when they stay. You'd think they'd have made them look different, but I guess grey stone's all they had when they built 'em.' Dom shrugged, then continued walking again. 'Could you open the door? Thanks... This is the Common Room, it takes up the whole floor. It's pretty much where we chill out.' He started gesturing to different sections of the room. 'There're games, books, a couple fireplaces and lots of comfy lounges. First Years usually hang on the left side and Second Years on the right. Don't worry though, it's not a rule or anything, we'll still get to hang out if you want!'

I nodded along as I absorbed all the information Dom was throwing my way. When I eyed the shelves of books I nearly squealed with delight. 'It looks great!'

'Yeah, mostly. Sometimes it gets a little crowded, depending on the company. Let's put your bag away, the rooms are up the stairs over there.'

At the top of the stairs I slowed to get my bearings. I stood on wooden floorboards and looked down both sides of the thin corridor, hoping the insides were more inviting than the outside seemed. There were maybe sixteen rooms in total.

'First Years are on the left this year, Second Years on the right. It'll be the opposite next year, so you won't need to move rooms. Number thirteen should be on the left. Yeah, there it is.'

It was my turn to stifle a laugh. Dom sounded like he was starting to get puffed out. Probably from the pile of thick books I had sitting at the base of my suitcase. I was lucky they hadn't fallen out when the clips burst open in the foyer. He propped the suitcase in front of my cupboard and then moved back to the door.

'I'll give you five to set up, then come back and take you to Axel if you like?'

'Sounds great, thanks.'

I hastily placed my suitcase on my new bed and unclipped it. There was a small dent from the stone floor, but nothing too bad. I doubted Dad would even notice. I picked up a few of my favourite books and turned to survey the room. Aside from the bed with a small built-in side table and lamp, there was a cupboard for my clothes and a small bookcase. Carefully, I lined the shelf with my favourite books, spines out in perfect alignment and alphabetical order. There weren't enough to fill the shelf, but the prospect of borrowing some from the library when I got a chance was an exciting one.

I positioned my favourite childhood family painting on the bedside table. I loved the obvious resemblance between me now and my mum back then: I could see the similar shape of our faces and our matching amber eyes. A familiar swell of misery built in my chest, wishing I could remember her better. Dom knocked and burst in the door, eyes moving straight to the portrait. He gave it an odd sort of look. Before I could ask about it, he shook his head a little and gave me another of his friendly smiles then immediately led the way back out the door.

We made small talk as we walked up to the top floor of the Academy, where the library was located. Dom was fascinated by the fact that I'd lived in a human settlement in the mountains south of the Academy. I supposed it was pretty unheard of.

'Why'd you live with the humans and not around here with the Pack like us?'

I shrugged, disconcerted. 'I don't know. Dad would never tell me why, just insisted we couldn't. I eventually stopped asking. I had to fight tooth and claw to get him to let me come to the Academy this year—hence my arriving almost mid-way through!'

I was more intrigued by his life. He had a whole bunch of Shifter friends. He'd even made his first Shift to full wolf on his sixteenth birthday, towards the end of last year (as was expected). I was excited and anxious for my birthday; it would be here in no time, just like winter. When we arrived at the library doors, I still had a million questions boiling away in my brain. It's wasn't like Dad hadn't told me anything, but it was so much better to hear about it from someone my age.

I took one step inside and stopped dead. It was as though I'd walked into an extraordinary dream. Floor-to-ceiling shelves lined every wall, and all were filled with books. There was a sliding ladder that had a kid standing on it, reaching for a thick volume. The scent of the musty pages mixed with smoke from the wood slowly crackling away in the fireplace had me feeling super excited.

Oh, I can't wait to explore every inch of this place!

'You must be our newest student,' boomed a deep voice to my right. I turned to look at the man, whose presence alone told me he was the Pack Alpha. He sort of reminded me of my dad. The man was tall and had giant muscles. His hair was mostly black with a bit of grey mixed in. He looked and sounded like he could either be your best friend, or your worst enemy. Etiquette drilled into my brain, I bowed.

'Yes, sir. My name is Elita White.'

'No "sir" here. Axel will do. You certainly show good Pack etiquette for someone who is new. This is your first Pack, correct? It's a shame your parents didn't bring you sooner. You'll have missed a lot.'

I bristled but bowed my head again before looking him in the eyes and answering. 'Probably, but I think I know enough. My father made sure to teach me everything I needed up until this point.'

He tilted his head to the side just a little and looked as though he was examining me. Finally, he nodded and beckoned me closer. 'We'll see. Since Dom has missed most of his last class for the day now,' he briefly moved his focus to Dom and gave him a hard look, 'he can take you to the Food Den for dinner. I expect I'll be seeing you soon.'

We both bowed our heads, but my gaze lingered a little longer, wondering how I could prove how much I already knew. I didn't move until Dom gave me a little shove. When we made it out the door, he looked at me like I was crazy.

'What?'

'That's the Alpha, you can't stare at him like that. You'll end up having to clean a whole floor with a toothbrush!' Then added quickly, 'Or something.'

I thought that was a bit of a strange choice of punishment, but I shrugged.

Dom rolled his eyes. 'Even so, I'd watch it next time. You might have gotten away with it today 'cause you're new, but I doubt you will again.' He started moving back towards the stairs, a giant grin on his face. 'Come on. Dinner time!'

I laughed and followed along, a comfortable silence settling between us. When he stopped I came to a halt beside him. Realising we'd made it back to the entrance, I looked at the Food Den door, then at Dom.

'Do you like the wolf?' he asked. 'One of my friends drew it in our first week.'

'Yeah, it's a real work of art,' I said dryly.

He chuckled and led the way through. I followed eagerly; I was starving after too many emotions in such a short amount of time. The room was almost full of kids eating and chatting. The smell of wolf and meat was potent, and it only got worse as we moved deeper into the den. We were almost to the front when it really hit me. Blood. Blood and uncooked meat. Like someone had punctured a cow and drained it into a cup and stuck it under my nose.

I'm gonna be sick.

'Hey, are you alright?'

'I don't do raw meat,' I muttered. 'It makes me wanna puke.'

The look of shock that flashed across Dom's face might have been priceless if I wasn't just keeping in last night's meal. Not that the expression lasted long. He smoothed it out and then pulled me forward and ordered something for us while I looked away and tried to hold my breath. Once he was done he led me outside to fresh air. I breathed in deeply through my nose and out through my mouth until I felt my stomach settle a little. Relieved, I turned to Dom and let him know I was ready to find a seat. He led the way over to some logs and we made ourselves comfortable.

It looked beautiful outside with the sun going down, if you ignored the gloomy looking Academy anyway. The grass was bright green, like the inside of a delicious lime, and spread out for about a mile before it reached the tree line of the forest. The trees there were gigantic and formed a barrier around us, as though this section had been cleared just for the Academy. I breathed in again, this time taking in the scent of freshly cut grass and pine from the forest trees. Once I was more relaxed, I tuned out the sound of all the kids chatting and heard some running water nearby, a stream maybe.

'So,' Dom said. 'No meat? Bit funny for a wolf!'

I turned back to look at him. 'Yeah, I know. But I haven't really liked it since I was little. I don't know why.'

'Huh. You might want to keep that aversion on the down low. A wolf not eating meat will cause quite a stir. But hey! I'm happy to eat yours and mine!'

I smiled at his enthusiasm; he clearly loved his food. He stabbed his chunk of dripping raw beef with a fork and started ripping it apart. I looked back to the forest as I ate my dinner. A stabbing sound caught my attention and I laughed when I noticed that Dom had just started stuffing in a second steak and still had some large chunks of bread lined up to eat. Thankfully the freshly baked bread had masked the scent of the meat a bit.

So I could avoid watching him devour the bloody carcass, I looked around at the other kids. They mostly looked normal, though I could lightly smell the Shifter scent in the breeze. I took in the faces of kids my own age, and those who seemed noticeably older. There seemed to be the same variation in looks as the humans I lived near: in skin colour, height, clothing styles. Unmistakable though, was the slight sharpness to their movements, their faster reflexes as they lobbed a ball around or dodged one as it flew near their food.

Enthralled but exhausted, I decided it was time to call it a day. On my feet once more, I turned to Dom who was stuffing in the last of his bread.

'Mind walking back to the dorm with me? I'm pretty tired after the trip and everything.'

'Sure thing.'

He grabbed all the plates and rubbish and disposed of them on our way back inside. I walked as quickly as I could to avoid the stench left over in the air, which was stronger now that we were back inside again.

'You really don't do raw meat, do you? You look like a ghost.'

I smiled faintly and shook my head.

When we walked in to the Common Room, I felt the warmth of the fire cocoon me. I looked forward to curling up in front of it with one of my books. It would be a perfect place to read.

'You wanna hang out down here for a bit?'

'Not tonight, thanks. I'm pretty exhausted.' Then, suddenly worried I'd lose my only friend so far, I added quickly, 'How about tomorrow?'

'No probs, I'll take you up to your room.'

'Thanks.' I smiled. Dom was good company.

When we made it to my new room, I opened the door and walked inside, ready to say goodnight. But when I looked at him again, he was staring at the portrait of my family with the same puzzled look as before.

'That's me with my mum and dad,' I explained. 'Everything okay?'

He hesitated a moment then said, 'It's nothing, sorry. It's a cool painting. I'll meet you at the Food Den for breakfast?' He waved and hurried back down the hall before I could answer.

Weird.

DIFFERENT

T HE SOUND OF THREE deafening bells woke me up. I opened my bleary eyes and tried to blink them clear. The puzzled look on Dom's face last night had kept me up and the little bit of sleep I'd managed was fitful. There was only one thing that would wake me up properly: a nice hot wash.

Soap and towel in hand, I made my way to the washroom at the end of the hall. The door opened as I went to enter and a tall girl with tanned skin walked out.

'Hey, you're new right?' At my nod, she continued. 'You might want to hurry a little. Those bells were signalling that breakfast is being served in the den.'

'Oh, thanks! I didn't know.'

She nodded and smiled. 'No worries.'

Once she'd left, I rushed inside. I was a little miserable about the lack of time to heat my water to the temperature I liked it and at having to wash and leave immediately.

Back in my room, I put my clothes and shoes on and hurriedly pulled my hair into a ponytail. I yanked my bed cover up, snagged my timetable then rushed downstairs. Frustrated with myself, I walked doubly fast from the dorm over to the main Academy building and into the Food Den entrance. I paused to look for Dom and spotted him bouncing from foot to foot near a stone pillar. He rushed over when he saw me.

'Come on Elita, I'm starving!' Dom urged, leading me right up to the serving area, which was mostly empty since I'd made us so late.

Despite my queasy stomach, I laughed. Dom looked like drool was about to start dripping from his chops. I was sure it would have been if he were in wolf form.

I felt relieved to smell no bloody carcasses as we approached the serving area this morning. Though the tubes of lard—otherwise known as sausages—were almost equally as unappealing. Ah, porridge! I asked the server for some with peaches added in. I looked up when I didn't sense him moving; he seemed confused.

'No sausages?' His voice was edged with concern.

I shook my head quickly as my cheeks heated. When he offered my bowl, I reached up and took it with a slightly shaky hand. Keeping my eyes averted, I moved to the doors to wait for Dom. I grinned when I saw his over-stacked plate and the piece of toast already hanging out of his mouth. I was surprised he didn't always have a stash of food on him, considering how much he seemed to love it. I pointed outside to let him know I wanted to sit on the same logs as yesterday.

And away from the watchful eyes in the Food Den.

After we'd both scoffed our food, Dom scanned my timetable and dropped me at my first class as the bell rang.

'Just ask the teacher or one of the other kids how to get to your next lesson. Have fun!'

I called out thanks, but he was already halfway down the hall. He'd mentioned something at breakfast about not being late to another class. Excitement bloomed as I faced the door to my first-ever class at the Academy: "Sorceress Lore". Upon seeing a full classroom, a touch of nervousness joined the excitement.

Okay, you can do this. Just get in there.

I knocked quietly. Not that it would matter. The superior wolf hearing would mean no one would miss it. The door opened, and Miss Stone stood on the other side. I immediately gave a small sigh of relief.

'Hi Elita,' she said with a smile. 'Come on in.'

I nodded, my heart racing once more. I was about to walk into a class full of Shifters who had already been learning together for the first half of this year! Talk about nerve-wracking. If only Dad had let me come at the beginning. Though, I suppose I should just be grateful he'd agreed to let me come at all.

She smiled kindly at me, then opened the door wide and faced the class. 'Everyone, this is Elita. Please do your best to make her feel welcome.' As everyone said hello to me, the teacher turned back and lowered her voice a little. 'There are two seats left. One at the front and one at the back; you can choose.'

'Thank you.' I smiled at her, relieved that, at the least, I knew her already. I quickly checked out all the kids and the two chairs.

Walk past everyone or quick dash to the front and look like a nerd? Who am I kidding?

I sat right up the front, just like I would in all my other classes at the Academy. Learning new things was exhilarating and I didn't want to get distracted by people who liked to have not-so-secret chats when the teachers talked. Miss Stone gave an approving nod and smile before she continued with the lesson.

'Okay, let's pick up where we left it last lesson. Ah, yes... Crones of Old. Natasha, tell me the names of the three original Crones.'

Everyone's heads, including mine, whipped around to look at Natasha—it was easy to find her with everyone else staring. She appeared put out. It seemed as though the teacher had interrupted one of those "chats".

'Yes, Miss Stone. Their names are Narcissus, Belladonna and Dracaena.'

'Well done, Natasha. And perhaps you could finish the rest of your talk after class?'

Natasha nodded back with slightly pursed lips. Once the teacher had looked away to address the whole class, she rolled her eyes.

Definitely not my kind of person.

'The Crones of Old were born of the hate, fear and discord in our world. They have been in existence now for millennia. They, of course, were the reason the ancient Pack split—one becoming three. The Crones used their powers to cause rifts between Pack members. The Pack leaders, who were strong and least affected, made the decision to split the Pack when deaths started to occur. Who can tell me what became of the original Wolf Lords?'

I saw a few kids put their hands up and turned to look when she called on one to answer. 'Yes, Harper?'

'They are said to rest beneath our Academy, in the stone tombs. And that if you need guidance, you can pray to them and they may answer you.'

Snickers broke out from some kids at the back, including Natasha. Poor Harper turned bright pink. Miss Stone gave them a withering look and they stopped.

'That is correct. Thank you, Harper. In response to the destruction the Crone's caused, The Seer began creating new Sorceresses, originally The Ladies of Light, who in turn made more. These Sorceresses, while never welcome on our lands as law dictates, do liaise with us in order to protect the world from the Crones and their darkness and have vowed to support us should the Crones or *their* Sorceresses invade us again.' Another bout of talking broke out at the back of the class and Miss Stone sighed. 'Since everybody seems so well versed, I won't bother going over the rest of the origin stories for your essay due at the end of next week, I'll just give you time to work on it. There are some books up the front for you to look through and borrow, or you may continue with those you already have.'

As the class bustled to begin the essays, I approached Miss Stone at the front of the room. 'Hi, Miss Stone. Could I record a copy of the essay question please?'

'Oh, yes. Here," she said, showing me the essay question scrawled on a piece of paper. 'It is due at the end of the week, but you can have an extra—'

I interjected quickly. 'I don't need any extra time. Thank you, though.'

'Okay. Let me know if you change your mind.'

'I will. Can I go and get started?'

She nodded and indicated the left-over books at the front of the room. I quickly read through the assignment and wrote out the question on my own paper. As I made my way over, I decided it wouldn't be too difficult. Definitely interesting, though.

I perused the books until I found the title that looked most useful, even if it was a little basic: *Sorceress History: Volume I.*

I placed the book flat on my table, rested an elbow next to it then wrapped my right foot around my left ankle and began reading. It seemed no time at all had passed when the bell sounded. Happy with my half-page of notes, I slid my paper inside the book and closed it, then made my way back to the teacher. I got jostled a few times by kids making their way out the door.

'Hi again, Miss Stone. Do you think you'd be able to tell me how to get to my next class?'

'Of course.' She took my timetable from my hand and scanned it. 'It looks like you have Weapons Basics next. Natasha. You have Weapons Basics now, yes?' The girl nodded and her lips pursed slightly once again. 'Wonderful. You can show Elita where to go.'

Great.

'Thank you, Miss Stone.'

She nodded. 'You'd both better hurry along or you'll be late. Master Ira won't be impressed.'

I smiled weakly at Natasha as she gestured grandly for me to walk through the door before her. She didn't say a word until we'd made it to the end of the hall. I'd have preferred she hadn't said anything at all.

'Ugh. Stone's such a cow. Don't you think?'

I paused, unsure what to say.

'Well? Isn't she?' Natasha demanded.

She doesn't really expect me to agree with that, does she?

She stared, expectation clear on her face.

I sighed. 'Um, not really. She seemed kinda nice to me.'

Feeling the impact of the glare coming from beside me, I kept my head forward.

Natasha was silent for the rest of the walk but stopped dead outside of what I assumed was our next class. 'Do you have any idea who I am?'

'Uh, Natasha?'

She rolled her eyes and crossed her arms in front of her chest. 'I'm the Alpha's daughter, so you'd better think twice before you disagree with me again. Got it?'

Just let it go. Just let it go.

A man who I assumed was our teacher, Master Ira, appeared out of nowhere and told us both to get inside. Natasha dropped her shoulder into me as she walked past.

'Keep it on the mats,' the teacher barked.

Fuming, I followed behind them both and made my way slowly to the rest of the group. There seemed to be a few kids like her no matter where I lived; she reminded me of the mean girls from the small village near home, they never had anything nice to say. I guess I'd hoped things would be different here with the Pack; that everyone would be more mature and get along.

So much for a pack mentality.

The cavernous room held the familiar scent of a training arena. Sweat, rubber and fear.

I wonder how little Miss Alpha's Daughter goes in here?

'Warm up. Five laps, now!'

The class didn't need to be told twice. I joined in from the back and then set my pace around the middle.

As I ran, I surveyed the room. There were fighting squares marked, mufflers for boxing, a range of weapons and some weights. I hoped we'd get to use the weapons today; I enjoyed the short sword most. By the time we reached our final lap, the myriad of small open windows that lined the basement were barely keeping the sweaty wolf stench at a tolerable level.

Unfortunately for me, the rest of the hour was going to be spent fighting one on one. And, of course, I was paired up with Natasha.

Master Ira whistled sharply to get everyone's attention. 'Combination one: straight punch, right elbow, left uppercut, then swap sides. Other person blocks. Mufflers on and start.'

'I'll go first,' Natasha said.

Never would have guessed that was coming.

She hit pretty hard, but I was able to keep my stance steady. When it was my turn, I began by focusing on my technique rather than strength. I ground my teeth together when she sniggered.

Technique solidly in place, I put a little more muscle into it. Natasha took a step back. I couldn't stop the smirk that lit up my face, or the laugh that escaped when she glared at me.

'Combination two: left front kick, right knee, step back and right outside kick. Then swap. Go.'

By now we were both drenched. Between the technique, strength and speed, I was sure we were a sight to see.

After six sets of combinations and a lot of sweeping glances from the rest of the kids, Master Ira ended the session. 'Class dismissed. Go back to the dorms and get clean. You have half an hour before lunch break, as usual. Do not be late or you will not eat.'

Drenched in sweat, I walked out behind everyone else and followed them back to the dorms. I grudgingly admitted to myself that Natasha actually had pretty good technique, not that I'd ever say that to her face. Outside, the breeze felt refreshingly cool against my sweaty body and being out of the suffocating wet-wolf smell was pretty great too. Master Ira was a tough teacher; I was sure Dad would approve.

SECRETS

I WALKED OUT OF my bedroom door and almost straight into one of the other girls. 'Woah! Sorry. Hey, it's Harper, right? We had classes together this morning.'

'Yes, that's me. Sorry, I didn't mean to get in your way. Also, all First Years are in the same classes. There's not that many of us here.' She flushed bright red. 'Sorry. I didn't mean to correct you; I know people don't like that.'

I smiled in what I hoped was a reassuring way. 'It's fine, seriously.'

She nodded. 'Listen, the bell is about to go and I don't want to be late for lunch. Did you want to, maybe, go together?'

I offered a smile, trying to reassure her. 'Sure, I'd love to. My friend Dom might meet us there.'

Her cheeks went a little pink again. 'That's fine,' she muttered.

We made our way back across the grounds and past the creepy wolf sentinels in an awkward silence. As we neared the Food Den, I looked around hopefully for Dom. He was nowhere to be seen. My lips puckered into a small pout. I really didn't want to have to go near the blood bath or the watchful food server. My stomach gave a little flop as I tapped my feet.

New plan.

'Hey, Harper. Any chance you'd grab a salad for me and then meet me on the logs outside? I'm starving but need to pop in to see Mrs R.'

She looked at the ground. 'Uh, I don't really like sitting in the sun.'

'That's fine, there're some in the shade. How about one of those?'

She gave me a proper smile. 'Okay, great. I'll meet you there.'

'Thanks!'

I made my way back outside the Food Den and loitered in the entrance for a few minutes since I didn't actually need to see Mrs. R.

Once I thought enough time had passed, I hurried back inside then walked along the back wall until I reached the door to go outside. I paused and took in the view as I breathed in the crisp air. It was still beautiful, and even more vibrant during the day than it was at sunset. There were so many kids out chatting and soaking in the sun that I realised I couldn't hear the rippling stream that was hiding in the forest. When I approached Harper, she passed me my salad.

'Thanks.' I smiled.

The silence while we ate was a little more comfortable than before; I guessed she figured I wasn't here to make fun of her like Natasha and her little cult. It was as though my thoughts summoned her; I spotted her nearby talking with the girls and cosied up to the boys. I rolled my eyes.

'Hey, Harper? What do you know about Natasha?'

'Oh, her. She pretty much thinks she's queen around here, with her Dad being Alpha and all. She spends her time showing off, trying to make fun of people and bossing everyone around. I saw you two fighting pretty hard in Weapons today. I take it the trip down from Sorceress Lore didn't go too well?'

I stared at Harper for a moment before answering. It was the longest, most unapologetic speech she'd given so far. Clearly she had a bit of a history with Natasha.

'Yeah, you could say that. She kindly said that I shouldn't cross her right before she barged into me. In front of the teacher.'

Right at that moment, Natasha looked at both of us and sneered. Harper put her head down and turned her body to one side. I took my time averting my eyes. The status had obviously gone to her head. Dismissing her, I looked back at Harper, determined to salvage our previous better mood, and started making small talk.

Harper had us packed up and back to the Food Den door by the time the bell tolled. I wondered why they didn't get a quieter bell. With the superior hearing, I was surprised everyone hadn't gone deaf; even after my short time here, there was a ringing that seemed to linger in my ears.

Eyes on my timetable, I followed Harper. After reaching the staircase and studying the schedule in front of me, I realised she was leading me to the library. We had a double study period. The thought of being able to get a real start on my Origin essay for Miss Stone's class was pretty exciting, though the feeling may have had more to do with where I'd be studying.

Inside the doorway, Harper paused and looked at me. 'I've got to find some books for an essay for my Hunting and Gathering class. I'll catch you later.' After she'd taken a few steps, she suddenly turned back. 'And thanks for hanging out.'

'It was great,' I said. 'I'm looking forward to next time. See you later.'

As Harper wandered off, I closed my eyes and inhaled the scent of old books; biblichor, it was called. Knowing there must have been a name for it, I'd looked it up and found out it was based on the Greek words "biblio", meaning book, and "ichor", the fluid that flows like blood in the veins of Gods; pretty fitting, I thought. Relaxed, I moved into the library. After a few more steps, I noticed Miss Stone standing near a bookshelf.

Ah, brilliant!

'Hi, Miss Stone. Is there any chance you'd show me a good section to find some more books for my Origin essay?'

She smiled kindly at me. 'I'd hoped I would see you in here, Elita. This is actually the section right here, though some of the more ancient handwritten accounts are in a special room. Perhaps you will be able to visit there soon. After you earn the librarian's trust, that is. Let me pick you out a few to start.'

She looked as if she were waiting for me to protest, like earlier, but I was happy for some help with book selection. I could always pick my own later if the ones Miss Stone gave me weren't helpful. Realising I wasn't going to argue, she turned and picked three books off the shelf and then turned back to me.

'Here you go. I trust you'll read them carefully and treat them well.'

At my nod, she handed them over and began to walk away. I quickly realised she'd given me one too many books.

'Miss Stone! You've accidentally given me your book too.'

She looked over her shoulder at me, winked, and then kept walking.

How strange.

I looked at the title of her book—The Seer—and then at the others I'd seen her pull off the shelf. The rest were just books on The Crones of Old, The Ladies of Light and The Wolf Lords.

Hmmm. Why does Miss Stone secretly want me to know more about The Seer?

Fascinated, I went and found a comfy lounge and curled up with my books. The fireplace, crackling away merrily in front of me, kept me warm in the cool air of the dank stone castle. Unable to contain myself, I placed the origin books down and cracked open Miss Stone's older book.

The spine made a slight crinkling sound as I pulled back the hard, patterned cover.

It's handwritten!

The script was surprisingly clear, considering the obvious age of the book. Its yellowed pages were worn from being turned by many fingers.

Reading the first pages, it became clear that this was an origin story too. The origin of magic, written by The Seer.

"I sat and prayed to the Earth Mother for kindness to reign once more with our people, and for the souls of those who could have still been with us if not for the hatred of man. I prayed, then lightning struck. From the middle of the noonday sun did it come and strike the tree, causing it to splinter and bleed. Blue seeped from its insides, and a voice did whisper in my mind.

'Drink of the tree, my daughter. Drink of the ichor so that I may help my people. Drink and be saved.'

The voice in my mind did not scare me, for with it came the comfort of a mother's embrace, of kind words on a dark, stormy night. Without question, I leaned forward and drank of the tree's blood.

The world before me turned blue and I fell gently to the ground, as though laid to rest by one who loved me, though I had no such person besides the Earth Mother. Head down, my eyes fell shut.

Gentleness and peace were torn away. In their place I saw horrors too many to count. Death. Deaths of those I knew, and of those

I was yet to meet. On and on it went, until without warning, it ceased.

Face wet with tears I did not recall shedding, I sat, shaking. The tree before me looked bereft, broken. I couldn't bear its pain, too. As if in a trance, I approached and laid my tear-stained hand on its trunk, wishing it better. A coolness that somehow left a warmth in its wake moved through me, and into the tree's wound.

Shocked, I pulled my hand away. The tree was healed.

My jaw dropped open, astonishment colouring my thoughts. *I wonder if Dom knows about this?!*
Enraptured, I flipped to the next page and continued to read.

A hand shaking my shoulder startled me awake. I opened my bleary eyes to see Dom standing over me, an exasperated grin on his face.

'You really weren't kidding about loving books, were you? You've been up here for ages.' He laughed. 'Dinner's over and everyone's heading to the Common Room. I got a bit worried at dinner when I didn't see you, so I checked your room and when you weren't there either, I came looking. Here.' He handed me the book I'd been reading.

I'd managed to get through most of it before I had apparently fallen asleep. I placed the book down, rubbed my eyes and stretched out. There was a familiar tightness in my muscles from falling asleep upright. Feeling somewhat human again, I answered Dom. 'Sorry, it happens to me a lot! Thanks for coming to find me. That was really nice of you.'

Right at that moment, my stomach decided to embarrass me with a deafening rumble.

A human could have heard that from a mile away!

Dom burst out laughing. My cheeks got so hot they must have looked like ripened tomatoes.

Gee, could this get much worse?

As if on cue, my stomach made another thunderous grumble. I clutched my stomach to try and make it stop. By this point, Dom was clutching his own sides and tears had sprung up in his eyes.

Ugh, boys!

I think he finally caught the embarrassment and exasperation I was feeling because he tried to pull himself together.

'Sorry, sorry! Come on, I know a back way into the kitchens. We can grab you something to eat.'

Irritated but starving, I decided that taking him up on his offer would be better than being laughed at again. Books in hand, I gestured for Dom to lead the way.

The corridor outside the library was cast in shadows and the cold had well and truly seeped in. Without the warmth of the library fire, I shivered. I quickened my pace a little to keep up with Dom. When we started down a set of service stairs at the far end of the hall, Dom put his finger up to his lips to shush me.

'These stairs go past the staffroom. Some of them will still be in there, and we aren't technically allowed down here,' he whispered.

I nodded and indicated for him to keep going. It was creepy in the stairwell with only the moon lighting the way. I could see okay but all the shadows creeped me out. I shivered as I imagined the stone wolves from the front doors chasing me through here.

Once we'd reached the bottom landing, Dom pushed a splintered wooden door open a crack and peered out. After a few moments of me anxiously bouncing around on my toes, he pushed it wide open.

'Follow me. I can't see or smell anyone nearby, but we'd better keep it down anyway,' Dom whispered, and then muttered what sounded suspiciously like, 'I don't want to do any more cleaning than necessary.'

My chest ached. The last thing I wanted to do was get into trouble when I'd only just arrived. If I hadn't been starving, I'd probably have chickened out. Instead, I tiptoed along behind Dom, using my years of stealth training to keep quiet. A couple of times Dom turned around, as though he was checking if I was still behind him.

We reached another door. He held up a hand to stop me and then peeked around it.

'Hello, Dominic. Come on in.'

My knees almost buckled when the deep voice echoed from inside. This was it; I'd be in so much trouble. What would Dad say? I'd told him I would be so responsible. I was just about to go into complete melt down when Dom said, 'Come on, you can meet my dad.' Catching sight of my face he added, 'Relax! You won't be in trouble... though I might be.' Then he turned and walked in with me close on his heels. 'Dad, this is Elita.'

Inside the kitchen, Dom's dad stood near one of the benches. He had a tall, muscular frame and brown hair that resembled his son's. His head was tilted to the side, much like Axel's had been in the Library.

What is it with these Pack leaders?

He nodded once. 'Nice to meet you.'

Once I registered his friendly tone, it was like my heart decided it could resume its normal pattern. I really needed to give the poor thing a break.

I bowed my head, almost as low as I had for Axel. 'Nice to meet you too, sir.'

'Call me Corbin.'

I flushed and nodded, not sure if that was a good idea.

He turned to look at his son. 'I'd ask why you're here when you should be in the Common Room, but the answer seems rather obvious. You're just lucky it was me in here and not someone else. You know better.

My shoulders slumped. This was all my fault. I didn't want to get Dom into trouble. I opened my mouth to take the blame but, once again, Dom answered before I could.

51

'Yeah, sorry Dad. I was just starving. You know I'm always hungry. I'll just grab something and get outta here, 'kay?'

Corbin sighed. 'Hurry up, son. I'm going. You two better be out of here before Master Ira does the night rounds.'

Corbin sounded disappointed and resigned. I looked to Dom to check if he was okay. I could just make out a slight slump to his shoulders and a flush to his cheeks before he turned away and started rummaging quietly through a few food trays. By the time he turned back with some bread to offer me, he was almost back to normal. I wanted to ask him if he was okay, but thought he'd probably say something if he wanted to. Instead, I smiled and took the food he offered. He smiled back; it almost reached his eyes.

'I'm sorry, Dom. I can go tell him it's my fault. Honestly, it's okay,' I whispered.

'Naw, don't worry about it. Let's just get outta here.'

I still felt horrible but followed him anyway. Secretly, I was a little glad he hadn't made me turn myself in. I hated disappointing my dad too.

We made it back to the Common Room without running into anyone else, and thankfully with no more grumbles from my stomach. Most of the kids had gone up to bed already so there was space on the comfy lounges by the fire. I placed my books down on a small table then curled up on one of the couches and opened the food Dom had given me. We both ate in silence for a few minutes, Dom lacking his usual gusto.

While I finished the last of my food, I watched the flames dance in the fireplace. The blues and oranges weaved and swayed; they looked the way I imagined elemental wind and fire magic might if they joined together, similar to Shifting but with different colours. Thinking of magic reminded me of The Seer. I looked up at Dom.

'Hey, have you learned much about The Seer?' At his slightly confused look, I added, 'You know, the original Sorceress?'

Recognition flooded his face, then what looked like guilt. I tilted my head and surveyed him before I pulled myself up.

Huh. Must be a wolf thing, not a Pack-leader thing.

'Yeah, I've heard of her. She was here before the Crones and gave the elemental magic to the Ladies of Light, who used to be human, so they could try and stop the Crones, y'know? Didn't quite work like she'd hoped, obviously. I am surprised you know, though. I didn't learn about her until this year.'

'Hmm. Well, Miss Stone gave me a book about her. I don't know why she wanted me to know. I mean, it seems like I would have found out next year anyway. Any ideas?'

Dom shifted uncomfortably in his seat. His odd behaviour reminded me of how he'd acted in my room. I sat up in my seat.

'What's going on with you? Is there something you're not telling me?'

Dom looked like he'd swallowed a rock. He turned his eyes away, hesitating for some reason. My heart went back to racing in my chest.

'Dom?'

He sighed and looked back at me. Anxiety and worry were plain on his face, but it looked like he'd made a decision.

'Yeah, I guess there's something, but I could be wrong about it and I didn't want to worry you for nothing.'

He stopped as though he wasn't going to say any more, but I waved my hand to indicate he should continue.

'It's about your mum. It's just, I think I've seen her before.'

I sat up further, my back ramrod straight. How would he have seen my mum?

'Look, it'll be easier if I just show you what I mean, but we'll have to go back into the Academy. Let's go.'

I was dizzy. Something about my mum? Why wouldn't he have said something before? I stood up and followed him out the door and along the path. I stuck close by him, walking in the darker shadows of the trees. My head was reeling. Why would we need to sneak in to learn about her? Something wasn't right here. My heart began thumping erratically.

The glare of the stone wolves followed us through the Academy doors. I could still feel their eyes on my back as we snuck up two flights of stairs and down a corridor. My breathing had turned shallow; it was all I could hear besides the pounding of my heart in my head. I was so focused on sticking close to Dom that I bumped into his back when he stopped suddenly outside a door. He turned to look at me, eyebrows drawn together in a worried frown, then looked back at the door to open it. My eyes followed and I saw the sign for the first time: "Sorceress Records—Staff Only".

Oh, Salvatore.

My stomach felt like it had fallen down to my feet. I trailed into the room behind Dom and stopped dead. Dozens of sketches lined the walls.

My head shook back and forth like it was on repeat as he made his way over to a section of the wall directly in front of us. He looked at the sketches for a moment, then pointed to one. He turned back to me, watching and waiting.

My legs had turned to lead. I swallowed the lump in my throat and forced myself to walk forward. I could hear the deafening thud of my heart picking up pace. It was like it wanted to escape. I wished I could escape. I stopped next to Dom and looked him in the eye, a cold dread filling my body. He gave me a tight smile and a small nod then squeezed my shoulder with his other hand. I absorbed the courage he was offering and turned to look where he pointed.

No!

I gasped, hand clutching my chest. It was her. My mother. On the wall of Sorceresses. My knees smashed into the solid stone floor. This couldn't be true.

A Sorceress cannot be the mother of a wolf.

SHOCK

I COULD HARDLY BREATHE. My short, rapid breaths matched the thumping of my heart. The world was closing in around me and my face was wet with tears that wouldn't stop rolling. The same thing kept running through my head: there was no way my mother was a Sorceress.

Through my haze of roaring thoughts, I vaguely registered Dom sitting down on the floor beside me. He put his arm around my shoulders and pulled me into his side. I think he said something, but I didn't hear it. I couldn't hear anything over my erratic breathing. I felt like I was going to pass out.

'Hey!' Dom shouted in my ear.

It was enough to jolt me from the spiral of despair I'd found myself in. I looked at him in panic. The sympathy on his face was evident, and while my breathing had calmed down a touch, it just made the tears fall faster. He pulled me closer and gave me a tight hug. I finally heard him speak.

'Hey, it's okay. Everything will be all right.'

How will it ever be all right? My mother is a Sorceress. Oh, Salvatore! Is she a good one or a bad one? I mean, they're all our enemies, but please, don't let her be a Crone Sorceress, they're evil.

'Come on, we need to get out of here before someone shows up.'

I pushed my shaking palms into my forehead as I forced my breathing to even out. He was right, I needed to pull myself together. Get back to my room. I couldn't stay here like this.

Dom leant back and looked at me as though assessing my mental state. I supposed that was fair considering what I'd just discovered. It seemed reasonable to assume I was one inch away from laying down and never getting up again.

Dom's brows furrowed. 'Let's move. I had to shout pretty loud to get you to snap out of it before. I doubt anyone was around to hear it, but just in case...'

I nodded. I couldn't speak right now, there were just too many thoughts rushing around, but I could move my head up and down. I watched him stand, then hold a hand out for me. I looked at it for a moment before realising that I should take it and get up. I grabbed his hand and he hoisted me to my feet.

On the way to the door, I stopped. My mother. I looked back to the wall where her sketch was and took a step back towards it. It looked much more recent than the painting I had.

'You can't, Elita. I'm sorry. They'll notice and you'll draw attention to her.'

I didn't think my heart could hurt any more than it already did, but I was wrong. Despite my devastation at finding out my mother was a Sorceress, and at the cold hard betrayal I was beginning to feel, I still wanted the picture. I couldn't move myself away, but Dom gave me no choice. He grabbed my hand and gently pulled me towards the door.

I followed him in a daze, pausing and moving when he did. I still couldn't speak. This was too much. The unwelcome feeling of betrayal began to bubble over. But not at my mum. This time, it was towards my dad. How could he not have told me that my mum was a Sorceress? It's not like he could have mistaken her for anything else with his sense of smell.

My thoughts spun around in my head. I only realised we'd made it back into the Common Room when the warm dry air encompassed my body. It was then that I noticed I was shivering.

Dom must have seen the shivers wracking my body because he led me over to the chair closest to the fire. My earlier questions about The Seer were miles away but, once the fire had warmed my outsides and insides enough, questions started to flow.

'How could they do this to me, Dom? Why were they even together? It's not like we live or stay anywhere near Sorceresses. They're our enemies, for Salvatore's sake! Even the Ladies of Light are still considered enemies and we only work with them when absolutely necessary. She'd better not be a Crone Sorceress! Ugh! How did they even meet? How could my dad not have told me?'

I gulped in a massive breath of air, my chest protesting the onslaught of questions. As soon as I drew breath, Dom tried to reassure me.

'Hey. Hey! It's all right! We can figure all this out. I'm sure when you speak to your dad, he'll tell you. I'm sure there was a good reason or something, y'know?'

I stared at him blankly.

A good reason? What could possibly be a good enough reason for this?

I guess my thoughts came through loud and clear, because he answered me.

'Yeah, you know, like he probably met her doing official Pack duties or something. And I mean, I guess, they were probably in love, or whatever.'

The pink tinge that popped up on Dom's face caused me to give a hysterical giggle, which then turned into another barrage of tears. This time he just put an arm around me and let me cry it out.

Once all the tears had dried on my face, a new set of worries arose. It was too much. When Dom felt me shift, he moved back and looked at me. His concern cut me further but I didn't have enough left in me to offer a smile of reassurance.

'I'm gonna go to bed now,' I said, my voice raspy from crying.

Dom just nodded then hopped up and grabbed my books from the table. He led the way upstairs to my room, stopping once he'd reached my door. He turned to look at me, and I could see he was trying to think of something else to say.

'Don't worry, Dom. There really isn't anything to say about it. I need to sleep.'

He nodded again and handed me my books, worry furrowing his brow.

'I'm in number five upstairs, if you need anything.'

I dredged up all the energy I could manage and pulled up the corners of my lips in thanks, then turned and let myself into my room. I closed the door gently behind me, though slamming it would have been more reflective of how I felt.

Then again, maybe not. My insides felt dead from the shock of this new knowledge, and even slamming the door seemed too hard.

I placed the books on my shelf then laid on my bed and let my worries flow through me.

If Dad is a wolf and Mum is a Sorceress, what does that make me? I know humans and Shifters just make Shifters, but I bet this won't be the same!

What will happen when I Shift for the first time?

Will I even be able to Shift?!

What happens to me if I can't Shift? Will they make me leave?

What will happen if anyone finds out my mum is a Sorceress?

Could she... maybe... be alive?

Why didn't Dad tell me about all this?

Feeling overwhelmed and exhausted, I rolled over, buried my face in my pillow and closed my eyes.

I woke to the sound of loud knocking on my door. I quickly rolled out of bed but as the events of last night hit me, I staggered to a halt. When the knocking turned to banging, I forced myself to continue to the door. I pulled it open to find Natasha. She looked me over from top to bottom, making me feel unusually self-conscious.

Can she tell I'm not a real Shifter?

Before I could drift into full-fledged panic that I'd been discovered, she spoke, her usual snarky tone turning my mood from misery to irritation. 'You're late. Stone sent me to find you. Hurry up.'

'I'm not ready to leave,' I ground out.

She glared at me. 'Obviously.'

I shut my door in her face and gave a satisfied grin at the "Bitch" I heard come from the other side. I considered taking my time, just to annoy her more, until it really hit me that I was so late I'd missed breakfast and part of the first class for the day.

I wonder why Dom didn't come and get me? Maybe he doesn't want to be my friend anymore. Can hardly blame him now, can I?

I sighed and quickly changed into my training gear, feeling somewhat glad I'd get to hit something today, then I sucked in a deep breath and let it out. On the other side of the door, Natasha looked irate. If those daggers she stared were real, I'd be shredded.

Maybe I'm not the only half-breed after all. Natasha looks like she could be part Crone.

I gave her a grand wave, to signal that she could lead the way. She ripped herself away from the wall and stormed off. She kept up a wicked pace, clearly trying to keep ahead of me. Not that it did her any good since we were about the same height.

When we got to the class, she charged straight in without knocking and went directly to her friends. I briefly wondered why she'd been picked to come and get me, but my anxiety at being so late caught up with me and forced me to focus on entering the room. I looked at Miss Stone, who stood at the front by the slate on the wall. She gestured for me to go to her. The concern on her face brought the tension running through me down a notch.

'Good morning, Elita. Are you feeling okay? Since the bells are about to ring for next period, I thought I'd send someone to get you.'

'Morning, Miss Stone. Sorry, I'm not feeling great today.'

Not really a lie.

She nodded. 'If you need to go back and rest, you can do that. You just need to get a slip from Mrs. Randolph, in the Administration Office.' She then added gently, 'You should also do that from the beginning of the day in the future, if you're not up to classes, or ask one of the other girls to do it for you.'

I nodded, heat rushing to my cheeks.

'Sorry, Miss Stone. I'll be sure to do that next time. I think I'm good to go onto the next class though.'

She nodded again and sent me to wait at my desk for the last part of our lesson. I purposefully ignored Natasha's filthy look when I sat. To pass the time, I scrawled absentmindedly on a page.

When the bells sounded, I looked down and saw what I'd drawn. The blood drained from my face. Despite its simplicity, the image was clear. A wolf shrouded in magic. A haze of interwoven lines surrounding the wolf, coming from its centre. As discreetly as I could, I shredded the paper then stuffed it into my book.

I walked into Weapons Basics behind the rest of the class and joined into what appeared to be the usual five-lap warm up. Today, I didn't pace myself. Today, I needed to run. In no time at all, I'd well overtaken almost everyone, including the boys. The only one who really managed to keep pace was Natasha. Irritated, I increased my speed, causing my lungs to protest. Apparently it was a competition, because she moved faster too. We were neck and neck for the last lap, only a foot in it by the finish. I launched myself over the line. Victory. I threw myself on the floor and attempted to catch my breath as I waited for everyone else to finish.

Once the last of the kids crossed the line, my breath was mostly back to normal and Master Ira instructed us to pair off with this week's partner. That meant Natasha, again. I glared as I squared off with her. Normally I disliked boxing, but today I was glad.

We spent the last hour going through the combinations Master Ira barked out at us. I used as much strength as I could manage for each hit and kick. Every impact sent a question jolting around my head about my mother and father, and about the new uncertainty that clouded my life. Inside my head was a vicious tornado; questions, worries and emotions flinging around in an ever-increasing spiral. Each hit Natasha made was like a knife through my body, widening all the wounds this new revelation had caused.

By the end of the session I was drained. My body barely had enough energy to move and my mind was a blur, unable to hold onto a thought for more than a moment from the sheer exhaustion. It was time for a wash.

When it was my turn, I waited for the water to reach scalding before I filled my jugs. As I poured each one over me, I felt the heat work its way through my aching and thrashed muscles, slowly restoring them. When I was almost out of water, I quickly lathered myself with soap and used the last jug to rinse the suds away.

Back in my room, I changed into some fresh clothes and did a short set of stretches; I knew my muscles would scream at me later if I didn't.

I'd learned that lesson when I'd trained with Dad. We'd done a particularly gruelling workout and I was annoyed at him for pushing me so hard, so I'd refused to stay and stretch. The punishment for that choice: I could barely walk the next day.

As I stretched in my exhausted state, my mind stayed blissfully blank and allowed me to just feel the pull of my muscles. I changed stretches after I felt each muscle begin to relax. By the time I'd finished my set it was time for lunch. I raised myself up from the floor and gently shook out each limb, relishing in the feel of my worn body.

Walking down the stairs with my bag over my shoulder, a pit began to build in my stomach. I wondered if Dom would want to see me after finding out about my mum. The thought hollowed me out. I couldn't take much more right now.

Please, please be waiting for me.

UNEXPECTED

RELIEF SURGED THROUGH ME when I spotted Dom's concerned face waiting outside the Academy doors. As soon as I reached him, he enveloped me in a tight hug.

'Don't worry,' he whispered, 'I'm here for you.'

I was glad he was holding me at that moment because otherwise I may have fallen.

He stepped back and looked at me, a troubled smile on his face. 'Why don't you go sit outside? I'll bring lunch out for you.'

I sat and stared, unseeing, into the forest across the field as my worries returned one by one. Dom sat in silence beside me, though I could feel him watching me pick at my food. He must have been extra worried because I realised he hadn't even gotten himself any meat today.

In no time at all the bell rang, signalling the end of lunch. I looked down at my barely touched plate and sighed. I knew I needed to get moving, but the idea of going inside was just too much.

'Hey,' Dom said, 'do you want to go for a walk in the forest or something? Get away from here for a bit.'

I turned and stared at him for a moment. 'What about classes? I mean, I just have personal study until I get my specialist class assignments, but don't you have a class?'

'Yeah, but don't sweat it.' He looked at the emptying area then back at me. 'Let's go—we'll have to be quick. We're really only supposed to go into the forest during lessons with the teachers.'

Before I could say anything else, Dom grabbed my plate and disposed of our uneaten food inside. As he exited again he waved me over. I knew I should just go inside, but the idea was suffocating.

I followed Dom at a run. We stuck close to the wall of the Academy. When we reached the end, he peered around the corner, gave me a nod and sprinted off towards the forest. I followed, pushing myself to keep up with his longer legs. It felt good, like I could breathe a little easier.

Dom continued through the tree line, only slowing a little as the trees became denser. He came to a stop once he reached a rippling stream and I followed suit. A small smile rose on my face at finding this little treasure; I was sure it was the one I'd heard on my first day. I bent down and put my hands into the icy-cold water, forcing it to part around me to continue its journey.

I turned and looked up at Dom. 'Thank you. For bringing me out here.'

He nodded. 'Do you think it'd help to talk about it?'

I looked away. *Would it help? Can't hurt to try... can it?*

As I watched the water trickle by, I took a deep breath in through my nose then released it slowly. 'I'm just so upset and confused. I feel really betrayed by both of my parents. I can't understand why my dad would lie to me about my mum! It's just crazy. Every time I've tried to bring her up, he won't even talk about her. He gets upset. Is that why? And my mum... I thought she was dead. Is she dead? I don't even know. She disappeared when I was little, so I thought she was dead, but maybe she just went back to be with the Sorceresses. I don't even know what to think about her. And I am just so angry with Dad! He could have told me anytime in the last, like, almost thirteen years! And now, Salvatore knows what is going to happen when it's time for me to Shift! Will I even be *able* to Shift? Gah! No wonder Dad was talking to Miss Stone about something maybe going wrong. I can't believe him! How could he not have warned me? Everyone is just going to hate me, I won't fit in anywhere. Am I Shifter? Am I Sorceress? Am I just some weird hybrid cross-breed who no one will like or talk to, with crappy parents who obviously don't love me?'

Panic kicked in and I started taking deep, gulping breaths. I sensed Dom move closer and sit by my side. He snaked an arm around my shoulders as tears began to build and then fall.

This is too much. How could they do this to me?

Eventually my breathing started to slow and the tears dried up. I looked up at Dom.

'Do you feel a little better?'

I huffed. 'Maybe a tiny bit to have said it all, but I don't think it solved any problems—'

'Well, hold on a minute. First up, I may not know all about your mum and dad, but I do know that your new friends aren't going to hate you. Harper will be fine and there's no way I could hate you! You can't choose who your parents are.'

I sniffed. 'Well I guess I know you two won't hate me, but can you imagine what Natasha will say when she finds out? And her friends? I'm sure she'll make a big deal of it. Hell, it is a big deal Dom! I don't even know what I am.'

I jumped up from the ground and started pacing along the stream, trying to calm myself down again.

'Elita?' I looked back at him. 'I'm sure your parents still love you. You said your dad was talking to Miss Stone or something before you came. I'm sure he only did that because he was worried. I don't know what happened with your mum, but I'm sure she had a reason. Maybe the best thing to do would be to just speak to your dad? Or send him a letter with one of the crows?'

Motionless with thought, I watched the water ripple down the stream.

Am I being over-the-top? Surely this reaction would be normal if anyone else actually had this problem, which I doubt they do. Send Dad a letter. I guess I should give him a chance to explain. What about Miss Stone?

'I guess you're right. I could at least give Dad a chance to tell me his side of things, though I really don't see what he could say that would make this right.' I sighed. 'And I think I should go and see Miss Stone, too. She knew my parents when I was a baby.

I think they used to be friends. Maybe she knows more than she was letting on. Actually, I want to speak to her now.'

I turned around and started walking briskly back towards the Academy.

Dom hurried to catch up. 'Hold on. Now? It's the middle of class!'

'So? I think she would understand. This is important.' I jerked to a halt and looked at him, frustrated and doubtful. 'Isn't it?'

'Oh, well, yeah—'

I turned and kept going, once again on a mission to get answers.

He rushed back to my side. 'But, considering, you know, that this is about Sorceresses, shouldn't you wait till her class is finished?'

'Fine,' I grumbled. 'But I'm going to tell her I need to see her urgently.'

'Yep, okay. Sounds like a good plan.'

Dom trailed just a little behind me once we made it into the Academy. At Miss Stone's classroom, I rapped on the door three times and tapped my foot impatiently.

Miss Stone opened the door and looked at me. 'Elita, hello. Can I help you? Shouldn't you be in class?' She glanced behind me. 'And you too, Dominic?'

'Yes. But I need to talk to you urgently. About... my parents.'

Her brow furrowed. 'It can't wait until this evening?'

I felt the heat rise in my face.

Unbelievable.

'No.'

She nodded. 'Very well. Meet me in my office after this class.' She looked back at Dom. 'I trust you can show her the way. Then you can return to your lesson.'

I glanced at Dom in time to see him nod and then looked back just in time to see a shadow of worry cross Miss Stone's face.

Good.

I turned to Dom and waited for him to lead the way to the level where the staffroom was. Once we were on the right floor, he led me past three doors and then stopped and pointed to a pale wooden one. 'This is her office.'

I nodded. 'Okay. I guess we wait.'

He shifted his weight and scuffed his shoe against the floor.

A pit started forming in my stomach again. 'Do you... Do you want to go?'

He looked at me for a moment, then shook his head. 'Nah, it's cool. I'll wait here with you.'

Eventually, light footsteps sounded along the stone hallway and I looked up towards the corridor entrance to see Miss Stone staring at the pair of us.

'Dominic, what are you doing here? I told you to return to class after you showed Elita the way.'

I cut in before Dom could speak. 'I want him here.'

'Do you really think that is the best idea, considering what your father said before we left for the Academy?'

I gritted my teeth. 'I don't care what he thinks. Dom is my friend. Besides, he knows anyway.'

Miss Stone raised her eyebrows. 'He knows?'

'About my mother. We both do.'

The colour drained from her face as she opened the door wide. 'Very well.'

I edged inside quickly, followed by Dom. Miss Stone walked in behind us and pulled the door shut. The room consisted of a packed bookshelf, a desk and three wooden chairs. She indicated that we should take the two seats across from hers. The moment I sat down, my feet started tapping.

'So, what has happened?' she asked.

I looked her dead in the eye. 'I found out my mother is a Sorceress.'

She paused for a moment. 'And how did you find that out?'

'I found her picture in the Sorceress Records room.'

'And how exactly did you end up in that room?' She looked at Dom.

When I glanced over to him, I saw that he'd slouched down in his chair and averted his eyes.

'I showed it to her,' he muttered.

She heaved a sigh. 'And how exactly did you know that it was Elita's mother?'

'I saw Elita's family portrait and recognised her mum because I had to, uh, clean the Sorceress Records room from top to bottom not that long ago.'

'I see.'

It seemed like the small talk had given Miss Stone a chance to pull herself together, because she sat a little straighter in her chair and looked back at me.

'What do you want to know, Elita?'

'How this happened would be a good start. They're our enemies! How did they even end up together?'

She stared at me for a moment, her thoughts clearly churning through her mind. She gave an almost imperceptible nod, maybe to herself more than me.

'Your father and I both used to be liaisons to the Ladies of Light for this Pack. We often travelled to meet their representatives, one of which was your mother. This job started when your father and I were quite young—around your age now. Your father and mother, over time, fell in love. Eventually, they decided to run away and be together, since they knew they couldn't do that here, for obvious reasons. Then,' she smiled gently at me, 'they had you.'

I stared. Floored.

'Do you want to know anything else?'

I needed time to think, to pull myself together, but I knew if I left I wouldn't get such a good opportunity again. There was one thing I really did need the answer to. My stomach turned, nauseated.

Just ask. You need to know.

'What am I? A Shifter? A Sorceress? Is there anyone else like me?'

'I'm not certain, Elita. I have searched high and low for any sign of others like you, but there have been none. You definitely have Shifter in you, I can smell that clearly and so can everyone else. Your father definitely would not have let you attend if you didn't smell of Shifter. But, I can also smell slight traces of Sorceress.'

I sensed Dom turn and stare at me; when I looked at him, I noticed the shock on his face.

'But as you can see by Dominic's reaction, it wouldn't register to anyone who is unfamiliar with Sorceresses. And I'll be perfectly honest, we won't know for sure until you are seventeen, because that is when a Sorceress gets her powers. Your scent will change again if you do obtain magic.'

'I might get...magic?'

Miss Stone nodded.

Magic. Wow.

'What about my mum? What happened to her?'

Miss Stone shifted uncomfortably in her chair.

'You need to tell me! Someone has to tell me! She's my mum. Even if she is a Sorceress!'

'Well, first, you need to understand, she is a good person. She's not evil and she loved you a lot—'

'Loved?' My heart felt like it was stabbed by a sharp, hot knife.

'I'm sorry Elita, I don't have a definite answer for you about her now. But... I will tell you what I do know, though I am positive your father won't thank me for it. I've already meddled enough by giving you that book.' She grimaced. 'When your mother was pregnant with you, a few of the Crone's Sorceresses came looking for her, to kill her. Your parents managed to capture one of them and discovered they were sent there because of a prophecy about her unborn child. But the one your parents captured didn't know much about it. After that, they moved further away from the Sorceresses and Shifters to where you live now, in the Sovereign Mountains. Your mother stayed as long as she could but knew the Crone's and their coven could track her using blood magic; the elemental talismans she used to shield herself from The Ladies of Light would not protect her from the Crones. When you were about three, she decided she would leave and try to discover more about the prophecy. Your parents were both heartbroken. She managed to send some information back to your father about it, but no other reply came and she never returned. I believe the sketch you discovered of her was after she had left you to seek out the prophecy.'

'So, no one knows if she is alive or not now?'

Miss Stone shook her head. 'I'm sorry, Elita.'

'Did anyone even look for her?'

'They did, but she had already been missing for so long from the Ladies of Light that everyone had stopped looking. Your father couldn't risk leaving you to go and search.'

I clutched my churning stomach.

I need to get out of here soon.

'What about the prophecy?'

'I honestly don't know much about that. You will need to ask your father. All I know is that it involved the Crones.'

Dom shifted in his chair. 'Well, that's kind of cool. Must make you pretty special, huh?'

I stared at him blankly. 'But I'm nobody. I'm not special. Why would I have anything to do with the Crones?'

'Well, it sure sounds like you're special. Half Shifter, half Sorceress. You could even have powers.'

I struggled to understand the tone in his voice. It sounded maybe a little awed.

Miss Stone interrupted my wandering thoughts. 'Elita, you mustn't tell anyone else about this. Your mother. The prophecy. Anything. And you mustn't look into it. It is dangerous for you and the Pack.'

'You must be crazy! Of course I need to know what it says!'

'It would be safest if you just asked your father.'

'I'll send Dad a letter to ask for his side of things, but I won't promise not to look into it. I need to know more.'

She nodded at me, but she didn't look happy. 'You can use my personal crow to send your father the letter. Just bring it to me, I swear not to read it. It will be safer than using the school crow, particularly if it returns with a letter for you. You really must be careful, if the Crone's discover your existence here, they will come for you as they did for your mother. I'd say the only thing that has stopped them is they are searching for a Sorceress and you are not only that.'

I nodded and stood, unable to stay any longer. 'Okay. Thank you. We'd better be going now.'

'Yes, it is time to get back to class. Make sure you both go there now. I'll be checking. And be very wary if you discuss these things. You know how good everyone's hearing is. My room has charms I was gifted during my time as liaison to The Ladies of Light, to protect from prying ears, but nowhere else in this castle is a safe place. Understand?'

After getting an affirmative from us, Miss Stone got up and let us go. Despite my original idea of talking with Dom, we decided to head straight to class so we didn't draw any more attention to ourselves.

FORBIDDEN

I SPENT THE NIGHT in my room trying to write my dad a letter. In the end, I scrunched up about six versions before I thought one was clear enough for him to understand. The rest I burned in the fireplace downstairs.

Dear Dad,

I'm sending you this letter because I need answers. And to tell you that I'm so unbelievably mad at you. How could you lie to me for all these years about mum? I found out that she is a Sorceress. A SORCERESS!

My friend showed me a sketch of her in the Sorceress Records room at school. He recognised her from our family portrait. It was drawn after she LEFT US.

I saw Miss Stone after I found out and she told me about how you and mum met and what happened. But I want to hear it from you.

Can you tell me what you know about mum? And why you lied about her? And why she left us in the first place? And about the prophecy?

None of this makes any sense, Dad. I'm no one. I shouldn't even be in a prophecy, let alone one about fighting the Crones!

I wasn't going to say I love you. But, I guess I still do, even though I am furious.

I hope you answer this soon.

Elita.

I tucked the letter under my pillow and went to sleep. It was fitful but I got enough. The next morning, with the letter stashed in my bag, I ate breakfast outside on the logs with Dom. After I said goodbye and we went our separate ways, I headed straight to Miss Stone's office. She took the letter from me with a tight nod just as the morning bell rang. I ran off to my first class, determined not to be late again.

By the time lunch came around my brain was a disorganised mess spinning on repeat about my mum being a Sorceress and whether I would be one too, or if I'd be a Shifter. Or maybe even just a human.

I ignored my usual sick feeling and grabbed a plate of lunch; just salad and bread today, which was enough to satisfy my hunger, but some well-cooked steak (prepared nowhere near me) would have been more fulfilling. I gave Dom a half-hearted wave when he showed up to eat with me.

'Hey, how was your morning session?' he asked. 'Mine was okay. I did Weapons and Sorceress Lore with Miss Stone. That was pretty awkward!'

I laughed a little. 'I bet it was. Mine was fine. I had Hunting Strategies and Shifter History. My head is a mess, to be honest.'

'Hey, it'll be okay. You have library time after lunch again, right? It's my day for that as well. Maybe we should check around for some of that stuff we learned about with Miss Stone?'

'Yeah, that's a good idea. Do you think it would be okay to ask the librarian?'

Dom scrunched his face while he thought. 'I don't see why not. As long as we're pretty vague. Just prophecies in general, about Sorceresses and stuff. We can always say it's for Miss Stone's class.'

Energised at the thought of getting answers, I stood up. 'Yeah, good idea. Okay. Let's go.'

'Woah! Hold up, I want to eat my lunch first!' When I looked at him, he gave me a big goofy grin and started scoffing his bloody chunk of meat. I looked away so I wouldn't have to watch it ooze, and could focus on the scent of the pine trees rather than the blood. Shocked, I realised I must be getting used to the scent a little because until I focused on it, I hadn't really noticed—or maybe I'd just adapted to the constant nausea in my system.

Now that I'd made a decision, I bounced my legs up and down as I waited for Dom. Not that he took ages or anything. Within a couple of minutes I heard him licking his chops. I could picture him doing that in his wolf form and was sure it would look just as hilarious.

'Okay, ready!'

When we entered the library, we stopped and looked around for the librarian. Dom spotted her in the scrolls section. The all-too-familiar feeling of butterflies returned to my stomach. I looked up at Dom.

'I'll do the talking, if you want?' he offered.

I nodded, relieved, and followed him to the librarian. I stood to his left and a little behind him.

'Hi, Miss Deerling. I was wondering if you had anything in here about prophecies?'

She clutched a dark stone around her neck and gave Dom a sharp look that caused the butterflies in my stomach to increase their flight speed.

'What sort of prophecies?' she asked sternly.

'Oh, you know, ones with the Crones in them. It's for a task for Miss Stone.' Dom grinned easily at the librarian. I envied him.

'Everything we have on prophecies is in the scroll section. If you want to look in there, you'll need written permission from one of the teachers, as usual. Miss Stone, in this case.'

'Okay, no worries. Thanks, Miss Deerling.' Dom turned to me and raised his eyebrows. 'Let's go sit down and do the rest of our assignment.'

I nodded and led the way back towards the chairs by the fireplace. I curled up on the one closest to the fire. Dom sat down opposite me.

It took a little while for the librarian's eyes to stop wandering over to us.

Over the following week, Dom and I looked around the rest of the library with hopes of finding a mention of the prophecy. When that hadn't worked we had decided to sneak into the library in the evening but, to our dismay, the librarian had locked the scrolls away. We'd even asked Miss Stone for written permission to access the scrolls, and were met with a resounding no, along with a stern lecture.

On a dreary Monday afternoon, I was sitting by the fire in the library doing my best to forget about the prophecy and get some work done when all hell broke loose.

BANG!

Glass and stone were blown everywhere. Part of the roof and wall had exploded. I hissed as shards dug into my arms, stinging. Kids and teachers screamed and coughed all around me. I looked through the haze and saw a group of shadowy figures right underneath the hole, standing on the debris.

'We're being invaded!' screamed one of the students.

I crouched behind the end of the sofa, heart thudding, trying to stay out of the way as I watched what was going on. My heart stopped when I realised that one of the invaders was a Crone. Her wraith-like appearance was exactly as Miss Stone had described it in the story. I sucked in a ragged breath; she was terrifying. Shock froze me in place for a moment as I realised that meant there were Sorceresses in the Academy.

Please don't let this be my fault!

The invaders wore cloaks that looked as though they were dipped in dark blood. The red lines that were smeared across their faces transformed them into a vicious vision of death. Potions were thrown and spells were cast; they looked like black and red lights weaving together then colliding as they sped through the air. The wolves touched by the magic froze or collapsed, their faces masks of fear.

A string of screamed instructions came from behind me, telling students to leave out the back exit, when suddenly the doors to the Library crashed inwards. More wolves flooded the room and attacked the Sorceresses. Teeth and claws and weapons flew everywhere. The Sorceresses were nowhere near as competent with their weapons and were not able to protect themselves once the wolves got close enough to attack them physically.

Forcing my heartbeat to slow by breathing deeply, I kept watch from my position, trying to take in all the details of the fight. The Sorceresses's magic reached the Shifters within seconds of being cast. They needed to get closer. Too many of the Pack were being killed and injured.

After yet another wolf was blown away, most of the dust with it, I saw her.

Mum!

I stood and blinked, unable to believe my eyes. She was standing in the middle of the fight with her hands bound in a thick cord.

Look at me! Mum!

As if by magic her amber eyes turned and locked with mine. They widened, panic flooding her features. Within seconds she whipped her head away. A hand tugged on my shoulder. I ignored it, waiting to catch my mum's gaze again.

Look back at me! Why'd you turn away?!

I started forward, desperate to regain her attention, when a hand pulled at me again. Furious, I turned. It was Miss Stone. Fear and concern were etched into her face.

'You can't, Elita. We need to go. I'm sorry.'

'I'm not leaving her!'

'You need to. Now. Our Shifters are starting to make traction. But her being here can only mean one thing. They know. They know you're here. The Pack is being hurt and killed and they are looking for you. We need to go. Now.'

I squeezed my eyes shut tight, guilt filling my insides. Unable to help myself, I turned back to look at my mum, but immediately noticed she was looking at a wolf. A wolf that wasn't moving. One with the peppered hair.

No! Our Alpha. Natasha's father.

I allowed Miss Stone to pull me away, my gaze alternating between my mum and Natasha's father. He'd Shifted back to his human form, but he still didn't move.

Is he... dead?

'Come, Elita. Now.' Miss Stone hissed in my ear. 'Your mother isn't going to be happy if you get hit by a spell simply because you didn't want to leave her there. Move!'

Painful as it was, I knew she was right. I forced myself to follow my teacher quickly towards the exit at the back of the Library.

Before we went out the door, I took one last look back at the scene of chaos. The Sorceress's numbers seemed to be dwindling as they backed towards the hole they'd come in through. Wolves surrounded them from every angle now. I knew they'd make their escape soon; the Crone seemed to be hovering from the floor already. I paused as I saw my mum being dragged aggressively backwards by her dress. Right at that moment she turned her head and met my eyes for a brief moment, relief flooding her desperate features before she looked away again.

She was watching. She really does care about me.

My heart swelled, though guilt soon followed when I thought about Natasha's father and the other five or six Pack members who probably wouldn't be walking out of here today.

I followed Miss Stone down the corridor and into what looked like a hall. It was cavernous and full of Shifter kids and teachers.

'I need to go to the other teachers, Elita. Stay with Dominic.'

My head whirled around; I hadn't even noticed that he was with us.

'Where'd you come from?'

'Miss Stone called me over when you came into the room. Didn't you hear her? I mean, it's pretty loud in here... but you know, Shifter hearing?'

I shook my head. 'My mum is alive, Dom! I just saw her, just now!'

'Your mum?' His brow furrowed, concern covering his face. 'But... I heard it was the Crone Sorceresses and one of the Crones. Does that mean...?'

Shock hit me when I realised what he must have been thinking. 'No! No, she was a prisoner. Her hands were tied up with something. No, she's good, like Miss Stone said, and she *looked* at me, Dom! I mean, she didn't look for long, I guess she was trying to protect me, but she saw me. And I saw her!'

He grinned. 'That is awesome! Well, awesome that she's alive. Not so much that she's a prisoner and probably gone again. But...'

My smile faltered a little and my heart started to plunge. I'd been so excited that my mother was alive and here that I hadn't really thought about the fact that she was about to be taken away again, that the Shifters wouldn't try to rescue her. I turned for the door and started weaving my way through a different kind of chaos, one where fear and grief reigned and kids shouted and sobbed and held onto each other. Within a minute, I'd slipped past a teacher and back out the door, Dom close on my heels.

He tried to call out to me but I didn't have time to talk. I had to get back and stop my mum from being taken away again. They couldn't take her. I ran up the stairs, two at a time. On the library level, I came to an abrupt halt. The sound of fighting was gone and there were Shifters everywhere, some in human form, some as wolves. Small moans escaped some of them as words of comfort were offered by those who kept them company. Others looked dead.

I felt all the warmth leave my body. There were too many dead. *This is all my fault. It's my fault they're dead.*

I felt Dom's hand on my arm, he was saying something but I didn't understand. My vision began to waver and the ground rushed up to meet me.

A series of gentle taps landed on my face and a voice called out to me.

'Elita? Elita, can you hear me?'

I blinked repeatedly and my vision slowly came into focus. Miss Stone was leaning over me with a worried look on her face. Dom stood behind her buzzing with tension.

'What... happened?'

'You fainted!' Dom called over her shoulder. 'As soon as you saw everyone in the corridor.'

Miss Stone shook her head. 'Do you think you can sit up?'

I thought about how I felt; besides being massively anxious and a little out of it, I thought I was okay.

The corridor was almost the same, but a few of the Pack had been moved.

The dead ones.

'You look like a ghost, Elita. You need to move away from here and go downstairs with everyone else.'

I shook my head and looked at the Library.

'She's not there, Elita. I'm sorry.'

'But surely someone saw she was a prisoner? Didn't anyone try to help?'

'I don't know. I had to leave and take you and the last of the other students downstairs. Everyone who was left behind was fighting for their lives and the lives of the Pack. I doubt they considered any of the Sorceresses.'

'Did she... make it out?'

Miss Stone looked me in the eyes as she spoke, her tone soft but reassuring. 'I think so, Elita. She wasn't here when I got back. I'm sure she's okay.'

Yeah, she'll be fine. She's survived for this long. She's okay.

Even as I tried to convince myself, I felt my body begin to shiver and my teeth chatter.

'Dom, can you please take her back downstairs? I really need to see what I can do to help up here. We have a lot of Pack issues right now because...' She looked away without finishing her sentence, but I knew.

'Axel didn't make it.'

Her head whipped back to me, surprise clear on her face. She obviously didn't think I'd noticed with everything going on and my mum being in the room, but I'd been trained to notice.

'Yes, and that means...' She turned and looked at Dom.

'My Dad is Alpha now,' Dom said quietly.

When Miss Stone nodded, he looked grim. Dom straightened his shoulders a little and thanked her before turning to help me up.

'Come on, let's go Elita. We'll be in the way up here. They'll fill us in later.'

Seeing that I was on my way, Miss Stone left and disappeared into the Library.

'You okay, Dom?'

He smiled tightly at me. 'Yeah, sure. Things will probably be a bit different around here now. This wasn't really meant to happen. A Beta has only ever needed to be initiated into the position once before. This will only be the second Alpha not of the original lineage.'

'What do you mean, the original lineage?'

'It was a pretty big scandal, Dad told me. It happened when he was younger. The Alpha of this Pack has always been from Salvatore's line until, like, fourteen years ago. The Alpha's heir ran away and hasn't been heard from since. When his father—our Alpha—passed on, Axel took the position. He was the first Beta to take it. My father was made the new Beta because our family lines have also been around since the beginning, though I think our families used to be sentinels. But now Dad will take up the position.'

'He'll be great at it. Don't worry,' I said.

Dom gave me a small smile and nodded. 'Thanks.'

EMOTIONS

I NSIDE THE HALL, THE teachers had managed to rein in the chaos. Students sat quietly in small groups and comforted one another, but I was sure that it would get crazy again as soon as they heard the news.

I spotted Natasha sitting with her friends, looking irritated as usual.

She doesn't know.

My stomach twisted. Naturally, she chose that point to meet my eyes and give me a sneer. I couldn't even manage to make myself return it. Instead, I felt like crying. I saw a puzzled look on her face as I turned to Dom. I tugged frantically on his sleeve to get his attention. 'No one has told her, Dom. Who is going to tell her? She can't find out in the general announcement.'

He gave me a small nod and looked around the room. When relief crossed his features, I followed his gaze. His father had come in.

'Give me a sec? I'll find out before he makes it to the front.'

Before I had time to reply, Dom shot off to his father. I watched from a distance as they spoke. There was no chance of overhearing a specific conversation in this room. When Dom came back, he let me know the plan.

'Since we know what's happened, we need to take her to Miss Stone.'

I sighed. As cowardly as I knew it was, I didn't want to be there when she found out. I'd already had a slice of losing a parent in my life, and I wouldn't wish it on anyone. Not even Natasha.

Dom led the way and I trailed a little behind him until we reached her. I glanced at his Dad and realised he was looking this way, probably waiting for us to take her before he addressed the Pack.

Natasha scowled. 'What do you two want?'

'We need you to come for a walk with us,' Dom said, a serious tone in his voice.

A look of incredulous disbelief crossed her face. 'I'm not going anywhere with you two.'

When she turned back to her friends, Dom tapped her lightly on the shoulder. 'I'm afraid you need to. It's Pack business.'

I didn't know how Dom was keeping his voice so even. My thoughts were in turmoil and my dad wasn't even the new Alpha. Natasha huffed and rolled her eyes at her friends before directing us to lead the way.

I walked beside Dom, but I couldn't help glancing back at Natasha a few times. When she started to lose a bit of her usual snarky demeanour and began looking concerned, I scolded my-self.

Eyes forward. Stop looking at her. This will be horrific enough.

She followed us without a word until we got to the library corridor. When she saw where we were, she stopped abruptly. Even those who hadn't been involved had now discovered there had been an attack of some sort.

Natasha stopped and looked at us with wide eyes. 'What are we doing up here?'

Dread had crept into her voice and I couldn't stop the tears that started to form in my eyes. I kept looking ahead and let Dom speak to her.

Gently he said, 'We need to take you in to Miss Stone.'

When we didn't move, I turned a little to look at her, trying to hide my tears. But it was no use. She knew something was wrong now. There were tears on her face. She shook her head back and forth. Stuck. I reached out a hand to her, but she shoved it away.

'No. No, no, no.'

Miss Stone walked out of the library doors and over to us. The look on her face was heartbreaking, but it was nothing compared to the horror on Natasha's. Natasha dropped to the ground and screamed. It was a sound so desolate and loud that I was sure every Shifter would hear it and feel her pain.

I went to step forward again, but Dom grabbed my hand and held me back. Miss Stone knelt down on the floor and embraced Natasha.

'I'm so sorry, Natasha. He fought bravely and saved many lives of the Pack. He protected us fiercely from the Crone and her Sorceresses. I'm sorry.'

Natasha howled and sobbed and clung on to Miss Stone for dear life. I was glad I had Dom there. I looked up at him through my tears and saw them trailing down his cheeks as well. I hugged him and rested my head on his chest. This was going to be a devastating day for the whole Pack, but not as bad as it would be for Natasha.

We stood there for what felt like an eternity. Then suddenly Natasha shot up out of Miss Stone's arms, her shirt wet from the tears still streaming down her face.

'I want to see him. I want to see my father.'

'Natasha, I don't think that is a good idea.'

'He's my father. I want to see him. I—' Her voice broke. 'I need to see him.'

Miss Stone looked conflicted but, after a few moments, decided to take her in. Natasha walked past us without making eye contact, but after she'd gone a few feet she stopped and looked back. 'Thank you,' she said quietly, then turned and kept going. I knew the haunted look on her face would stick with me for a long time to come.

Feeling shaken, I turned back to Dom. 'Come on, let's go back down. We aren't needed here now.'

He nodded and led the way. We walked slower than usual and I wondered how much his life was about to change with his father being Alpha.

I wonder if that'll mean he'll have other duties now. Surely not. Natasha always seemed to be around.

I was shocked I could even think about that right now.

Stop being so selfish. Natasha lost her dad, Dom's life is changing. Hell, I have enough on my own plate with my mum and everything.

Before I realised it, we were downstairs and back in the hall. It looked like the speech had finished and Dom's dad had left the stage; I looked around but couldn't see him anywhere. What I did see was sadness. So much sadness. All the kids, and even the staff, were mourning their Pack leader and the others who had died. I began to feel a little glad that I hadn't been here for very long and that I didn't know any of them as well as the rest of the Pack did.

Dom told me he'd catch up with me later then disappeared to find his dad. I thought about sitting with Harper, but I needed some time in my own head, so I left.

After I pulled on my training clothes, I left the dorm. Sticking to the tree line, I started jogging. When it wasn't enough, I ran. Once I cleared the Academy grounds and made it to the forest, I let instinct take over and sprinted, weaving in and out of trees, ducking branches, jumping off rocks.

I stopped at the stream and splashed water on my face. The icy temperature broke through my feelings. It felt so good, I took my shoes off and walked in.

Feet planted in the centre, I breathed in and out as the icy water rippled around me. With each inhale and exhale my thoughts turned to focus on my mother. Her sandy-coloured hair, her amber eyes and how she'd widened them when she first saw me. Then how she'd looked away almost immediately after recognising me. My heart swelled.

She recognised me. Even after all these years, she knew it was me.

I touched my mouth as I felt my lips curve up into a smile for the first time since the break in.

My mother is really alive. And she actually recognised me.

I turned and sat on the edge of the stream with my feet in, and began running my hands through the water. Replaying the moment over and over in my mind, I recalled things I'd noticed: her eyes; the shape of her face; that we were almost the same height.

But then my mind strayed to reality: the ties around her hands; how worn and skinny she'd looked; how the loose, pale dress hung loosely on her body. I saw the two Crone Sorceresses that clung to her, making sure she couldn't escape.

Over and over, I saw the Shifters in my Pack hit what looked like an invisible wall and get thrown back. I remembered seeing Axel, hit by the Crone's magic and shifting back to human form, never moving again. Dead.

I touched my face when the cool air hit it. Tears. Again. All I seemed to do lately was cry.

At least Dad would be proud that I noticed everything in the invasion, that I didn't lose focus. Well, mostly.

I pondered what would happen with Dom's dad and wondered if there would be some kind of ceremony for the new Alpha, and if anything would change at the Academy.

Does it matter? I need to leave and rescue Mum.

I considered all the things I would need: maps, internal drawings of Crone Keep, food and weapons. Then I wondered about Dom.

Don't be ridiculous. I can't ask Dom to go with me for something like that. He could end up dead. And his dad just became Alpha.

The sky through the trees had darkened. Reluctantly, I pulled my feet from the water and put my shoes back on, hating the wet feeling. Feeling somewhat calm now that I had a basic plan, including the knowledge that I was definitely going to rescue my mum, I walked back to the Academy. Judging by the sky, it would be about dinner time, so I made my way through the tree line then along the building to the Food Den. Ignoring my now-faint nausea at the scent of cooking meat, I lined up behind some kids.

'Hey, Elita. How are you doing?' said Harper.

I smiled. 'Oh hey, I didn't see you there. I think I'm a bit out of it, with everything going on. You?

'Yeah, same. It's crazy. I can't believe our Alpha is gone, though the ascension ceremony tomorrow will be interesting.'

Her cheeks turned a deep rouge when the Shifters next to us turned and gave her a sharp look.

'Hey, back off,' I said to them.

They eyed me, but turned around. I gave her hand a tight squeeze.

Yeah, there's no way Harper could go with me. At least she'd probably just be interested if she found out about me and my mum, not hate me.

Ignoring the concerned look of the server, I ordered salad and bread then followed Harper outside to eat. She knew that I didn't like to eat inside. I remembered when she'd asked me about my aversion to wolf-style meat, curious as ever, and her shocked face when I'd told her how sick it made me feel.

'How are you doing, Harper? I feel like I haven't seen you much lately.'

She laughed quietly. 'You've only been here for, like, almost a couple of weeks! But thank you for asking. No one ever does. I'm doing okay, keeping to myself like usual, and studying. I was in the library, when, you know...'

'Ah, yeah. I was there too.'

'It was so scary. I was lucky that I was right near the exit. Can you imagine if they had busted in on the other side? We'd probably be dead. What about you?'

'I wasn't too scared,' I said quietly. 'I'm not trying to be brave or anything. I was just distracted, I guess. Taking notice of what was happening with the Crone and her Sorceresses. The magic, all the colours as they cast spells.'

Harper looked shocked. 'What do you mean colours? I didn't see any colours.'

My stomach twisted. 'Oh.'

She shook her head. 'It was probably just the light reflecting from the stained glass window or something.'

Trust Harper to explain it away. I'll have to ask Miss Stone about it later.

'Yeah, probably. So what time is the ceremony tomorrow? I missed it because Dom and I had to take Natasha to... Miss Stone.'

Harper became solemn. 'To her father?'

'Yeah.' I shifted on the log and crossed my legs, then picked at more of my food.

'The ceremony will be out on the lawns behind the Academy at midnight tonight and there won't be any classes tomorrow so we can rest. In the afternoon, the funeral will be on.

'Right, that makes sense.'

We sat in silence for the rest of our meal, caught up in our own thoughts. When Harper finished, she took both of our plates and disposed of them.

'Ready to go?'

'Yeah, sure. You haven't seen Dom about have you?'

She raised her eyebrows. 'You guys have something going on there?'

I felt my cheeks heat. 'No! Of course not! We're just friends!'

She smiled and started walking. 'No, I haven't seen him, sorry. He might be with his dad or back in the dorms.'

'I'm serious, there's nothing going on!'

'Yeah, yeah. Come on. I want to have a wash.'

I grumbled as I caught up with Harper.

Like Dom? Sheesh. Can't we just be friends? Do all girls and guys have to be together?

I walked into the Common Room behind Harper and waved as she left to go upstairs. My eyes combed the space in search of Dom. Nothing. I decided to check up at his dorm room before I settled on the couch by the fire. Taking the stairs two at a time, I reached the second floor in less than a minute. I found his door, number five, and knocked.

I heard someone moving around inside, steps coming closer, and then the door opened. Dom looked sad and serious.

'Hey. You doing okay? I couldn't find you at dinner,' I said.

'Oh, yeah. Sorry. I just didn't feel up to it after this morning. Then I had to go and spend time with my dad. We had a *chat*.'

My brow furrowed. 'Oh. Did you want to talk about it?'

'Nah, not really. Do you want to head downstairs and just chill out? Maybe play a game with the guys or something?'

I hesitated, then shrugged. 'Yeah, sure.'

'Unless... is there something that you wanted to talk about? I know you've had a crazy day, too.'

Even though I did want to talk to him about my plan to rescue my mum, I knew now wasn't the time.

'Maybe later. Let's go hang out with the guys.'

It turned out that the guys wanted to play a kicking game, so we went out to the field behind the dorm rooms.

'Hey, how are you?' I asked them all.

Why is it that I'm more comfortable with boys than girls?

I got a chorus of hellos in return before most of them rushed to the field. Oliver stayed behind to walk with me. I looked up at him by my side and noticed a whitish glow on his inky black hair from the moonlight. His deep blue eyes met mine. 'Hey, I heard you were up in the library today, when the explosion and stuff happened. You 'kay?'

I smiled lightly. 'Yeah, sure. I'm all good. Were you in the hall when Dom's dad made the speech?'

'Yeah, I was there. It was pretty miserable. Some kids were taken outside and then he told us that the Sorceresses had invaded. He let us know who was injured and who... didn't make it.' His face was marred by a concerned frown.

I swallowed the lump in my throat and nodded. 'Yeah, Dom and I took Natasha upstairs to Miss Stone. It was pretty horrible. I didn't realise they'd waited and taken the others out too. That's something.'

He looked into my eyes. 'It'll be okay. I'm sure those scum Sorceresses won't be back. They might have killed the Alpha but we won't be blindsided again.'

What had started as a tingly feeling at his protectiveness immediately turned into a scowl and me shrugging him off.

That's my mother you're talking about.

Kicking the ball around suddenly felt like a good idea. I ignored the shocked look on Oliver's face and ran off to join the game.

I might have been a little less strong than the guys, but I was certainly as quick, if not quicker, than most of them. It was a breeze compared to training with Dad. I raced along the field, kicking the ball in between them. I had to jump to miss a few slide tackles. I grinned and laughed when they groaned about it.

By the end of the game my team had won seven to three. Once we were back inside I was ready to have some time to myself. I gave Dom a quick hug goodnight and headed upstairs to wash off the stress of the day.

ASCENSION

JUST BEFORE MIDNIGHT, WE were all called to go to the field. I pulled on some of my nicer clothes, not knowing what to expect. When I walked into the hall and Harper saw me, she gave a little chuckle. Apparently I'd overdressed.

'Should I change?'

'No need. We won't be Shifting or moving around like the others anyway.' Her brow furrowed. 'Unless you can Shift already?'

I shook my head, feeling excited and nervous about my birthday almost being here, then followed her down the stairs and outside. All of the kids merged together as they made their way around the side of the Academy. Everyone was creating a giant circle; it looked like a replica of the full moon above us.

I wonder if this was prophesied?

I walked with Harper, and sat between some of the other First Years and looked around, noticing for the first time some adults I hadn't seen before. Once we were all seated, a woman I hadn't seen before moved into the centre of the circle and began to talk.

'We are here, under the light of the full moon, to share in the Ascension of our new Imperial Pack Alpha: Corbin Silva. I stand before you as a descendant of the first Pack Medicine Woman. It is my sacred duty to reside over this ceremony.

'Corbin Silva, please step forward and place your hand on the Book of Wolves.'

Dom's dad stepped forward, face grim under the light of the moon. He placed his hand on the tome and looked at the Medicine Woman.

'Repeat after me: I, Corbin Silva, swear my loyalty to the Pack. I will put the interests, wellbeing and safety of my Pack above all else. I swear to support all women, men and children to the best of my ability. To seek and provide care as it is needed. I will protect my Pack, if needed, with my life. In the names of Salvatore, Mikhail and Demetrius, The Great Wolf Lords, I do so swear.'

Dom's dad repeated each line, looking around at the Pack members as he did. Once he'd finished, the Medicine Woman spoke again.

'All rise, and hail Corbin Silva. Imperial Pack Alpha.'

I was not prepared for what happened next. Everyone stood up and Shifted, including Dom's dad. For a few moments, it was like an explosion of shimmering earthy tones, weaving between one Shifter and the next. The circle remained but was now full of wolves standing on all fours in shades of black, brown, grey and the occasional white. Their faces tilted up to the sky as they bayed in unison at the moon. The sound of so many wolves howling was deafening.

How did they all know to do this?

I looked around and took in the sight of the Shifters. Because everyone had sat in year order around the circle, I was able to pick out Dom, his dark brown coat a perfect match for our new Alpha's. Corbin was huge, but Dom was already almost as large as him. I watched him howl along with the rest but while everyone else howled to the moon, Dom and his dad looked to each other.

Once the howling stopped, our new Alpha took off to the east, leading the Pack through the open field and into the forest. The howls and yips could be heard even after they'd breached the tree line.

I watched them for a moment and then turned to Harper. 'So... what do we do while they're gone?'

She shrugged. 'Just wait, I guess. They won't be gone for long. From what I've read in the Pack history books the kids don't normally participate in this, but because it's a bit of an emergency situation, I suppose it had to happen this way. The Pack run is an important part of the ceremony to show our unity and togetherness. Our new Alpha must also show that he can lead us.'

'Who normally participates then?'

'All the adult members of the Pack. It's actually meant to be quite a big and prestigious ceremony, with a hunt at the end. The books state it must be on a full moon, so I suppose they would normally wait for the next one to prepare, but given the attack I assume they wanted someone in the position immediately. It's been a long time since we've had an Alpha killed, especially here. At least some Pack members from the town outside the Academy are here.'

'Oh, well that makes sense. Do you think they'll do another ceremony for him?'

'No, I don't think so. Though I'm willing to bet we'll have more Shifters arrive soon to greet him and offer their support and allegiance. Plus, plans will need to be made for the Pack and what not. Dom's dad has been involved since he was chosen as the Beta though, so he would know pretty much everything.'

Harper was quiet for a few moments as she surveyed the other First Years left behind. 'Natasha isn't here. I mean, it makes sense with her dad and everything.'

'Yeah. I can't imagine she feels like celebrating right now. Will her mum come to see her?'

Harper looked away and shuffled her feet. 'She doesn't have a mum. I heard she passed away during childbirth.'

I was floored. My insides turned cold with dread.

Poor Natasha.

It wasn't a thought I'd ever anticipated having, considering she'd been so nasty since I'd arrived. Maybe this explained why. I didn't want to really think about it.

I should check on her... Who am I kidding? She hates me! I'm probably the last person she wants to see. But still...

'Harper, do I need to stay here? For when they come back.'

She looked shocked. 'Well, no. I guess not. But, where are you going?'

'I'm just... tired. I'm gonna go and lay down.'

Her eyes bored into mine. 'You're going to see her, aren't you?'

I dug the toe of my shoe into the ground. 'Yeah. I feel like someone should. This has to be so hard for her. She has no one.'

'But *you*?'

'Yeah, I know. She hates me, but I feel like I need to do it.'

'Do you want me to come?'

I thought about it. Having company going to see Natasha could be a plus but, considering how things were between them, I decided that would be too cruel.

'That's okay. You stay. I'm sure they'll be back in no time at all and then everyone will head in for bed anyway. I'll see you in the morning?'

'Okay. See you then.' She sounded a little disappointed.

I gave her a quick hug and was happy to see her face lighten up before I turned and headed back to the dorms to find Natasha.

I glanced quickly around the Common Room, expecting it to be empty, and was surprised to see Natasha sitting on the couch by the fire. Her back was to me, but I knew she'd have heard me come in. We were the only ones here. I walked over and sat down opposite her. Her face was dry, but her eyes were rimmed with red and looked bleary from crying.

'Hey,' I said quietly. 'How are you doing? I mean, I know bad. But...?'

She sneered. 'What do you care? Why aren't you out there celebrating like everyone else?'

'I care because you just lost your dad. Look, I know we aren't friends, and that you hate me or whatever, but I still wanted to check and ask if there's anything I can do.'

She stared at me for what seemed like an eternity, looking as though she was trying to decide what to say. Eventually, she pulled her legs up tighter against her chest and leaned her head on the thick arm of the lounge.

'Miss Stone said he fought really hard but died protecting some of the kids who were there.' She sucked in a broken, angry breath. 'But I wish he'd just let them die so I could still have him.'

The tears had started streaming down her face again.

'You don't mean that. He was strong and brave and the best protector the Pack had. You wouldn't have wanted him to let others die.'

She didn't answer, the tears making her face shine in the light of the fire.

'Do you want to tell me about him?'

After another few minutes of silence, I was getting ready to leave, but then she spoke again. 'He was the best dad. Even though he was Alpha, he still always made time for me. We did lots together. He took me hunting in the forests, and fishing in the streams and rivers. He even took me to visit the other Packs, once he'd become Alpha and before I started here. He was kind and fair to everyone and never turned a Shifter away. Whenever I'd get into trouble at school, which was a bit too often for his liking, he'd just hug me and ask me to come up with what I could have done better. He was always trying to get me to be my best self.' She stopped and looked me dead in the eyes. 'And you're right. He'd be disappointed that I said that. He wouldn't have wanted it.'

I gave her a genuine smile. 'He sounds like an amazing dad. It's great that he spent so much time with you, even after becoming Alpha. It would have been hard to share him with everyone else.'

She nodded. 'That's why he took me on the trips, I think. Always tried to include me in everything. He certainly didn't pull back any stops in training me.'

We both laughed. 'My dad never has either. Training is serious business.'

'It is,' she said quietly. 'I'm... going to try and sleep. Thank you, though. For talking with me.'

My lips curved up, glad that I was able to help her a little. When she'd almost made it to the door, she turned back and gave me a half-hearted sneer.

'Don't think this changes anything though. Got it?'

I grinned and shook my head. 'Yeah, I got it.'

Once I heard the yips and howls die down outside and footsteps and voices heading this way, I escaped to my room upstairs, thinking as I went.

Okay. The plan: Get maps from the library, ask Dom for help to find the internal drawings for Crone Keep, then pack and leave. Find mum, rescue her and come back to the Academy. Easy.

I knew everything would be much harder than my simple outline and that it would require more planning and details, but it felt good to have a plan.

I laid back in my bed and closed my eyes. After the craziness of the day, I knew it wouldn't take me long to fall asleep.

After my morning wash, I waited for Dom on our usual couch in the Common Room. The atmosphere in the room was sombre as everyone waited for the funeral. When he came into the room he looked... different. He stood a little taller and even his clothes seemed to be cleaner and straighter. He was more serious.

'Hey, Dom,' I said hesitantly as he approached. 'How are you this morning?'

'I'm all right. You?'

'I'm... good. Okay.'

He tilted his head at me. 'Want to go for a walk?'

'Yeah, sure. Sounds good.'

I wish I could go for a run.

I followed Dom out the building's main door, along the tree line and into the field. He didn't talk until we'd passed the Academy. He kept looking back at it, frowning.

'What is it, Dom?'

'Uh, I guess I just don't know if I'm meant to be out here at the moment or if I should be in with Dad. Preparing, you know?'

'Oh. Right. Do you want to go back?'

He shook his head. 'Nah. I need a walk. Besides, I want to know how you're doing. I feel like you got the biggest shock ever yesterday, on top of everything else that happened, and I haven't had a chance to ask about your mum.'

'Oh. Well, uh, don't think I'm crazy but...' I looked around '...I'm going to rescue her.'

He looked shocked, and I quickly added, 'That is, if the Imperial team won't go and rescue her. Obviously I won't say she's my mum, but just "their prisoner".'

He shook his head and then was quiet for a few minutes. As each one ticked past, my chest felt tighter and tighter.

Relax. It's not like he'd turn you in or anything. Would he? His dad is Alpha now. No. Don't be ridiculous. He was your friend before he was the Alpha's son.

'How about I ask him about rescuing the prisoner? I don't think you should draw attention to yourself. Just in case, you know, someone puts things together?'

It was like my heart melted into a pool of mush. He was just so thoughtful. 'Are you sure? I mean, that would be so amazing! But I don't want to cause trouble with you and your dad again.'

'Nah it's all good. I'll ask him. Tonight or tomorrow, yeah? I don't want to bring it up before the funeral.'

'Of course! It can wait. There are some things I'll need to do anyway before I leave, if they won't go. It'll probably take me a bit to organise. Speaking of, I hate to ask but, do you know where they keep the internal drawings for Crone Keep?'

'Uh, well, yeah. But do you think maybe we could wait until I see if Dad will send a team first?'

I sighed. 'Yeah, I suppose, but I won't wait too long. I need to get her back. I don't want them to hurt her because they didn't find me when they attacked the Academy.' I was quiet for a moment, then added in a hushed tone, 'I don't think I could stand one more death happening because of me. This was all my fault. Natasha's dad, everyone who died or got hurt, it was because of me.'

A chill came over me and I wrapped my arms tightly around my chest.

'Hey. Stop. Look at me.'

I turned to Dom, tears partially blurring my vision.

'It is *not* your fault. None of those deaths are your fault. Not even your mum being a prisoner, or failing to stop her from being taken away. How could you possibly know that looking for information about a prophecy would lead to that?'

I shrugged. 'You know, I spoke to Natasha last night, to see how she was doing. Her dad, her only parent left, is gone and he wouldn't be if I hadn't looked into that prophecy. The prophecy that Miss Stone told me *not* to look into.'

'For all you know, they would have attacked the school any-way. They obviously already knew about the prophecy and they might have come looking eventually. And hey, I was looking into it as well so if you're determined to take the blame for this, then you at least have to share it with me.'

I sniffled, feeling a tiny bit better. 'Thanks. Let's just forget about it for now, until you can ask your dad about rescuing my mum. Then I guess I'll figure it out from there.'

'We'll figure it out. Not just you. Okay?' At my questioning look he said, 'Elita, this place never felt so much like home until you got here. I'm here for you okay?'

Heat rose in my cheeks at his declaration and I was sure the colour of mine matched his own. I gave him a small smile and nodded. I knew I needed to focus on other things to distract myself, though where we had to go next was certainly not going to help.

'Shall we get going?' I looked up at the sky to hide my feelings. 'It has to be about time to go to the funeral.'

He sighed and looked a little less determined, a little more sad. 'Yeah, let's go.'

I sat with the other First Years at the burial ground not far outside of the Academy gates and watched Dom trail off to the Second Years.

The Medicine Woman was up the front with Dom's dad, Miss Stone and Natasha, next to a wooden coffin. There were a few other adult Shifters I didn't recognise that stood close by them.

Friends of Axel's maybe?

The teachers were dispersed throughout the rest of the students, probably to keep them in line, though it certainly looked unnecessary, and other Pack members were at the back of the students. Everyone was quiet, waiting for the burial ceremony to start.

Harper sat on my left and Ingrid, one of the other First Years, on my right. Before the hush had settled, Harper had told me that this was really understated compared to the usual fanfare that was made to celebrate the lives of Alphas. I really hoped they'd do a bigger celebration of his life when more Shifters could make it here. It wasn't fair.

'Welcome, thank you all for coming to celebrate the life of our former Alpha, Axel Meier. Beloved Pack Master, father, friend and protector. We give thanks to Axel for the love he gave to this Pack and, ultimately, his life, with which he protected many Shifters. Without his brave efforts, we would have lost many more and the Crone and her Sorceresses may not have been forced to retreat.

'I now call on Axel's daughter, Natasha, to speak before the burial commences.'

Natasha walked forward, her slow steps mirroring the pain that was clear on her face.

'My father is... was a loving and caring father. He always made time for me despite his duties. He took care of me, played with me and trained me to be the best I could be. He always made choices to make life better for me and for the Pack. It was clear in his every decision....'

Miss Stone moved next to her and wrapped an arm around her shoulders.

Tears blurred my eyes as she spoke. Each time Natasha had to pause and suck in a breath, the knife dug in just a little further.

Following Natasha's speech, the Medicine Woman addressed everybody again.

'As we lower Axel Meier into the ground, we celebrate his life and offer a prayer to the great Wolf Lords to care for him as he cared for us. Through their creation he was made and into their love he will return. Please offer your prayers now as we complete the burial.'

Thank you, Axel. I hope you see your wife again and are happy. Thank you for being a great protector and... I'm sorry.

Once the burial was completed, everyone was told to go to the Food Den, where a special meal of Axel's favourite foods had been prepared. I stood with the rest of the First Years and looked over to Natasha as I wiped my eyes. She looked so lonely.

'Elita, are you coming?' said Harper.

'Uh, in a minute. I'll meet you there, okay?'

Harper looked over to where Natasha was, then turned her head back to me. 'Okay.'

I gave her a small smile and left to see Natasha. When I approached, she remained looking at the plot her father had been lowered into. I spotted Miss Stone nearby; she was talking with some of the other adult Shifters who had come to attend the funeral.

'Natasha... hey.'

'It's weird, you know. I guess I thought he was going to just be around like normal. Even though I know that's crazy, I hoped it would happen.'

I nodded. 'It doesn't seem crazy to me at all. Of course you'd want things to be like normal. Hey, I, uh, was wondering if you wanted to walk with me over to the feast they have planned?'

'I'm not really hungry.'

'Even so, it's probably a good idea to try and eat something small. You still need your energy.'

After what seemed like an eternity, she turned and walked past me, towards the Food Den. I followed behind her. When Miss Stone caught my eye, she mouthed a thank you. She knew we weren't friends, despite her best efforts to stick us together.

I caught up and walked beside Natasha all the way to the feast. When we got inside her two friends, Maja and Olivia, found us. A little more like herself, Natasha walked away with them, without so much as a word to me.

Maybe she will be all right after all.

CONTINGENCIES

B Y THE TIME Dom returned, I'd moved outside with some First and Second Year guys to kick the ball around. When I saw him approach, I waved at the guys and ran off. A couple of them wolf whistled and I felt my cheeks heat up so much that I knew they'd look like ripened tomatoes. When I reached Dom I saw that his cheeks were flushed as well.

So embarrassing.

'How'd you go? What did he say?'

'Let's walk for a bit?'

I swallowed the lump that had formed in my throat and nodded. When we'd reached halfway back and could no longer hear the conversations from the guys or from inside the dorms, we slowed to a stop. I looked at Dom, eyebrows raised. He sighed and the look he gave me made it quite clear what the answer was.

'I'm sorry, Elita. Dad said no. Pretty much because Sorceresses are not our business and, in case we have another attack on the Academy, the Imperial team needs to stay in place here. I'm sorry.'

'It's okay,' I said quietly. 'I didn't really expect that they would do it. I know they don't really have a reason to care about her. But... you understand I'm going to go and save her right? That I need to go?'

'Yeah, I know. But, do you think maybe you should wait to talk to your dad and see him about it? I'm sure with all his years of experience, he would be able to help.'

I shook my head. 'He is over with the Trevini Pack. I mean, if he shows up before I'm ready, maybe.'

I looked away. I was still angry with my dad for lying to me, and while Miss Stone's explanation made sense, it didn't take away the hurt from what he'd done.

'Have you heard back from him yet?'

'No, but I need to go check with Miss Stone. She mentioned her crow returning this morning in passing, so there may be some news, but she also made it clear I wasn't allowed to go to see her today.' Frustration leaked into my tone.

He looked at me sympathetically. 'In the morning then?'

'Yeah, but I'm not holding my breath. And I won't wait for him, Dom. I won't leave her there any longer than I have to.'

He looked to be thinking really hard about something. Eventually he spoke again. 'Look, if he won't be there, I want to come with you. I'm *going* to come with you. You can't go all the way to Crone Keep by yourself and rescue your mum. You need help.'

'Really? You'll come with me? Are you sure? I mean, your dad just became Alpha and everything.'

'Yeah, I'm sure. Part of being an Alpha is protecting the members of the Pack. That includes you. When are you planning on leaving?'

'As soon as I can get everything we need. Maps, internal drawings, weapons if we can find some, and definitely food.'

'Okay. Well, how about we start with the maps and internal drawings because they're easier to access. The food, I reckon we get on the way out of here, but if we run into any trouble I can always do some hunting for us.' Disgust must have shown on my face, because he laughed and said, 'Don't worry, I'll make sure it's well cooked!'

I laughed too. Dom was always good at lightening the mood.

'Okay. So where do we get the maps and internal drawings?'

'Maps you can find in the library, internal drawings in the Archive room. But with the extra people around and the attack that just happened, we may need to wait a couple of days to hit that room to borrow the internal drawings. Maybe start with the maps? I'd say the library is shut right now, so maybe we can sneak in tonight?'

'Perfect. When should I meet you?'

'Let's say about midnight, under the trees outside the dorm?'

'Thanks, Dom, really. I'm so glad that you're here for me and that I don't need to do this alone.'

Dom's cheeks went a little pink again. 'Don't sweat it.'

The rest of the day passed with quiet games and food. I hung out with Harper and Dom and his mates, mostly outside. When evening came, I read one of my books to pass the time, though I had to work hard to keep my attention on it. Way harder than usual.

Peeking at the moon's position outside for about the hundredth time, I realised I could go. I pulled on my darkest outfit and snuck downstairs. I figured I must be a little early since I didn't see Dom on the way down.

Quietly I opened the front door, pushing it towards the hinges a little in case the door decided to pick today to start squeaking, and slipped out of a gap just big enough for me to pass through.

Sticking to the front of the building, I moved swiftly to the trees then slunk beneath the canopy in case one of the teachers or other students looked outside. After a few minutes, Dom arrived. I knew because he was crumpling every leaf he crossed.

How the heck has he been topping stealth classes walking like that?!

'Hey. You're being a bit loud!'

'Oh, yeah. Sorry. Not like anyone is out here anyway.'

I rolled my eyes and chuckled quietly. 'That's not really the point.'

He laughed even louder than I did. 'Guess not. Come on, let's do this.'

I trailed behind him, sticking to the darkest shadows cast by the trees that loomed above us. We moved along the tree line and in through the doors to the Food Den. About halfway up the stairwell on the staff level we heard voices and froze. It was Miss Stone and Dom's dad.

'...needs to be more responsible now. Things have changed.'

'He's still just a kid, Corbin. I know you think he needs more responsibility, but he also needs time to be a child and grow up with his friends.'

'Yes. I know that. But things have changed. He may even become the Beta, Genevieve.'

'Corbin, you know that's not likely. Someone of age will be voted into the position, just like you were, in case something like this happens again.'

There was silence for a moment. Then, 'Either way. I want to give him some more responsibilities. Work something out that would be of help and report back.'

'Yes, of course.'

Footsteps sounded and then a door opened and closed. We waited another few minutes and, when we couldn't hear anything else, I looked to Dom. His face was serious once more.

'You okay?'

'Yeah, sure. Just forget it. Let's get going before we run into someone else.'

He kept walking up the stairs. We were almost at our floor when I had the sudden realisation that he was actually now moving so quietly I couldn't hear him. I wondered if he felt the need to prove himself after overhearing the conversation.

He pushed lightly on the door and peeked out of it. Once he confirmed it was all clear, he opened the door further and moved out into the hall. Sticking to the wall, we continued along to the library. The doors were still missing. We listened for a couple of moments and then moved inside.

My feet jolted to a halt. The room was half destroyed. There was a giant, gaping hole through the roof and one wall. Shattered glass and chunks of stone sheeted the floors and furniture, and there were so many ripped and destroyed books that it hurt. I looked to the spot where my mum had stood and felt myself drift closer, needing to be where she was.

Despite Dom's quiet protests, I waded through the debris to stand where she had, picturing her as she'd looked at me, even as she was dragged away. I looked down at the ground, seeing faint footprints in the dust and wondering which belonged to her. As I took a step to my right the moon shone down past me and I noticed a glint of silver.

Chest tight I bent down to get a closer look. The edge of a silver pendant stuck out from beneath a piece of wall. I shoved it aside and rescued a delicate, silver bracelet. The pendant had a pentagram on the front and the back was engraved with the letter "M".

It must be my mum's!

I clutched it tightly then walked over to Dom to show it to him. 'I think it's my mother's bracelet.'

'Oh, wow. Are you sure?'

'Yeah, I think so. It's right where she was standing when she was here and it has the letter "M" on it, for Margot. Maybe she slipped it off?'

'Yeah, maybe,' he said quietly. 'Come on, we need to get moving and grab the maps.'

I nodded and waved my right hand to indicate he should go ahead while I looked again at the bracelet in my hand. I held it up, letting the moonlight shine onto the pentagram. I smiled, excited at the prospect of owning something that belonged to my mum, then tucked it into my shirt pouch and followed Dom.

Thankfully, the map section was on the opposite side to the blast and was easily accessible, unlike the scrolls that always seemed to be locked away. Dom rifled through the maps quickly and pulled out a couple that showed both the Academy and Crone Keep in the Mortis Mountains. He pointed each of them out to me on the clearest maps.

I swallowed hard. It looked like a bit of a trip. We needed to pass through a lot of forest and cross a mountain range before we'd make it there. I looked up at Dom and saw a grim, but determined, expression on his face.

'Don't worry. We can do it, but we should definitely pack some warm sleeping gear in our packs and pick some good resting places before we leave, so we don't get caught out in a storm or anything.'

I opened my mouth to answer and quickly snapped it shut. Footsteps. They were coming from the hallway outside the library. I shooed Dom towards the entrance we'd used to escape the Crone and her Sorceresses. He quickly folded up two maps as quietly as he could while he walked. The footsteps were closer.

Come on, come on… We need to go.

I stepped through the door behind Dom just as the footsteps entered the library entrance. I shut the door very gently behind us and breathed a silent sigh of relief. I waved to Dom to get moving, but there was no need; he was already way ahead of me.

I moved lightly along behind him, taking care not to lose my footing on the dark staircase. I was relieved when we finally reached the bottom and made it out onto the corridor landing.

We moved along to the back stairwell and I was grateful to discover that there were no teachers hanging around having conversations; it made slipping through the bottom door and outside much easier. In the open air, we moved directly back into the shadows of the trees and slowed our pace.

'Did you see who was in the Library?' Dom asked.

'No. I was too focused on trying to shut the door quickly and quietly. Did you?'

'Nah, but I must say I'm pretty curious about who would be in the library at this time of the night, and why.'

I laughed. 'You mean, besides us stealing maps?'

He smiled. 'Yeah, I guess so. Though I'd be pretty surprised if someone else decided to *borrow* maps.'

When we were almost back to the dorm, Dom paused. I stopped and looked at him. 'Have you been back to Miss Stone today, to ask about your Dad's letter?'

'No, I said I'd go tomorrow, remember? Why?'

'I just wondered, is all. I'm kinda hoping he'll show up so we don't need to go do this on our own, since the Pack can't help.'

I tried my best to smile, but I knew it looked forced. 'Come on, let's get inside before someone sees us out here.'

A branch snapped in front of us. My head whipped up.

Natasha?!

'What exactly are you two doing out here?'

My brain went blank. 'Uh, nothing—'

Dom cut in. 'What are *you* doing out here, Natasha?'

She shrugged, her head tilted up in defiance. 'Whatever I want. Why do you care?'

'We don't,' he retorted. 'As long as you don't care what we're doing.'

'Fine,' she said, then turned on her heel and walked towards the dorm.

I exhaled deeply. 'Quick thinking, Dom!'

He coughed, sounding embarrassed. 'It's not the first time someone has caught me outside of the dorms at night.'

I smiled. 'That's not surprising, considering how you stomp around crushing all the leaves you can manage with each step.'

'Hey! I do not!' I could see his blush under the light of the moon. 'Hurry up, let's get inside.'

My smile stuck as I let him lead the way. As we reached the space between the trees and the front of the dorm, we both sniffed the air and kept watch. Sensing no threat, we stuck to the wall as we crept back to the door. Dom pulled the handle. It wouldn't budge.

I stared at him, dumbfounded.

She locked us out.

He muttered some curse words under his breath. 'Come on. Window at the back is kept open.'

I followed him around the building, irritated that Natasha would be so nasty after I'd gone out of my way to support her. Though she had said it wouldn't change anything. Looked like she'd stuck with it.

'Here it is,' he said. 'You go in first.'

I moved around Dom, feeling thankful it was a decently sized window, though how he was going to fit through unscathed, I wasn't sure. He gave me a hand so I could climb in, then he pulled himself up and followed behind, making a quiet hiss as he scraped his arms to fit through. I flinched.

Doesn't quite fit after all.

'You okay? That sounded kind of painful.'

'Yep. All good. Come on, let's go to the Common Room.'

I led the way in, wondering if we'd run into Natasha. Luckily for her, she'd gone straight to bed.

Sitting on our couch by the fire and after a quick check that the room was empty, Dom pulled the maps out and laid them side by side on the wooden table. I ran my finger over the images. 'Have you ever been out towards Crone Keep before?'

Dom shook his head.

I sighed and looked at the maps for a few minutes longer. 'Okay. I think the best route is to leave via the forest where we sat to talk by that stream, here.' I pointed to the map, then slid my finger across the page. 'Then follow it through here and into the mountains. I'm positive there will be plenty of caves, if it's anything like the mountains Dad and I live by. Then—'

'Wait, are you sure about going through the mountains and not around? The storms will be hitting a lot harder up there, and it'll be really rough. We'd have better protection in the forests, going around.'

I surveyed the map again, considering the other options once more. 'Yes. I'm sure. Your way will extend the journey even further, and it's already going to take us at least a couple of weeks to go this way.'

I looked at him and waited; when he nodded, I continued. 'So, through the mountains, staying in caves along the way, and then out through the forested section on the other side. That should take us pretty much to Crone Keep, though we'll obviously need to scout it a bit. Hey, would there be any sketches of the area around the Keep, maybe showing where they run patrols?'

'Hmm. Yeah, I'd say so. We should be able to get them with the internal drawings. But I still need to scope out the routine for the Archive room before we try and get in there. I'm willing to bet there is someone watching more often than in the Library now.'

'Okay, sounds like a plan. I think that's as detailed as we can get without the other drawings. When do you think you'll be able to scope it out?'

'I'll check the area a few times tomorrow during the day, and then at night. I'll meet you here around midnight to go over it.'

My chest tightened with worry. Daytime didn't sound like a good plan for scoping it out.

'Will you be able to do that without getting caught?'

'Don't worry. I'll pop in through the service stairs again. That way no one will see me and you don't have to worry about my loud, clumsy feet.'

I laughed, appreciating Dom's innate ability to keep the situation from getting too serious.

'Okay, fine. We should get to bed then, since classes are back to normal tomorrow. I'll take the maps and hide them in my room.'

Dom looked like he was about to argue. I tilted my head to the side and waited. Nothing. I nodded and picked them up.

'Okay, let's go.'

I walked up the stairs, trailed closely by Dom. When we got to my floor, I said goodnight and left to go to my room. When I glanced back he was still standing on the landing. I smiled and waved and then went into my room. He didn't move until my door was almost completely shut.

So protective.

FRUSTRATION

WHEN I ARRIVED AT my first class of the day—Sorceress Lore—Miss Stone started the lesson with a brief speech.

'Good morning, everyone. Now, I know that this has been a very shocking and difficult few days with the school attack, including the devastating loss of lives and the subsequent funerals. It's time now to try our hardest to focus on learning again. So...'

Being in class almost did make it seem like things were back to normal, though it was obvious that Natasha was missing. I wondered what would happen to her now that she had no parents, if she would stay at the Academy or if she would have to leave. I thought that was pretty unlikely since she was still just a kid—a teen—like the rest of us.

When the class finished, I felt bad. It was the least amount of attention I had ever paid to a lesson in my entire life, and between my primary classes in the human settlement and Dad's lessons, I'd had some pretty boring ones. On my way out, I asked Miss Stone if I'd be able to see her later in the day. She didn't ask me why, but I assumed she knew, and she said I could visit during lunch in her office. I gave her a tight smile and continued onto my next lesson.

The day wore on and I barely saw Dom, but I knew that while he was doing his part of the job, I needed to do mine.

Time to find Miss Stone.

I walked up the stairs to her door and knocked. After a few moments, she opened the door.

Huh, maybe the sound spell means I couldn't hear her say "come in" even if she had... Cool.

My cheeks heated and she gave me a questioning look. When I shook my head to let her know that it was nothing, she pointed towards a chair. I walked past and took a seat. After closing the door, she walked back and sat down.

'You're here for your father's letter?'

'Yes.' I sat up straighter in my chair. 'Is it here?'

'It is. But first, I want to ask you about Natasha. How is she doing?'

My mouth dropped open. Realising how ridiculous I must have looked, I snapped it shut. 'Why would I know how Natasha is doing? It's not like we're friends or anything.' I shifted uncomfortably.

'I did notice that you left the Alpha ceremony together. You went to speak to her, yes? And again at the funeral?'

'Oh, well, yes. But, I mean, she said she doesn't want to be my friend or anything, even though she spoke to me.'

Sheesh, why do I feel so guilty about this?

'Even so, I am sure since you have spoken to her, you could let me know?' She raised her eyebrows.

I sighed and thought about it for a moment. 'She's sad. Miserable, really, but she hides it really well. She seems to be doing pretty well, considering.'

Miss Stone nodded, seemingly satisfied and reached into a drawer. Before she managed to collect my letter, I interrupted.

'Ah, Miss Stone. I know she's not my friend and it's really not my business, but what will happen to Natasha. You know, now that her parents are both gone?'

Miss Stone paused for a moment, considering, but thankfully decided to indulge me.

'She'll stay at the Academy and will essentially become a ward of it. The teachers and the Alpha will take care of her, and make decisions and the like until she turns eighteen and is able to make choices on her own. She will be well cared for Elita, do not worry. I know you were not brought up with the Pack, but we do take care of our own.'

I smiled faintly. *What about the ones that are half your own, like me?*

'Have you got my letter?'

She reached back into her drawer and pulled it out. My stomach fell. It was tiny. There was no way it could have held much detail. As I reached for the letter, I saw Miss Stone's look of pity and felt even worse.

I snapped the small wax seal, the tiny wolf imprint cracking down the middle. As I unfolded it my hands began to shake.

Dear Elita,

I'm sorry that you had to find out that way about your mum,
I know that must be hard and I understand that you are really
angry and want answers from me. It is something I will have to
talk to you about in person, I can't answer it via letter. It isn't safe.

I love you always,

Dad

I read the letter over and over, looking for some extra information or a sign or hint of anything, any reason. But there was just nothing. I crumpled the paper. My chest thudded and my hands continued to shake. I looked up at Miss Stone again and realised my eyes had become blurred.

'Are you okay?' she asked.

I shook my head. 'He told me nothing. Absolutely nothing. "Not safe", he said.'

'Well, it is certainly risky. I'm sure he'll tell you when he can. You are welcome to send another message back with Xavier,' she said, indicating her crow's empty cage, 'as soon as he returns. I did already send a quick message regarding the invasion... and about your mother. I'm sure he will write back very soon.'

I thought it over briefly, but I was just too angry and devastated at his response—or rather, his lack of one. I shook my head. I wasn't ready to send him a message now. Maybe he'd change his mind after discovering that mum was alive.

I stood, the chair scooting back with a loud scrape on the stone floor. It echoed harshly in the room.

'Thank you, Miss Stone.'

I turned and walked to the door. Before I could open it, she called out to me. I paused with my fingers resting on the handle but didn't look back.

'Elita, I'm sure he has his reasons and will explain them as soon as he sees you.' Her voice was weighed down with concern.

I turned the handle and pulled it toward me, stepped through and gently pulled it shut. Wishing instead that I could slam it repeatedly. I was really glad I had weapons training coming up. Hitting something in that class would seem perfectly reasonable.

Plus, it'll be a good opportunity to check out the weapons available, see if there are any that might not be missed.

Master Ira began barking his usual set of instructions to prepare. Since I had arrived early, I'd spent my first few minutes looking over the weapons rack. There was a range of practise and actual weapons. Everything from ropes, to archery gear, to knives and swords. I carefully considered which weapons would be helpful, balanced against those that would be too heavy to carry or get in the way when travelling for so long.

I decided on a rope, a bow and arrows, a couple of throwing knives and a short sword, though I knew I'd need to check with Dom what he thought and what he wanted.

I was so intent on the weapons that I completely missed the fact that Natasha was already back in class. When Master Ira told us to get moving for our warm-up run, I dodged around the rest of the students and up to Natasha, who had already started running. Despite her gruelling pace, I caught up and stuck with her. She acknowledged my existence with a purse of her lips and an increase in her speed. I dug my toes in and kept going.

I'd given up trying to reason with myself about checking on her and just resigned myself to the fact that I cared. When we got to the end, we were once again the first there.

'Natasha,' I huffed. 'What are you doing back in class already?'

She took a couple of gulps of air. 'Well, I couldn't very well get out of shape and let you take over, could I?'

'No, of course not.' I shook my head and looked at the rest of the group who were close to finishing. 'You're really okay to be here?'

She gave me a hard stare but chose not to answer. Worried, I continued to watch her throughout our lesson, which today included using throwing knives to hit a target. A small group of us, thankfully including Natasha, were allowed to practise on moving targets powered by a pulley system. Even upset, she maintained her skill level. I briefly wondered if she was good at all forms of weapons before focusing on my own turn.

At the end of the class, I watched her leave and considered if I should check in on her again later. I turned to her usual crew and noted that none of them had rushed off after her, and even seemed to be avoiding her a little. It was weird.

When it was finally time for dinner I was pretty thrilled to see Dom sitting outside. I rushed over to see if he'd had any luck.

'Easy, there. I still need to check later tonight to see what time will be the best, but I've noticed a couple of windows we could use.'

'Actual windows, or...?'

He laughed at me while stuffing in some food. 'No, I meant times.'

'Oh, right.'

'You hear from your dad?'

'Yep. Wouldn't say anything. Said it wasn't safe, 'cause, you know...'

Dom nodded and continued scoffing down more food. I couldn't ever figure out where he put it all; he must run it off or something.

'Uh, Elita. Why are you staring at me like that?'

I looked up at his flushed face and laughed. 'Sorry. Was just wondering where you keep stuffing all that food!'

'Oh.'

He turned a deeper shade of crimson and looked away as he finished his food.

I coughed to interrupt the now awkward silence. 'So, uh, I'll meet you in the Common Room tonight, near midnight?'

'Yep. Sounds good.'

As the bells tolled I tried to think of something to say to him to break the new awkwardness, but nothing came to mind. Once we'd finished eating I gave him a tight smile then said goodbye and rushed over to join Harper who was standing by the door.

At about an hour before midnight, almost everyone had left the Common Room. Everyone besides me and Natasha. She sat curled up on the couch across from me, just staring into the fire. I'd been reading a book and was glancing up occasionally, but every time I checked, her eyes were still there, unseeing.

I put my book down beside me and waved a hand in the air. Nothing. I coughed loudly. Still nothing. Starting to get a bit more concerned, I gave a half-shout. 'Hey!'

'There's no need to shout at me. I'm not deaf, you know. And you can stop staring at me now. I've felt your eyes on my head for, like, the last hour. I'm fine.'

'Oh, right. Well, sorry. You just didn't seem to be noticing anything.'

A few more minutes of silence went by before I got up the courage to talk again.

'Did they speak to you about what you do now? I mean, I was talking to Miss Stone and she said something about you living here.'

The silence was deafening. I fidgeted in my seat, waiting.

'Yes. The new Alpha—'

'Dom's dad.' I interjected.

She scowled. 'Yes. The new Alpha spoke to me and told me I was a ward of the Academy now and that he and the other staff would take care of me until I'm old enough to make decisions for myself.' She scoffed. 'As if I'm not already capable of that. Anyway, I just keep living here, like I have been.'

'Well, that's a good thing, right?'

She looked at me condescendingly. 'Sure. I suppose if being controlled by people who aren't your parents because they're not here anymore is a good thing.'

I felt heat flush my cheeks. 'Right.'

Just mind your own business next time.

As it got nearer to midnight, I started getting more agitated, shifting my feet up and down off the couch, and opening and closing my book. Natasha needed to get out of here before Dom got back. I'd resigned myself to the fact that she wasn't going to move and had started formulating excuses to give her when she abruptly stood up.

'Your fidgeting is really irritating. I'm going to bed.' Without another word, she stood up and walked out of the room and up the stairs. I leapt up, with my feet lightly touching the floor as I moved and listened until I heard her door shut. I exhaled deeply, walked back to the couch and curled my feet up to wait for Dom.

In no time at all, I saw the Common Room door creep open. Dom walked inside and over to me. I watched as he looked around the room, checking for anyone else. When he got to me, I expected him to sit down but instead he told me to follow him.

I stood anxiously and trailed behind him, back out the front door.

When we'd made it into the shadows of the trees, I tapped his arm to get his attention then stopped. 'What's going on?'

He looked around quickly. 'We need to go now. I overheard a conversation between a couple of the Shifters who run the Archive room. They said they were taking a bunch of files to my Dad in the morning to run over their options. If they take something we need, we're screwed. There's no easy way to get it from my dad's office. This is definitely our best chance.'

'Okay, let's hurry. Was there anyone there when you left?'

He shook his head. 'They left before I snuck out of where I was hiding. I was lucky they didn't smell me.'

He looked a little pale. The Alpha's son being caught listening into secret conversations wouldn't be good, though getting caught stealing plans would be even worse.

'Dom.' I stopped again. We were almost at the end of the tree line. 'Are you sure you want to do this? I mean, what if you get caught? This should be on me.'

I thought I saw a light pink touch his cheeks again, but it was hard to tell in the shadows. 'It's fine. I said I would help you and I will. Besides, you have no clue where you're going or what you're looking for. You need me.' He grinned.

Relieved that the awkwardness from earlier was forgotten, I smiled back at him. 'Thanks, Dom. Really.'

He nodded and turned quickly back in the direction of the Academy. I kept close behind him as he walked to the fountain in the courtyard, then from there cut across to the opposite tree line and around to the Food Den door.

They really should lock this thing. This is ridiculously easy.

Just inside the door, we froze. There was a rustling coming from the kitchen. I saw Dom inhale deeply then take off in the opposite direction to the service stairs. I stuck close to his heels. Once we were safely inside and up a flight of stairs, he paused and took a long, slow breath in and out.

'It was lucky the breeze was in our favour. It was my dad. He likes to go into the kitchen to get food when he can't sleep.'

I chuckled and gave him a pointed look. 'A bit like someone else I know then.'

'Yeah, yeah. Come on. It's on this floor.'

COLLECTION

DOM MOVED TO THE door, put his ear against it and listened. I stood impatiently, trying hard to resist the urge to tap my foot. When he started to crack the door, I leaned forward to peer out. I couldn't see or hear anything, so I shook my head. He nodded and pushed it further open.

We walked out onto the landing, sticking by the wall. I followed Dom until he reached another room. This one needed a key. I looked at him with wide eyes, but he just grinned, reached into his shirt pocket and pulled out an old metal key.

My chest, which I didn't realise had squeezed tight, relaxed and I breathed normally again. The thought of being stopped now was almost unbearable. Luckily, he hadn't left me any time to panic about it.

He put his ear to the door, double checking there was no sound on the other side. When he decided it was all clear, he opened it. We snuck inside and I looked around the room. There were wooden shelves lining the walls and a large oak table in the centre, surrounded by chairs. On the table were a range of maps that looked to be of the Academy grounds and surrounding land.

A few sketches had been pinned on one of the walls. All women. Sorceresses, I assumed. I wondered why these ones were hanging up in here but not others. I walked over to them and looked while Dom rifled through the shelves. When I heard an "Aha", I turned away from the photos and walked over to him. He spread one of the drawings across the table, taking care not to budge the maps beneath it. It was of the Crone Keep building. The bottom layers were clear, but as the levels went higher the details became less specific.

I guess not many who made it up that far actually made it back out.

I swallowed a lump in my throat, realising for the first time what I planned on doing, and what I was dragging Dom into. Shifters with a lot more experience than me had obviously gone into Crone Keep and not returned.

'Hey,' Dom said, noticing my worry. 'It'll be fine. The prisoner area is not that far from the bottom. There are plenty of details for down there. See.' He pointed to the spot labelled "Prisoners".

I nodded. At least he seemed positive that we could do it.

'Come on, Dom. Fold that up and hide it. Let's get out of here before we're caught. There aren't exactly a lot of hiding places in here.'

I watched as he folded up that drawing and a couple of others we needed and then tucked them into the back of his pants. I hoped they wouldn't make too much noise when he moved.

We triple checked that everything remained as we'd found it and went back to the door. I put my ear to it this time to listen; sensing nothing, I opened it and stepped out. Dom followed behind. When we were a few metres from the service door, my heart stopped.

Footsteps sounded behind us, then a voice.

'What are you two doing here?'

How the hell did she sneak up on us? More charms?

I breathed a small sigh of relief when I realised it was Miss Stone and not someone else. The relief was short lived, however, because, when I looked at her, she was furious.

'I said, what are you two doing here? You should both be in bed.'

Dom and I looked at each other. I couldn't believe we hadn't thought of a plan, something to say if we were caught!

'Uh, I wanted to show Elita the Sorceress Records room again. She, uh, wanted to see her mum.'

I watched Miss Stone for any sign that she bought Dom's excuse. It was like I could almost see the thoughts crossing over her face. Anger, disbelief, worry. She settled on understanding, thankfully.

'I appreciate that you wanted to look at the picture again, Elita,' she lowered her voice so I had to strain to hear her, 'especially after seeing her recently. But you can't go back to look again. Particularly not in the dead of night, do you understand?'

I was crestfallen. I hadn't even thought of going back to see her picture again with everything that had been happening, but

I should have. I wanted to. I wanted to get it and keep it. Instead, I nodded and told her that I would stay away.

She shifted her focus. 'Dominic, more is expected of you, especially now. I am positive your father would be incredibly disappointed if he heard about this. Do not let me catch you taking other students around the Academy again. Even if your intentions are good ones. And stay out of the service stairs. They are closed for safety reasons, until such time as they are repaired. Go now. Down the main staircase. If you get caught by someone else, then I wish you luck. Do not say that you were with me. Understood?'

Wow, harsh. I guess after that chat with Dom's dad, she wasn't able to be quite so forgiving.

I nodded and walked with Dom to the end of the hall, avoiding her gaze as we hurried past. I was sure that she would tell my dad about this. I knew he wouldn't be happy with me taking risks and not following the rules. But I was also sure that I was still too angry with him to care.

I led the way down the stairs this time, keeping my feet light and my eyes peeled for any movement. I was grateful when we made it back to the dorms without attracting unwanted attention from anyone else. I had no doubt Miss Stone wouldn't have helped us get a second free pass for the evening.

I walked over to the lounge and collapsed onto it. Dom pulled out the internal drawings before laying back and putting his feet up.

'So. We have the maps and the internal drawings now. What else do we need before we go save your mum?'

I smiled. The idea of saving my mum gave me a warm and fuzzy sort of feeling.

'We just need packs with mats and blankets, our clothes, food and weapons. And then a plan to get out of here unnoticed. I guess, during the night would make the most sense?'

'Yeah, for sure, but we should probably go earlier in the evening, or as early as we can, because we'll need to cover a pretty good distance the first night. Once they realise we're missing, you can bet they're going to come looking for us.'

'You're right. Maybe around ten. Most of the kids go to bed around that time during the week.'

He nodded. 'Okay. We can just get mats and blankets from the visitors' lodgings. Do you have a pack that's easy to carry?'

'No, I just have dad's suitcase.'

'That's cool. I have a spare. I'll bring it to you before we go to bed tonight.' A grin lit his face from ear to ear. 'I'll get the food since I know the kitchens so well.'

I laughed. 'Makes sense. I think I can get the weapons.'

'Okay. I'll grab the mats and blankets during class break tomorrow and put them in our packs. There's rarely anyone in the visitor area during the day.'

'Are you sure?'

'Yep, I'm sure. Should we get the weapons and food tomorrow night then? Maybe after dinner, once everyone has headed off to their rooms?'

'Yeah, that sounds like a plan. I'd suggest going while everyone is at dinner but we all know you aren't going to miss out on that!' I chuckled.

'Too right! I'll be missing the dinners here for weeks. I definitely need to enjoy the final meal. And remember, when you go into the weapons room, there's only one door in and one door out of there.'

'Yep. Got it. I'll be careful. You watch out too. Won't do well for you to be caught again.'

'I will. Okay. So if everything goes to plan, we'll be leaving tomorrow evening, right?'

My stomach flopped and my chest tightened with the realisation that I was really about to do this. To leave without telling anyone. To run away after Dad had finally let me come to the Academy.

I heaved in a deep breath. 'Tomorrow. In which case, we should really get some sleep or we'll struggle to get very far.'

Dom pulled himself up off the couch and collected the drawings. He told me he'd meet me at my room and rushed off. A little weary, I walked at a slower pace. By the time I made it to my room and unlocked my door, he'd made it back. He passed me the pack and said goodnight, then headed off quickly to his own bed.

After I popped the pack in the corner of my room, out of the way but still easy for Dom to find tomorrow, I pulled on my sleep clothes and hopped into bed. Warm under the covers, I began to drift off in no time, my fading consciousness showing me amber eyes, a silver charm bracelet and our dead Alpha.

I trudged my way to dinner the next evening with Harper, who commented a few times about me being so tired lately. I was glad she seemed to accept the idea that I just wasn't sleeping well after everything that had happened.

We sat with Dom and his friends; everybody made comfortable small talk. It almost seemed like no one wanted to complicate life or talk about anything heavy after recent events. It suited me just fine and I was able to scout around and figure out where the teachers were dispersed among the students.

After I'd been looking for five minutes, my palms started sweating. If I couldn't find Master Ira, then I couldn't risk going into the training room to get our weapons. When I was about to say something to Dom, I spotted him through the Food Den door heading over to the kitchen server, presumably to get his dinner.

I exhaled, my shoulders relaxing. 'Hey guys, I'm gonna have an early one tonight. I'm really tired. I'll catch you all later.'

After a chorus of goodnights from the guys, I tried to reassure Harper that I could make it back alone. Dom eventually had to cut in and distract her so I could escape. On my way back inside,

I passed Natasha. I smiled a little when I realised she was back to sitting with her friends and being the centre of attention again.

Walking through the Food Den, I happily noticed Master Ira had gone to sit with some other teachers to eat. When I entered the foyer, it was almost deserted. I smiled briefly at anyone who met my eye and continued walking through, my heart racing. I bent down to fix my shoe so I could check that no one was watching me. Coast clear, I walked straight to the staircase.

I moved quickly, barely gracing each step with the presence of my boots before moving onto the next one. When I reached the bottom, I peered around. Empty. I walked slowly into the room, keeping my attention on the scents and sounds around me. Sure I was alone, I rushed over to the weapons vault.

I exhaled slowly through my mouth, feeling my chest relax when I saw it was still open. I carefully picked out the weapons Dom and I had discussed during lunch: a rope, throwing knives, a bow and arrows, and a few short swords. Then I grabbed a couple of weapons belts to secure them all.

As I closed the vault, I heard someone coming down the stairs. I looked around, my knees threatening to buckle from the panic. There was nowhere to hide. I was done for. Putting the weapons back now would make too much noise. After another look around, I spotted a window open near the wall to my right. I rushed over and climbed up. The footsteps were closer and gaining speed. I wasn't being quiet enough. I quickly shoved the weapons out of the window then jumped back to the floor and started running the track.

My heart thudded so loudly I had to focus to hear the footsteps entering the room. I slowed my jog and came to a stop as Master Ira walked in and glared at me.

'What do you think you are doing in here?'

I felt my face heat.

'Oh, I'm sorry. I thought I was allowed down here. I was just running some laps before I went to bed.'

The look he gave me was like daggers thrown at full speed. 'No. You are not allowed in here. Do it again after hours and you will have a punishment. Out. Now.'

'Yes, Master Ira. I'm so sorry.'

His sharp gaze followed me all the way past the weapons vault and out the door. I listened hard as I walked; his footsteps sounded again as I reached the stairs. Behind me, I heard the lock turn in the vault and nearly melted with relief. If he'd looked inside at the weapons instead of just locking it, we would have been done for.

I made my way back over to the dorm rooms slowly, stopping by the window outside to grab the weapons. The whole endeavour had taken longer than I'd thought because almost everyone was already on their way out of the Food Den and heading back to the dorms.

When I got there, I snuck in through the back window and went straight up to my room. Dom had been by. My pack was thick at the base with mats and a blanket. I pulled my warmest clothes off my shelf and put them in as well, then looked around my room wondering what else I should take.

I wanted to bring my family portrait, or my favourite book, but there was no space for things like that. I tried to focus on the fact that we would be back, and they'd be here, waiting. Once I had the few essential items besides clothes, I laid on my bed and waited.

I was startled awake by a loud knock. Looking out the window, I realised I'd been asleep for a while. I jumped up and rushed to the door. I pulled it open and felt myself relax when I saw Dom.

'Hey. Oh, were you asleep?'

I rubbed my eyes. 'Yeah, I guess so. Did you get everything?'

'Yeah, here. Let me pop this food in your pack. I've already done mine.' He walked over and opened the top and started placing it in.

'What were you able to get?'

'I got bread, fruits and dried meat. I got a little fresh meat for when we stop tonight, too, but I put it in my pack.' He grinned, seemingly happy with his selection.

'Great. Thank you. I have the weapons here too. Rope, throwing knives, a bow and arrows and short swords, plus a couple of belts. I wasn't sure if you had any. But I should probably tell you... Master Ira came in when I was there—'

He stopped putting the food in the pack. 'He what? What happened? Are you okay? Did he notice anything was missing?!'

'I'm fine, it was all okay. Though it probably won't be if he ever catches me in there again. Right before he came down, I managed to chuck the weapons out one of the windows. Then I pretended I was just running the track. He believed it, thankfully, though he did have a go at me anyway. I listened on my way out and I'm pretty positive he just locked the vault and didn't check it. I only heard the key turn, not the doors open and close.'

He heaved a sigh of relief and I felt a rush of happiness that he cared so much about me. Having friends was so important to me. I just hoped I'd be able to keep Harper and make even more after we rescued my mum.

'Okay, cool. Where are they? I'll take mine upstairs now.' He looked around.

'Wouldn't it be better for you to stop by here on the way out and just put them on then?'

'Oh, well yeah. I suppose that makes sense. Should we just go and hang downstairs then?'

'I said I was going to bed, so maybe if you go down and hang with the guys and I'll stay up here? Then when everyone has gone to bed, just grab your pack and come meet me here. You can put your weapons on and we'll go?'

'Okay, yeah, sweet. Good plan. I'll see you soon.'

I walked over to the door and he gave me a grim smile as he stepped out. The deep breath he took seemed to give him courage and I watched him bounce off down the hall.

After I shut the door, I sat on my bed and pulled out one of my favourite books. I tried to read it but struggled to focus and decided to put it aside. Instead, I stared at the portrait of my parents and me, wondering about my mum, and then about the relationship between her and Dad. When I wasn't thinking about them, I was staring out the window, watching the moon move across the sky.

It was getting pretty late, and Dom and I really needed to get going soon. I hoped he'd had a decent sleep last night because we were in for a long one tonight. When it seemed to be almost midnight, I couldn't stay still any longer. On my feet, I paced back and forth across my room. Too agitated to continue, I checked my pack to make sure I had everything I needed.

Finally, I heard a knock at my door and walked over to open it. I pulled it towards me enough to check that it was Dom and then opened it the whole way to make space for him to come in. He was wearing long pants with boots and a loose shirt, and had a warm coat tied around his waist. His pack was in place, but he pulled it off, presumably for the weapons. I pointed to the stash I'd laid out on my bed and shut the door.

'Sorry, the guys were in the mood for games tonight. Took ages before they went to bed!'

'Doesn't matter now. Let's get ready.'

PACE

I STRAPPED ON MY weapons belt and carefully tucked each one into a slot. After I pulled on my jacket, I secured the pack Dom had lent me, pulling it tight across my chest. My stomach was a mess of nerves. I'd be glad when this was all over and we were back safe and sound.

When I looked up, Dom was ready to go, too. I nodded to him and he led the way out of my bedroom door. After I stepped out, I locked up and tucked my keys into my pack.

Carefully, I made my way down the stairs, straining to hear movement or voices. I edged around the opposite corner of the Common Room to Dom, both of us looking at our own side to check for other kids. Nothing.

We walked quickly to the front door and opened it slowly. There were no shouts of protest so Dom pushed it the rest of the way and stepped out. I shut the door softly behind us. Snow had started to fall.

Of course.

We moved side by side across the lane and into the trees next to the teachers' dorms, careful to stick to whatever shadows we could. Once we reached the tree line of the forest, I led the way inside. We'd decided that since we were avoiding the Academy now, it would be best to stay completely hidden.

I moved about five metres in and then turned so I was parallel with the Academy, Dom by my side. We didn't talk. The bundle of nerves that was my stomach writhed around like angry snakes trapped in a pit. We made it to the end of the grounds and kept walking.

Once we reached the stream where we'd stopped to talk about my mum, I took a deep breath and looked at Dom. I'd never been further than this. I glanced back at my new home and a feeling of sadness overpowered my nerves for a moment. I'd worked so hard to be able to attend and now I was throwing it away, unsure if I'd even be allowed back in once we returned.

Don't be silly. Of course you'll be allowed back in. This isn't goodbye, just see you later. Pull it together.

Dom echoed my thoughts. 'Don't sweat it. We'll be back in no time and your mum will be safe. Everything will be all good.'

I nodded. I was surprisingly torn about the decision I'd been so sure about but really, there was no way I was leaving my mum to the Crones. Dom was right; we'd be back in no time.

'All right. You ready to run?'

Dom grinned at me. 'I'm always ready to run. It's almost as much fun as eating!'

I laughed. 'Okay. Let's go. Due north, right?'

'Yep. That's it.' He pointed directly across the stream. After I gave him a nod, he took off.

I followed close behind. It wasn't hard to keep up, though I had a feeling that he was going easy on me. Sprinting while weighed down like this was certainly different to running in a ball game.

Despite our love of running, we knew we needed to pace ourselves. We had a lot of distance to cover and the packs added extra weight to the trip.

The further we ran, the closer the trees became. This far into the forest the fresh snow was unable to break through the dense canopy, so the ground was dry and the fallen leaves had turned to husks.

After what seemed like both a long time and no time at all, we started to slow, exhausted. I thought we'd made it quite a distance, and the sky—what tiny peeks I could get—seemed to have lightened.

We slowed to a walk but continued on, looking for somewhere we could rest. It seemed to take an extraordinarily long time but, eventually, we arrived at a clearing big enough to lay out our mats, though we'd be pretty close together. I flushed at the idea of laying so near to Dom.

For the first time since we'd started running, I spoke. 'This looks like a good spot to sleep.'

'Yep, here's good. Let's set up.'

We laid our packs against a tree and carefully pulled out our supplies. I laid out my mat then rearranged it to make space for Dom's. They were so close that our hands touched when we were fixing them up. Dom dropped that part of his mat and a pinkness rose in his cheeks. I pressed my lips together to stop myself smiling. He was just as bad as me.

Nervous, I laughed. 'We'd better get used to close proximity. Who knows where this is going to take us.'

He seemed to flush more and focused on rearranging his mat so it was laid out straight. 'Yeah, for sure.'

I nodded and finished setting up my sleeping gear by adding my blanket. My vision started to blur with tiredness. 'Do you want to eat, or...?'

'Nah. Too tired. Let's just get some shut-eye. We should be safe enough here to sleep at the same time, but I wouldn't bet on it once we reach the mountains.'

I nodded, already packing the food back into my pack. I laid on my mat and pulled up my blanket, thankful that the trees were also keeping some of the cold at bay. I knew the snow would be worse when we reached the mountains. I muttered a goodnight and before I knew it I was asleep.

When I woke, my eyes were still blurry from tiredness but I could tell that, despite the tight-knit trees and semi-darkness, it was definitely daytime now. It was also a little warmer. I rubbed my eyes and looked over at Dom; he was still asleep.

Trying to be quiet, I pulled a little of the fresh bread from my pack, knowing it would be one of the first things to go bad if we didn't eat it. I opened my mouth to take my first bite.

'Hey!' Dom said.

I jumped and dropped the bread.

He laughed. 'Hope you weren't gonna eat all that bread without me.'

I grabbed mine off my blanket and laughed at myself.

Guess I'm a little more worried about being out here than I thought.

'Wouldn't dream of it.' I picked up the larger piece I had put aside and passed it to him. 'Here you go.'

'Thanks,' he mumbled over the hunk of bread.

I shook my head and started eating. As I looked around at the forest, all I could see were trees—not that I could see that far, since they were scattered all over the place. While I chewed, I took in the scents. Dom seemed to fit right in with his musky, woodsy scent. Around him I could smell the dry earth of the forest floor, with hints of the decayed leaves. There was an animal of some kind nearby, a bird perhaps. It was mostly silent besides the two of us eating, no trace of the gently rippling stream we had long since left behind.

After I finished my bread, I pulled out the map and spread it over the blanket covering my legs.

'If we ran according to plan, we should be about... here.' I pointed to a spot in the middle of the forest. It would take us at least another couple of days to make it through to the other side.

Then we needed to cross a field and enter another smaller forest before we would reach the mountains. Dom looked down after he finished chomping away at his food.

'Yep. That looks about right. Should we make tracks?'

I titled my head, confused. 'Why would we make tracks?'

He burst out laughing, clutching his stomach. By the time he pulled himself together, I was a little irritated. He'd tried unsuccessfully to answer me about three times.

'Sorry, sorry. I meant get going, not actually make tracks.'

He couldn't seem to wipe the grin off his face when I mumbled back that he could have just said so.

'Come on. Let's get going,' I muttered.

We stood and packed our things, making sure everything was secure. I decided to leave my jacket in my pack while we finished out the forest for the day, since it seemed a little warmer. Dom did the same.

We positioned ourselves facing in the same direction as where we stopped last night, to make sure we continued the same way. It was a lot harder to keep my bearings when I couldn't see the sky and, with the trees spread around in such a random fashion, there was no straight line to follow.

'Do you want to take the lead again?' I offered.

'Nah, you can this time. Easier if you set the pace, though you did a pretty great job keeping up last night.'

'Sure thing.' I gave him a small smile then took off. I loved to run. To feel the wind rushing through my hair and the ground disappearing and ever changing beneath my feet. I dodged easily between the trees, doing my best to keep our path as direct as possible.

As I ran I thought of my mum and dad. About what their life must have been like. How they'd had to run away from his Pack and their families to be together. I faltered a step.

Could I actually have more family than just my mum and dad? Maybe a grandmother or grandfather on my mum's side?

I knew my grandparents on my dad's side had passed, but we'd never spoken about mum or her side of the family.

I vaguely recalled a time when I was about three, my mum chased me around on her hands and knees as I squealed and tried to escape. I loved that she always caught me, picked me up and squeezed me tightly, before putting me down and doing it again.

Two days later we were running again, this time a little behind schedule. I led the way, my thoughts coming and going, when Dom called me to stop. I came to a halt and looked at him questioningly. His cheeks were flushed.

'I, uh, need to pee.'

I felt my own cheeks heat and I looked at the ground. It was still as embarrassing as the first time. 'Oh, ah, yeah, no worries. I'll wait here.'

I turned back to the direction we needed to run and leaned against a tree. I heard Dom running a little way back the way we had come. The superior hearing was great for some things, but it made others just plain awkward.

I zoned back into my memories. This time, to one of the first training sessions I did with my dad, back when I was five. He'd told me it was just a game of hide and seek, which had seemed fun.

That was the day I'd learned about Shifters for the first time.

Dad had told me to go and hide in the forest out the back of our house. He gave me five minutes so I could find a good spot. I remembered scrambling through the bushes and in between trees until I found a clever location. Then I waited. It had been pretty boring and I'd started to practise my counting using the little crawling ants.

I'd made it to twenty when all of a sudden the insects had disappeared and I'd heard the crunch of leaves and sticks. I'd peeked out and seen a giant white wolf, way bigger than I had been at the time, looking around with its ears lifted up. Listening. I laughed out loud at the memory. At the time, I'd screamed. The wolf came over to me, tongue lolling out of its mouth. It was scary but funny, and then the air around him had shimmered, browns and greens colliding all around him, and then he'd turned into my dad.

I remember being really cranky at him for scaring me. He'd said he was sorry and gave me a hug. Then he'd taught me how to practise staying really still so Shifters couldn't find me as easily.

'What are you smiling about?'

I jumped about a foot off the ground. That distraction would have cost me at least a hundred sit-ups if Dad had caught me out like that.

Dom had grabbed my arm to steady me, an amused smile on his face.

'I was thinking about my dad and the first time I'd found out about Shifters. The day I first became excited about when I would get to do it.'

Dom grinned. 'How'd it happen for you?'

I told him the story and he laughed. Then laughed some more as he told me his own tale.

'I was about four or five. I was playing with my wooden swing out the back and all of a sudden some giant brown wolf came walking towards me. Besides me being scared half to death, it was kinda funny 'cause he seemed to be smiling. Then he turned back into Dad. And you know, I don't even think I was mad. I just kept asking when I'd get to do that. It was pretty awesome when it happened, too. Are you excited for when you Shift? It'll be while we're out here, right?'

The smile slipped from my face and I looked away, tears building. Dom came forward and hugged me, squeezing tight. The tears fell even faster.

'Hey, I'm sorry. It'll be okay.'

'It won't. I probably won't be able to change into a wolf at all. Everyone will know that I'm not a Shifter and something is wrong with me and no one will talk to me again. I'll never fit in at the Academy and they'll make me leave.'

My sobs turned to gasps and my chest felt so tight I couldn't breathe properly. I wrapped my arms around my body, trying to hold myself together. I was going to break.

Dom pulled me to the ground. 'Hey, hey. You need to calm down. Slow down your breathing. Deep breath in. Good, now out. And in. And out.'

I inhaled and exhaled along with his directions. Slowly my chest seemed to relax and my breathing was able to return to normal. I sat for a few minutes, trying to pull myself together enough to get moving again. When I was ready, I gave Dom's hand a squeeze and stood up. He followed me.

'Okay. I'm good.' I breathed out in a huff. 'Thanks, Dom. And I'm sorry. I'm not normally this... emotional.'

I gave him a small smile when he told me not to worry, then said we should probably "make tracks", to which he laughed again, probably a little more than necessary. Neither of us wanted to be stuck in the open valley that was coming up. We'd be too easy to spot.

By the time we made it to the open area, it was getting dark and a layer of slush covered the ground. We stopped before walking into it.

'What do you want to do? I don't know if we should cross in the dark. Crossing in the light will mean we're easy to spot by any nomad Shifters or Sorceresses, but it will also mean it's easy for us to see anyone coming.'

'I agree. Let's stop for the night then leave at first light. I'm starving anyway.'

Dom had cooked the fresh meat on the second night we'd stopped, so we were down to eating the dried meat and fruits.

'Let's go back a few hundred metres from the opening. We'd be spotted here across the valley.'

Dom looked out over the valley and hesitated, then nodded his agreement and started leading the way back in.

'Hey, did you see something?'

He paused before answering. 'Oh, uh, nah. I'm sure it's fine. Thought I saw something, but then there was nothing there.'

Even though we were too far to really see, I turned back to look for whoever, or whatever, it was that Dom must have noticed.

Feeling uneasy, I continued to search behind us until I could no longer see any glimpse of the valley between the gaps in the trees.

INTRUDER

O NCE WE FOUND A spot we could agree on, we stopped and set up our mats and blankets. I was really glad we'd covered so much ground by now that I was sure no one was chasing us, or we would have picked up their scent.

Besides, I doubt anyone thinks we'd be running off towards Crone Keep. Well maybe Miss Stone but I doubt she'd share that information.

Dom pulled out the food for us to eat. We were both starving but knew that we still needed to ration ourselves so we didn't run out too soon. Dom had told me that once we got to the forest on the other side of the valley, there would be fruits to find and more animals for him to hunt.

I needed to relieve myself but talking about it always made me anxious. I looked at the ground as I mumbled to Dom. 'I need to go pee. I'll be back.'

'Okay.' His tone was a little embarrassed too.

I ran a few hundred metres back the way we had come and stopped when I couldn't hear him moving things around anymore. When I was done, I walked back slowly. I was sure Dom had seen something earlier across the valley and I desperately hoped that, whatever it was, it wasn't going to pay us a visit tonight.

Back in the small clearing, Dom was tucking into the food. Mine was laid out on top of my blanket, waiting.

He looked up at me. 'Hey, I was thinking, we should start taking shifts to sleep now that we are close to the valley. I know we agreed on the other side, but I think maybe we should now, just in case we run into trouble.'

I exhaled in relief. 'Yeah, great idea. Do you want to sleep first?'

'Nah, it's all good, I'll take the first watch.'

'Okay, cool.'

We chatted for a while, then I decided I should get some shut-eye so we could both have a decent amount of rest before we had to go in the morning.

Snug under my blanket, my thoughts drifted back to my family, but my last thought before I went to sleep was of how soon I'd be Shifting for the first time; it was almost my birthday.

Dom's face hovered over mine. His finger across his lips. I was instantly awake. I nodded and sat. He moved back a little, so I didn't crash into him. His eyes had left mine and were peering around. I listened. There was a rustling in the trees.

I looked at Dom and waved at the stuff around us. He shook his head. It'd be too loud, I knew, but I didn't want to lose our stuff. I pointed to our weapons. This time he nodded. We'd fight.

I picked up my weapons belt as quietly as I could and slipped it around my hips as I rose from the ground. I buckled it on slowly. The rustling was moving closer. I stepped behind a tree. Dom moved in the opposite direction and did the same.

The noise came closer again. A shadow moved. It wasn't human height. I took a gentle sniff, trying to catch the flavour in the air. Shifter. Dom had realised the same. He signalled me to indicate Shifting by pointing to himself and then lowering his hand down to a shorter height, a questioning look on his face. I shook my head. It would be easier with the two of us to ambush the intruder with our weapons.

The shadow was almost on our makeshift camp, which was just visible from the faint light of the moon. From my vantage point, I saw the large, black wolf step into our small clearing and snarl. I could hear the spittle fly from its mouth and connect with the leaves on the ground nearby. I looked at Dom. Our eyes connected. He gave a slight nod and I gently pulled one of my short swords out. He had pulled his throwing knives.

Dom took a swift step from behind his tree and threw a knife. The wolf was already moving. The knife missed. It pounced for him. I launched from behind my tree, sword already moving in a tight arc towards the wolf. It changed course at the last second, the fur on its haunches sitting on end. Drool slid from between its canines as it looked us both over. Sizing us up. Feral.

It catapulted from the ground, right at Dom. He'd been pegged as the bigger threat. I swung forward as the wolf connected with him and sliced its back open. It gave a snarl, abandoned him and came at me. I retreated, using my senses to avoid the trees. I could see behind the wolf that Dom had pulled himself up and was collecting the bow and arrows from the ground.

One step. Another. The wolf stalked. My mind flashed to my father stalking toward me in the cave, then back to the black beast in front of me. Its lips pulled up. The wolf's weight shifted. I held my ground, trusting Dom. Two noises sounded at the same time: the wolf shoving leaves into the earth as it launched from the ground, and the sound of an arrow being released from the bow.

I dropped and spun to the left. The arrow connected, the wet puncture hitting my ears as the wolf charged into my shoulder. I hadn't moved far enough. The impact was like being hit with a bag of stones. But the arrow had worked; it was embedded in the wolf's side. The animal snarled and howled. It snapped at me. Then, it ran back toward the valley and away from us.

I stood shakily, clutching my shoulder. 'I guess you did see something after all.'

Dom looked at me, face grim. 'I guess I did. We shouldn't stay here the night, in case he returns. Do you think we should go back or forwards though?'

I thought for a few moments. 'Probably best to continue ahead. If we have to face him again, at least we'll be going in the right direction. Turning back now will mean we won't make the mountains once the storms are in full force, and they never take long to hit once the snow starts in winter. We don't want to be trapped with nowhere to stay when that happens.'

'Yep. Makes sense. All right. Let's get our stuff.'

Back in the scattered camp, we repacked out bags. My face wrinkled with worry when I saw Dom flinch as he bent down to get his things. His shoulders were tight, bracing for the pain of each movement. It was lucky Shifters healed pretty fast, but we'd both need to walk instead of run for the next part of the journey, to give our bodies the best chance.

As the moon crept toward the horizon and the sun began to show its first rays, we trudged through the ankle-deep snow at a snail's pace. If anyone was watching, we were essentially sitting ducks. I looked around constantly and kept my ears focused on our surroundings. By the time we made it to the other side of the valley, the sun was well into the sky, making the frosty air more bearable.

The forest on this side of the valley was different. It was filled with a range of trees, like white oaks and green ashes, as well as some shrubs and plants. Vibrant flowers and fruits were scattered about. Even better was the sound of running water.

'There must be a stream close by,' I said thirstily. It had been a long time since the last sip of water. In anticipation, I pulled out my flask and upended the last of it.

'Yeah, probably. But you maybe should have kept that until we were sure the water was good to drink.'

'Oh, yeah.' I was a little dumbfounded that the thought hadn't crossed my mind.

'Don't worry,' he said. 'I'm sure the water will be fine out here.'

If only I could not worry. An extra thing to panic about was really just one more than I needed on this journey. I lifted my ear in the direction of the stream straight ahead.

Hopefully that Shifter didn't run for the same thing. Some water before another fight would be great, not to mention a bit of a wash.

I knew I stunk because I hadn't been able to bathe since we'd left. The only stream we'd passed was too close to the Academy to bother stopping at.

'Do you think we could head straight to the stream before we stop? I'd love a wash and a drink.'

He nodded. 'Yeah. Good idea. And hey, maybe when we get to the mountain, we might even find a hot spring! That sounds pretty great after the beating we just took. Not sure our dads would be too impressed with that effort.'

I laughed quietly. 'Yeah, I think you're right. My dad would be pretty disappointed, considering all the training I've done.'

We continued straight ahead until we made it to the stream. I was excited that it actually seemed to be quite deep. I leaned down and drank a few handfuls of water. My shoulder ached and I began daydreaming about finding a hot spring, like Dom had mentioned. A long sleep would work, too, but I knew that option was even less likely than the hot spring.

I peered up at Dom. 'I think we should use this water to bathe and wash our clothes. What do you reckon?'

'Yep, I agree. Do you want to go first?'

'Yeah, thanks! But, uh, would you mind not going too far, in case the Shifter comes back?'

'I'll just go behind the bush over there and set up some food, if you want?'

'Perfect.'

I filled up both of our flasks then took them to Dom before grabbing fresh clothes out of my pack as well as some soap. I walked back around the large chunk of greenery, then started stripping down. I kept my weapons close to the edge of the water, just in case.

I slid into the stream and felt the icy liquid envelope my body. It came up to my waist so I immediately lay back into the water so I could enjoy the feeling of floating. I exhaled loudly. Hot would have been better, but it was still bliss. I made quick work of washing myself and then my clothes, and spent a few minutes longer floating around, enjoying the feel of the water running over me.

'Food's out,' Dom called.

I dropped my feet down at the suddenness of his voice, my heart racing and my cheeks heated. Relaxed, I'd forgotten about him being close by. I looked over to where he was, but I couldn't see him there, nor did his voice betray having seen me floating about.

You're being silly. Of course he wouldn't peek.

Peering through the forest, I checked it was clear then pulled myself up out of the stream, managing to stay clean by using the leaves rather than the dirt. I towelled myself dry, grateful that I'd thought to stuff it in, then pulled on a new outfit almost identical to the old one. I strapped on my weapons belt and picked up my wet gear.

Once with Dom, I hung my wet clothes on a couple of low-hanging branches and sat down to eat.

'Feeling better?'

I smiled. 'Much better! Thanks for letting me go first and laying out the food. I suppose we should start collecting some as we go now, before we hit the mountains and it becomes sparse.'

'All good. I didn't mind, and besides, I got to sneak in a few bites.' He grinned.

We sat and ate mostly in silence. He looked preoccupied.

Noticing his distraction, I decided to check in. 'Everything okay? You're not too badly injured, are you?'

'Nah, I'll be right. Just a bit sore. I was thinking about my dad, actually.'

'What's up?'

He ducked his head a little. 'Just hoping he's not too disappointed or anything.'

'I'm sure he'll be okay, Dom. Don't worry. I mean, I'm sure both our dads will be worried about us, but they'll be fine once we're back. Well, after they chew us up, anyway. Hey, what about your mum?'

My chest tightened. I'd never actually asked about his mum. I hoped I hadn't upset him further.

'Oh, she's pretty cruisy about everything. She'll worry a little but she always thinks that I'll be fine.' He laughed. 'She's probably a little too chilled, really, but I guess with Dad being Beta, now Alpha, she has to be.'

I smiled. 'It's great to have at least one chill parent, I'm sure. I wonder if my mum will be like yours, or if she'll be more like my dad.'

He grinned. 'She'll probably be calm, like my mum. Surely you can't have two stressed-out, protective parents with super-high expectations!'

'I hope not! But really, I think I'll just be happy to have my mum back.'

'That makes sense. Worry about that other stuff later. Anyway, thanks for distracting me a bit. I'm gonna go have a wash.'

'No worries. I'll hang out here.'

He grabbed his towel and new clothes from his pack and walked off towards the stream. I kept my weapons close by, but laid down on my mat. I closed my eyes, focusing on sounds and scents.

The forest around smelled lush and green, despite it being a few weeks into winter. The flowers nearby had a sweet perfume, and I thought I could smell some sort of fruit nearby. These parts must have been inhabited at some point, for the food to be so plentiful. I'd spotted a section of banana trees back near the entrance, but only managed to grab one bunch on our way in.

At the end of each exhale I held my breath and listened, casting my senses out as far as I could. Dom moved through the water; it seemed like he was paddling along the stream. There was the sound of little feet moving, perhaps through the trees or over sticks on the ground. The squeak of a mouse or tree-dwelling animal.

My intakes of air kept drawing in the scent of food. After a few extra rounds of breathing, I could hear my stomach grumbling. Embarrassed, I sat up and clutched at it. Remembering the food I'd picked up and placed next to me, I started eating. The banana was mostly ripe and sweet. I devoured it in no time at all and peeled another one, hoping Dom wouldn't mind and that we'd be able to find some more on our way through to the mountain.

I kept the scents in my mind as I laid back down after eating. I'd need to discuss foraging for food when Dom got back from his wash. We'd have to collect a decent amount before we reached the mountain or we wouldn't have enough to make it through.

It would take us about a week from the base of the mountains, including stopping to sleep and preparing for Crone Keep. I sat up when I heard Dom on his way back from the stream.

'You look a bit more refreshed.'

A smile lit up his face. 'Yeah, I'm definitely feeling better after that. Amazing what a bit of water will do for you. Do you want to keep moving or rest a while? I don't think that Shifter will be back any time soon, not with the arrow sticking out of his side.'

'Rest, I think. We could both do with a bit of recovery time and to gather some food. Besides.' I looked at the ground. 'If I've been keeping track right, it's, uh... It's my birthday today. Well, tonight.'

'Oh, no way! Crap, I'm sorry Elita, I should have asked exactly when it was. Happy birthday! I can't believe I didn't know. And we've been attacked and everything. And you got injured.'

I peered up at Dom. 'It's okay. With everything going on, and me being unsure about what's going to happen when I have my first Shift, I haven't really been as excited about it as I used to be.'

He nodded at me, a serious expression on his face. 'It'll be okay. No matter what happens. Do you want to talk about it?'

I thought about it. On the one hand, it would be nice for someone to know what I was thinking. On the other, I didn't want to seem like I was just complaining. I knew there were worse things that could happen than me not being able to Shift.

Maybe. Well, talking helped last time. It's worth another try.

'I guess I'm still caught up on not being able to fit in with everyone at the Academy. And if I can't Shift, I don't know exactly what it'll mean. Will it mean I'm definitely part... you know, Sorceress? Will I have powers?'

As anxious as I was about not being able to Shift, I was also a little excited about maybe being able to do magic. Not that I could really tell anyone that. Or, could I?

'So what if you're half and half? That'd be pretty special. Maybe you'd even have some magic.'

The tone of Dom's voice hinted that he thought it would be cool. Could I dare to hope that he wouldn't be the only one? That maybe I could still fit in with my Pack—unlikely as it seemed at the moment, particularly given the animosity we had for the Crones and their Sorceresses?

I tried to keep the wonder and excitement from my voice when I answered him, but I wasn't sure that I really succeeded. 'I could have magic, couldn't I?'

I thought back to the blacks and reds weaving together in the Library attack. It was like a beautiful dance of death made purely of light. The idea of being able to do that was thrilling, but not if everyone would hate me for it. Not if I couldn't fit in or have my friends.

I shook my head and came out of my thoughts a little, then looked back at Dom. He was studying me. Had I given myself away? My heart began to race. The last thing I wanted to do was push Dom away while we were out to rescue my Sorceress mum by making him think I was a freak.

Maybe, after tonight, if things went wrong, he'd change his mind and abandon me. Leave and go back to the Pack without me. Tell everyone what I am, or what I'm not.

'Hey. Stop it. I can see you panicking. I'm not going anywhere. Even if you're a full-blown Sorceress, you won't get rid of me. I'm here for you. Though, honestly, you smell like a Shifter to me.'

I hoped he was right about me being a Shifter. But... a little magic wouldn't hurt, surely. Besides, would my mum even want me if I wasn't like her at all?

Ugh. This is ridiculous. Stop.

Dom apparently thought the same, because he got up. 'Come on. Let's do some sparring. You need a distraction.'

DISTRACTION

I STOOD IN THE small clearing next to the stream, facing Dom. We circled each other slowly, each step calculated. I watched the placement of his weight, the tensing of his muscles, to anticipate his movements.

His left knee gave him away. The slight bend showed that he was about to move forward. As he leapt, I took a step to the left and gave him an open-handed hit on the arm, then took a step back. He smiled wickedly. It was close to the target; his chest. But not close enough.

We continued our circular movements. This time he didn't make the first move. I did. Instead of pushing up to hit him in the chest, I dove down and took out his legs. When he came down, I leant forward and tapped him on the chest.

'One to me.' I grinned, feeling a little proud of myself for landing the first hit.

He laughed good naturedly. 'Again.'

We went back to circling. Dom dove towards me, but anticipated my move to the right and had his arm out ready for me. Tap.

I snarled. Surprised and embarrassed, I immediately stood up and covered my mouth with my hands. 'Sorry,' I mumbled.

His shocked look quickly became one of male superiority crossed with his usual laughter. I scowled at his macho behaviour, even if it was playful. I hated it when an opponent got cocky.

We circled each other again. This time I went straight for the chest. Surprised at my sudden straightforward approach, he didn't move in time. Tap.

'Two to one.'

This time Dom scowled at me a little. It seemed as though no one liked to lose. Particularly to someone younger than them.

'Again.'

The game went on for longer than it should have. The intensity increased as our strategies dwindled. After a few crazy dives, the laughter returned and our matches became light-hearted again, though I was willing to bet we'd be sporting a few extra bruises from the tackles that drove us into trees and bushes instead of each other.

'Okay. Enough! Enough!' I clutched my stomach, tears of joy leaking down my face at Dom's latest failed dive that landed him in the stream, completely soaking his fresh clothes. 'Let's call it a draw.'

He choked on the water and his own laughter. 'Sure, sure. A draw. But just so you know, I'd totally have won.'

I rolled my eyes, then grinned. 'Sure you would have. If you were versing the stream instead of me.'

We made our way back around the bushes and over to our stuff. There was a mouse on my blanket. I squealed. 'Get it off!'

Dom broke into laughter, clutching his stomach and scaring off the mouse with his big guffaws. 'You... are afraid... of a mouse. You're a... Shifter... a wolf... maybe even a Sorceress.' He sat down on a small rock to catch his breath.

I waited until he was done, much more relaxed now that the mouse had disappeared. 'Everyone is afraid of something, you know.'

He grinned, wiping the tears of laughter from his cheeks. 'Not me. I'm not afraid of anything.'

I rolled my eyes. 'Yeah, sure you're not.'

Too anxious to talk much more I laid down on my mat and pulled up my blanket. Once Dom had pulled himself together and changed his wet clothes, he snuggled into his own covers, too, though I noticed the smile hadn't left his face as he stared up at the traces of sky. I turned my gaze to follow his. The darkness betrayed the late hour.

I tensed where I lay. I would Shift soon.

Will I? Maybe nothing will even happen. No, I smell like a Shifter. Surely I'll change. But, if I change does that mean that I won't be a Sorceress? That I won't be like mum and won't have any magic? Ugh! I don't even know what I want.

As I sifted through my thoughts, my stomach felt more and more rocky, as if I was going to be sick. I could feel the change coming. I turned to Dom, my dad's instructions about Shifting alone for the first time running through my head.

'I think I might go for a walk.'

He looked at me, his expression serious again. 'Do you want company, or do you want to do it by yourself? I mean, when I Shifted for the first time, I had my family there. But, whatever you want is cool.'

I considered his words but what Dad said just kept coming back. I shook my head. 'I think I'll go myself. I just... Just in case, you know?'

He nodded and I started to stand up. Before I made it all the way, he reached out and grabbed my hand lightly. I paused and looked down at him.

'It really will be okay. And I'm here for you, no matter what happens.'

I felt pressure build behind my eyes and I smiled softly. 'Thank you, Dom. It means more than you know.'

He let go of my hand and I walked away, following along the stream until I found a large rock by the water. Bending my knees, I jumped up and sat on top of it with my legs crossed, then focused on my breathing like Dad had taught me. Centring myself. Inhale. Exhale. Inhale. Exhale.

Sitting with my eyes closed and hands resting in my lap, I began to feel a slight shiver over my body. It felt just like it had been described in a Shifter book I'd read. I opened my eyes and saw a shimmer starting to form in front of them. I closed my eyes, unsure if I wanted to see. The shiver became more intense. Not as though I was cold, but like I had too much energy trapped inside my body. I felt it to some degree all over my body, but mainly around my face and my hands.

Then, it stopped. Eyes still scrunched, I did a mental body scan. It almost felt like nothing had changed. Disappointment ripped through me and tears broke through my closed eyelids.

I'll never be able to run with my Pack.

I clenched my fists, hissed, and immediately released them as a sharp pain stung my hands. The smell of blood wafted to me. Eyes wide, I looked down at my hands. My fingernails had lengthened and sharpened. Claws. I had *claws*!

Dom burst into the clearing. 'I smelled blood! Are you okay?!'

I was clearly out of it. Surely I should have sensed he was coming before he crashed into the clearing. 'I, uh. Yes? Maybe? I don't know. I, uh, have claws?'

I held my hands up to show him. He walked closer, inspecting them. When he was a couple of metres away, he froze. 'Woah! You also have pointed ears, sharper teeth and glowing amber eyes. That's crazy!'

'I... do?' Instinctively I raised my hands to my ears. I didn't know what to think. I wasn't a wolf, but I was something. My earlier worry returned along with panic that I would look ugly like this. I tried to push the latter thought down.

'I'll never be able to run with the Pack like this.' My voice broke and my vision blurred through my tears as I resumed looking down at my hands, too embarrassed to keep my eyes on Dom.

'Well, you never know what could happen. Besides, you look like you have enough energy bouncing around that you *could* keep up. *Maybe*. Why don't you give it a try?'

I looked at him, confused. 'Give what a try?'

'A run. You know, get off that rock and see what other changes there are besides the physical ones?'

'Oh. Yeah, sure.'

Glad for the distraction, I stood, shooting up faster than I'd anticipated, but having no trouble keeping my balance. It was like I had more control or something, more awareness. I looked at my surroundings, then at Dom. I focused on his face. My vision was more acute. I had no trouble seeing the tiny smattering of freckles below his widened eyes, even while standing up on the rock and with him a few metres away.

Inhaling, I took in the scents. It was like an overload, the lush greenery hitting me with full force. I could smell our food, and other fruit. I scrunched up my nose. I could smell poop.

Dom burst out laughing. 'What do you smell that I can't?'

'Poo,' I mumbled.

He kept laughing. Clearly amused by either the poo or my face when I smelled it. When I realised I could actually smell and probably see things he couldn't right now, I became excited.

'Hey! I can smell stuff you can't, so my Shift at least did something. Do I call it a Shift?'

'I reckon so. You look like you could bite my hand off with those chompers.'

Embarrassed, I covered my mouth with my hand. They must look ridiculous and horrific.

He shook his head. 'Relax! They look cool, not weird or anything. You still look great!' At that he turned the colour of a tomato and ducked his head.

I felt my own cheeks heat in response. 'Thanks,' I mumbled back to him. 'So, uh, think we should have this race?'

He looked back up at me, his grin so big I could almost see his molars. 'You bet! To the valley entrance and back?'

I gave him a toothy grin of my own and, waving my hands as though I had a wand, gestured that he should change.

He laughed, then all I could see was the shimmer. This time when I saw it, it really was like magic. The light that covered Dom was like a billion tiny sparks of earthy tones—browns, tans and greens—colliding with each other in a magnificent display.

The brilliant colours faded out and then Dom stood in front of me in his wolf form. Up close, I could see that he was around half my height. Shorter than both my dad and his, but not by that much considering he was still growing.

Dom gave me a wolfy grin and shot off through the trees. I cussed, leapt down from my rock and launched myself after him.

It was as though I was flying. I felt light but sturdy at the same time. Movement through the forest was seamless; I weaved in and out of the trees and brush, able to study each piece of bark or leaf in my path as I moved. When it became too distracting and I heard Dom's footsteps begin to fade, I drew my focus back to the path ahead of me.

The light impact of my footfalls pulsed through me as I took each step. I barely touched the ground. The scents were a blur but I knew instinctively that, if I focused on them, I'd be able to separate them out easily. I needed to gain more ground so I concentrated on being light and throwing myself forward to reach a greater speed. If I had been in my human form, I'd have definitely smacked my head on a tree branch by now.

Talk about a headache!

The sound of Dom's paws hitting the ground came back into range as I began to gain ground on him again. The thrill of the chase coursed through me. The idea of catching him was magnetic. I was drawn forward.

Light filtered in through the trees ahead of me and signalled that we were close to the edge. I didn't think it was possible, but I increased my speed a little more, using the extra space between the trees to my advantage.

There you are! Almost got you!

The edge of the forest was visible now. I kept pushing myself, trying to make it despite the fact I knew it wouldn't happen.

I saw Dom's deep brown fur break through the tree line into the valley and I slowed, the instinct to conserve my energy taking over.

I broke through the clearing within seconds of Dom and saw him collapse on the ground, heaving in deep breaths, his tongue lolling out. He looked beat. I was pretty exhausted myself, but I wasn't too tired to register his shock as he saw me, standing and breathing only half as hard as he was.

I managed to pull my lips up into a quick grin before he began to Shift back. I stood, transfixed on the shimmer. Whoever thought Shifters weren't magic were crazy. The earthy sparks collided with each other, causing what seemed to be mini explosions of light that shifted and weaved around each other. Then Dom was laying on the ground, his breath returning to normal. He seemed so much clearer and more defined through my Shifted eyes. He stared at me.

'What?' I asked self-consciously.

He shook his head. 'Nothing. But, uh, do you want to Shift back before we return to the camp?'

'Oh. Yeah.' I stood for a moment and then had the embarrassing realisation that I had no idea how to Shift back. 'I, um, don't actually know how?'

'Oh, right. Sorry. You just need to visualise your human form and think about looking that way. It totally gets easier.'

I nodded and closed my eyes, my face scrunched up in concentration. Dom snickered at me. I stuck my tongue out then turned my back and tried to focus. Images flowed through my mind of shorter nails, flat teeth, rounded ears.

Then I felt it; the shimmer, the electricity spark through me. This time, I tried to watch. It wasn't the same as seeing Dom Shift; it was more like blurs of colours moving around. Definitely not the same as the magic I saw the Sorceresses casting in the Library attack.

Back to normal, I grinned and opened my eyes wide. I felt really proud at having Shifted back.

Dom spoke from behind me. 'So... what do you think? It's not full wolf, but it's pretty cool!'

I turned and considered it, but I didn't really know what to think.

'I'm a bit half and half, I think. I wish I could turn full wolf like the rest of the Pack. I mean, I'll never fit in with everyone else. They'll all know that I'm different. But you know, I'm glad I got to change a little bit. It's something.'

He nodded. 'Yeah, I get that. It's definitely cool. And hey, maybe one day you'll be able to change into a full wolf. Maybe you can cast a spell to do it or something.'

I grinned before I could stop myself and put my hand over my mouth. My eyes darted to Dom's. He'd seen. My stomach was a big twist of knots. It was one thing to have no choice but to be part Sorceress, but it was another entirely to want to be one, to have magic.

Dom's face scrunched a little, and he looked worried. He seemed to want to say something, but perhaps he didn't want to upset me.

My anxiety got the best of me. 'Out with it!'

He smiled, amused. 'Just don't worry so much. Shifters may hate the Sorceresses, but if they could have magic, they'd want it too. Well, that's what I think anyway.' He shrugged.

I wasn't convinced. 'Maybe. Anyway, we should probably start walking. Wouldn't want that Shifter to find our camp with us nowhere near it. And I don't want any of those little rodents thieving our food.'

He laughed. 'All right. Let's move it.'

The walk back was mostly quiet. I was lost in thought about what my life would be like with the Pack when they found out I couldn't change, whether they'd even let me stay. I mean, if the shoe had been on the other foot, I don't know if I'd let me stay. The Pack Alpha had to put the needs of the many before the needs of just me.

Maybe Dom will put in a good word for me or something. No. That wouldn't be fair to ask. He's already gonna be in enough trouble for having come with me. Especially once they learn what I am.

That led me onto another train of thought, about exactly what I was. I knew I was definitely part Shifter, because I changed, but couldn't have been a pure Shifter because I didn't turn into a wolf. Being part Sorceress seemed like something I was just going to have to deal with.

I'll probably be the weakest of both. Half probably means less power too, if I have any at all.

I fretted all the way back to our little camp. When we arrived, Dom decided he wanted another wash in the stream and, since I really wasn't that bad, I decided to just get some sleep.

I woke to a beam of sunlight shooting through the tree canopy. It shone almost right next to my face. I rolled my head to the side to see it hit the ground and squealed. The damn mouse was back again.

Dom shot up and had a knife drawn in no time at all. Having smelled the rodent the second he woke up, he flopped back down onto his mat and groaned. 'Aw, come on, Elita. It's just a little mouse. Not like it can hurt you or anything.'

The impact of his words were lessened by the fact that his groggy face was alight with an amused grin. He found the funny side of everything, which was equal parts great and frustrating. Though, maybe a little more on the great side, really.

Since the sun was now up, and so were we, I suggested we get moving so we could collect some food and make the mountain base today. It would be a long couple of weeks once we did. We ate a little food while we packed away our mats and blankets.

As we walked, we grabbed any fruit we came across. It made the trip slower, but it meant we could spend some quality time healing from the fight and our sparring match as we went. Ideally, we'd be back to one hundred per cent before we ran into any other problems, though I really hoped we'd stay safe until we made it to Crone Keep.

FREEZING

I T WAS FIVE DAYS into our mountain trek and we were starting to freeze. I'd resorted to pulling out several layers of my
clothes and wearing them together to keep the chill out.

Dom had discovered that it was less harsh in his wolf form
because of the thick fur coat, but that wasn't much help for me
because it meant I had to carry two packs while injured. Even
though I'd told him that he should stay Shifted, he'd refused.
He'd made me check if it was more bearable in my "wolf" form
but the cold still bit into me and, if anything, it was a little worse
because of my heightened senses.

Despite initially deciding that it would be safer to travel by
night so we were less visible on the snow-covered mountains, I
ended up suggesting we travel during the day so we at least had
the sunlight to warm us. Dom had begrudgingly agreed with
me, So each night we found small caves within the mountains
to camp in. Some had been so shallow that we'd nearly frozen
anyway, but others had been nice and deep, and had sheltered us
well.

I led the way along the mountain, keeping my head tucked down and my hood up to cover my ears from the icy smattering of snow. The incline was steep enough to make me stoop a little. I peeked up as the darkness started to descend, my stomach tightening.

I turned to Dom and shouted. 'We need to find somewhere soon. We don't want to be trying to make camp in the dark again.'

'Yep! Let's stop at the next one. I think I see a dark spot a little further along.' He pointed ahead, arm unsteady in the strong wind.

I nodded and turned in that direction. It was a good thing we could see pretty well because there was almost no chance of hearing over the howling winds if anyone was about to attack. We had to shout just to hear one another.

As we neared the cave entrance, I heaved a sigh of relief. We'd been hiking up the mountain almost since the sun came up. My legs were getting tired from travelling every day.

I turned back and looked at Dom, taking a quick step backwards when I realised he was watching his feet as he walked. He came to a sudden halt at my quick movement and looked up and met my eyes. His cheeks were flushed again, but this time I was sure it was from the icy wind whipping his face.

Once I was sure I had his attention, I pointed to the cave that was right near our current position then gestured to our weapon belts. Dom put his hand to his belt and pulled out the throwing knives. I pulled out my short swords.

Once we reached the flat landing outside the cave entrance, we carefully placed our packs on the ground to the right. We needed to be ready to fight if there were hostiles, and it was almost impossible to scent anything with the wind blowing in the snowstorm. We'd become a little more casual about it, figuring there would be no one around in these parts of the mountains, but carrying packs into a potential fight would just be a disaster waiting to happen.

It was Dom's turn to check the cave, so I stepped to the side and allowed him to pass. He slowly put his head around the corner to look inside. Within a second he had retreated, his face ashen. We had company.

I pointed behind us, asking if we could go. He quickly shook his head. They were coming. Knowing it would be easier to fight inside the cave then on the edge where we could be pushed, I gestured for him to go in.

We moved quickly into the cave front and braced ourselves. They were upon us immediately. There were three of them, two with weapons in front, and one sitting at the rear of the cavern.

Shit.

I had one short sword in each hand, using one to block and the other to attack. The numerous layers of clothes weren't convenient for a fight, but there wasn't anything I could do about it now. Seeing that I wasn't making much ground, I switched my attacking and blocking hands. I felt a rush of gratitude to Dad in that moment, for the gruelling hours he'd made me spend strengthening both arms for fighting with weapons.

It worked and I started making progress. I sliced the arm of the man in front of me. His brown eyes became furious slits as he tried to charge at me again. Anger was not his friend. It made his next movements obvious, allowing me to use my small size to dodge under his swing. But now I had my back towards the other Shifter at the rear of the cave. Not good. I focused on my hearing and realised he'd gotten to his feet, it sounded as though he'd staggered a little. Shocked, I realised he might be the wolf from the woods and he hadn't quite healed yet. I shook my head to focus, I was about to be surrounded. I'd be lucky to escape with my life.

I peeked at Dom between blows and was reassured that he at least seemed to be holding his own against the other Shifter, both of them still in human form. I suppose they thought the close quarters would be worse as wolves.

The Shifter from the rear was almost on top of me when I caught sight of another person in the mouth of the cave. A girl. I deflected another swing, this one making my arm shake. The sheer aggression of his hits were getting harder to take.

The girl had moved in.

We were done for.

There was no way we'd get out of here with both of us fighting two against one. I needed to move more quickly.

I ducked under the next blow and moved to the side, my back now to the wall. One sword faced each of my opponents. I'd trained for this once but it didn't make it any easier. I inhaled, ready to engage when I heard a massive thud and crash. My eyes flicked to Dom. It wasn't him. The girl had knocked out the other Shifter with a blow to the head. Relieved, I faced my attackers again, but one of them chose that moment to abandon me and attack Dom and the girl.

That left me with the injured guy. Piece of cake, right? Probably not. He swung his sword at me from the side, right at neck height. I managed to duck in time, but only just. I swung my leg out and tripped him. Before I could make another move, I heard another thud and then the girl was standing beside the injured Shifter in front of me, her sword poking into his neck, drawing blood. Clearly she wasn't afraid to slice him up. When he dropped the sword, I stepped back and leaned on the cave wall.

Suspicious, I turned my gaze to her. She looked maybe a year or two older than me and had light, straw-coloured hair—almost white. She wore leathers and a warm jacket, and chose that moment to raise her eyes to me. Hazel.

'Why are you looking at me like that?' she asked. 'I just saved your butts.'

I considered her for a moment. She had helped, and I had been sure we were done for before she'd arrived. I looked over at Dom and he shrugged. 'You did, thanks. But who are you exactly, and why are you here?'

She looked at the Shifters on the ground, two unconscious and one listening in to the conversation. 'Maybe we should take care of this and then talk about it later?'

Embarrassment flooded me at the realisation she was right. Determined to save face, I said, 'Yeah, fine. But take care of them how?'

She shrugged, flipped her sword, and before I had a chance to protest, she brought the pommel down on the side of the Shifter's head, knocking him unconscious too. His head slumped and when she released him he thudded unceremoniously to the ground.

Oookay, crazy. Well, I guess that takes care of that.

The girl's eyes flashed. 'Quit being so judgy. What were you gonna do about it?'

Lips tight, I shrugged. 'Let's just get out of here.'

She shook her head. 'Not until we tie them up. I don't want them waking up in five minutes and chasing after us. Not that they'd have an easy time following us in the snowstorm, but there are only so many caves to hide in around here.'

I looked at Dom, who was becoming more amused by the minute. When he saw my grimace, his grin swelled. 'Well, do you wanna see if they have some ropes? I don't want to use ours,' I barked.

He seemed to be trying to rein in his mirth as he walked deeper into the cave to search. After a few moments, he called out that he'd found some.

I looked back at the girl and she waved a hand at the men on the floor. 'Give me a hand with them?'

I gritted my teeth at being given instructions by some random girl I didn't even know, but moved to help anyway. Dom joined us too.

They were dead weight, and heavy enough to have us all breathing harder by the time we'd dragged them to the centre of the cave to be tied together.

'Either of you two any good with knots?'

I shrugged at the same time Dom did. She rolled her eyes and I bit my teeth together so hard I was surprised they didn't crack.

Who the hell does she think she is?

'Just pass me the ropes,' she said to Dom.

'Sure thing.' He fetched them from the ground and handed them over.

She gave Dom a double take as she took the ropes. I felt a flush of annoyance and jealousy run through my body.

Jealous? About Dom?

He gave me one of his goofy grins then turned to watch the girl. She expertly tied the ropes around each of the Shifter's hands behind their backs and pulled them tight. She finished by tying the ropes together. It looked like a pretty big mess of knots, though definitely the kind that would be hard to get out of.

Satisfied, she stood up and looked at us. 'Well? Let's get out of here. I spotted another couple caves further in the distance when I was scouting around earlier in the day.'

How long has she been following us?

Refusing to look like a fool again, I kept my questions to myself and indicated with a lavish gesture that she should exit first. There was no way we'd be walking in front of her when she seemed to have a thing for knocking people out with her damn sword. The giant smirk on her face irritated me as she turned and led the way.

Dom attempted to wipe the amusement from his face when I shot him a glare. Taking some things seriously would be a bonus, though he'd obviously decided that she wasn't a threat.

She exited the cave in front of us and picked up her own pack from the ground. It looked full to the brim with stuff, but she pulled it on like it weighed nothing. I bent down, picked mine up and slung it over my back. I watched Dom do the same from the corner of my eye while I kept a close watch on her.

Once she saw we were ready, she turned and took off without another word. It was like she was trying to make us rush on purpose. I rolled my eyes and continued on behind her.

We trekked for what felt like half an hour or so, and passed a couple of caves as we walked. The sky was a deep shade of blue by the time she found the one she wanted. She must have stayed in it before.

I sniffed the air. Water. Hot water. My eyebrows shot up in surprise and I looked hopefully at Dom.

'Hey, is there a hot spring in here?' he asked.

She gave a smug smile. 'Sure is. Worth the extra trek through the mountains, huh?'

I watched as she dumped her bag on the ground and took off her thick jacket to reveal a tight-fitting woollen shirt. Then she sat and pulled off her shoes, as though she were perfectly at home in some random cave. I tilted my head, wondering if she was from the Trevini Pack.

'Well, go on,' she said. 'I know you're barely containing the thousand questions you want to ask.'

I made a small scoffing noise and moved closer, then sat against the wall opposite her.

'Who are you?'

She looked right at me. 'Alessia.'

I waited impatiently for her to add some other useful piece of information, but it appeared that she was going to remain stubborn.

'And where are you from?'

She started rifling through her bag, no longer looking at me. 'Trevini Pack.'

I exhaled loudly and wondered if my dad had sent her somehow. 'Why were you following us?'

She snorted. 'Who said I was following you? Not that you weren't easy to spot, walking along the mountain in the middle of the day like you were.'

I gave her a hard stare and waited in silence until she spotted it, then she sighed.

'Fine. I was following you because I'm insane. Or I may as well be anyway. Our Pack Medicine Woman told me she'd had a vision of me needing to help two other Shifters in a cave in the Mortis Mountains. She practically pushed me out of the camp to go and find you two. Not really sure why she chose me but her instincts are usually right.'

'Right. Seems ridiculous.'

She shrugged.

'It seems as if you're telling the truth. Not sure why else you'd be on this snowy death trap in the winter storms. In saying that, it seems a bit of a stretch that you'd leave just because your Medicine Woman said so. Also, why aren't you at the Academy? You don't look much older than us.'

'Mum didn't want me to go. Don't really know why. But there are a few from my Pack who just get trained by our Alpha and the Medicine Woman, plus a few others with experience. Besides,' she laughed, 'seems like I'm not missing out on much. You guys were getting your asses handed to you.'

Dom piped in for what seemed like the first time since Alessia had shown up. 'Hey, that's not true. I was handling my guy just fine.'

'Yeah, you weren't doing too bad, but I don't think your mad fighting skills would have been quick enough to beat your opponent and save your girlfriend from being annihilated.'

Dom's cheeks turned scarlet. 'We're just friends!'

'Why does everyone keep saying stuff like that?' I muttered.

She gave me a look like I was some kind of idiot, which only fuelled my anger. I opened my mouth to say something else, but she started talking again.

'Anyway. Doesn't matter. So. My turn. What are you two doing out here in the dead of winter that is so important that I had to leave my cosy Pack fire and come and save you both?'

I pursed my lips, not convinced that I was interested in telling her anything, especially if she was just about to leave anyway. I didn't need my secrets being spilled. I looked over to Dom.

He shrugged. 'Your call.'

This conversation sucked. 'Are you even sticking around or are you just leaving at first light to go back to your Pack?'

Alessia looked like she was deliberating what she wanted to say. Eventually she answered. 'The Medicine Woman said that I'd need to stick around for a while. She said something about some crazy mission that would probably get us all killed, but that I had to be here, or you guys really would end up chopped liver.'

I bristled then looked her dead in the eyes, determined to see just how tough she really was. 'We're breaking into Crone Keep and freeing a prisoner.'

Alessia snorted. 'Crazy mission, all right. Understatement of the damn millennium. You guys even have a plan for that?'

Dom cut in, obviously put out by her lack of confidence in our abilities and forethought. 'Yes, of course we have a plan. We even have a set of internal drawings and a couple of maps of the surrounding area. We're not idiots or anything.'

'Huh. Well, that's something. A nice surprise, at least. I guess the few potions that my Medicine Woman gave me make more sense, now I know where I'm going.' At the questioning look I gave her, she continued. 'She gave me some kinds of magical sleeping draughts. A couple to put on a cloth and hold over their mouths and noses, and a couple more that you smash at their feet from the glass vials.'

I opened my eyes wide. I'd heard of such draughts but hadn't ever seen them in action. As I was pondering how we could make use of them, Alessia interrupted.

'Well, what's the plan?'

I pursed my lips. She was so abrupt and pushy! Unsure how much we should tell her this soon, I looked at Dom. He shrugged. I turned and stared back at her, eyebrows raised.

She stood suddenly. 'Ugh, fine. I'll go enjoy the hot spring while you guys get your story straight.'

PLANS

A LESSIA TURNED AND STROLLED right out of the cavern through a passage at the back. After a minute, I walked over and stuck my head in to be sure she wasn't eavesdropping.

Before I could say anything, Dom blurted out, 'Wow, she is all kinds of hot and crazy!'

I stared hard at him, not sure why I felt a little stab in the chest at his comment. It seemed more and more like I was jealous, which was ridiculous. I decided to ignore his comment.

'So do we trust her enough to share?'

He shrugged. 'Yep, I guess so. I mean, she did kind of save our butts back there and she told us why she's here. She even told us about the draughts she has. What do you think?'

I sighed. 'Yeah, I suppose you're right. I can't really see any other reason she'd be here. Do we tell her everything though? Like *who* we're going to rescue?'

Dom thought for a moment before he answered me. 'Nah, I don't think she needs to know that right now, especially if you're worried about how it might affect you. Let's just stick to saying that she's a prisoner.'

Grateful, I nodded. 'Thanks. I don't think I'm ready to share all of that stuff, but I'll probably have to say I can't Shift at this point. I fight well enough without Shifting. Though I did wonder, why don't you guys just Shift when you're fighting?'

'Oh, sorry. I forgot you haven't had to worry about it yet. When we Shift, we keep our clothes but not what we're holding. So if we have weapons in our hands, we're as good as passing them to our enemies to use against us since they'd just fall on the ground. If I'd had time, I would have left my weapons in my pack and just entered in my wolf form.'

'Huh. That makes sense. It never really came up with Dad in training because we were always doing specific drills and he was either in wolf form or we were doing weapons training, never really both.'

'Yep, sounds right. We never did both. It wasn't really until I Shifted and started taking intermediate weapons lessons that I really had to worry about it.'

I filed the knowledge away for later, along with the thought to try and see what would happen with my weapons when I Shifted since I didn't actually change that much, though it would be a waste of claws if I was trying to hold a weapon.

Maybe I could actually use a weapon in one hand and the claws with the other. I'm sure it would shock anyone I was fighting.

Apparently, I'd been off in my own little world for too long, because Dom suddenly coughed to get my attention. When I shook my head and focused, I realised he was waving his hand in front of my face.

201

'Oh, sorry. I was just thinking. Shall we go tell her the plan then?'

'Yep. Let's go!'

Someone's eager!

I followed behind Dom as he sped off down the path, following the steam that was making the air thicker and heavier. After a little while, I heard the water flowing from the hot springs and picked up my pace a little, excited to warm up my core.

I rounded the corner and nearly ran straight into Dom. He'd stopped dead in his tracks when he walked into the cavern. I gave him a little shove and he stepped to the side.

'Woah,' I muttered.

The cavern was huge and had stalactites hanging like giant icicles from every inch of the roof. The ground we were standing on dropped off just a few metres ahead of the entrance. So much steam rose from it that a haze covered the room. It was incredible. I turned to Dom and realised that it wasn't actually the space he was staring at, but Alessia. And her clothes, or rather lack of them. I looked around beside us and saw what appeared to be most of her outfit sitting on the floor.

'Seriously?' I called out to her. 'No clothes?'

'Gee, prude much? I still have my camisole on. Relax.' She raised her eyebrows at me, almost like she was waiting for me to make a fool of myself again. 'Are you going to wear all your layers in here?'

'Obviously not.' I turned to Dom and waved my hand in front of his face this time. 'Hey, Dom. You alive in there?'

I ignored her laugh and grabbed his arm and gave it a little shake. I raised both of my own eyebrows at him as he looked at me. He turned bright red. I just shook my head and started undressing.

'What are you doing?!' he yelped.

'Taking some of my layers off. We can't get in with all our warm clothes on.'

'Oh, right. Uh no, of course not. Yep, okay. Clothes off.'

He looked like he was concentrating really hard on the wall as he got ready. I turned back around and made short work of most of my outfit. I ignored Dom muttering to himself and went to climb in.

'There's a sort of step over near that wall,' Alessia called, pointing.

'Thanks.'

I walked along, looking over the edge until I could see the step-like piece of rock that jutted out under the water, and used it to get in. My body almost melted in relaxation as I slid into the softly bubbling, almost white water. I groaned and swam out towards the middle of the spring, feeling each of my sore muscles begin to relax.

When I made it to Alessia, I just floated about and waited for Dom. I looked over to see he'd gotten down to just under shorts and turned away. Noticing Alessia staring at me, amusement lighting her face, I said, 'What?'.

'Nothing,' she said, sucking her lips in to stop her smile.

We both turned away and waited for Dom to join us. When he made it over, I gestured that he could do the explaining. He nodded, a thoughtful look on his face.

'So. The plan. Basically, we need to break into the base level of Crone Keep, through the waterfall entrance, since it's the least obvious and doesn't have a constant guard, just patrols. Then we need to work our way up a few levels, free the prisoner then leave using the water system to head towards the Cladden Pack territory. Going that way means we might get some protection if we need it.'

She looked at us both deadpan. 'You're serious?'

Dom glanced at me and I looked back at her. 'That's definitely the short version, but yeah.'

She sighed. 'Well, since everyone seems to be enjoying the soak, how about you enlighten me with the longer version?'

I pursed my lips, irritated by her continual demands, but knew I needed to share the details if we actually wanted the help that she seemed willing enough to offer. Half of me was so eager to accept some help but the other half of me just couldn't wait to get rid of her.

'Sure. Why not? We plan to continue through the mountains, staying in whatever caves we can find for the next few days, which should take us right up to Crone Keep. We'll need to scope out the patrols they have running to make sure they are consistent with the information we have and check for any magical alarms in the surrounding area. Once we've done recon for a couple of days to get the lay of the land and their routines, we'll enter through the waterfall entrance at the base, like Dom said. After that, we'll follow the internal drawings to where the prison area is and break her out. Then we'll leave the way we came and head towards the Cladden Pack before making our way back inland and going home.'

She waded through the water as she considered our plan. 'So it'll be a woman we're rescuing. Don't suppose you'd like to tell me exactly who it is that I'm going on this stupid, insane mission for?'

'No,' I said.

'Didn't think so. Well, the plan seems decent enough. At least you factored in a couple of days to scope the place out. I guess you've put some thought into this suicide mission you've organised. I'm assuming this is someone that the Pack doesn't want to rescue since you both seem to have gone rogue to do it yourselves.'

I considered what she said. 'That's about the size of it. So you'll be coming with us then?'

'Emmie seems to think that I need to go along, and if I return without doing it then I'd be up shit creek. So yes. I'll be going along.'

'Emmie?'

'Ah, Emerilla. The Medicine Woman for our Pack. You'd be insane to argue with her about anything. I've seen her idea of punishment for ignoring instructions and I certainly won't be on the receiving end. Surely your Medicine Woman is the same?'

'I'm not really sure,' I said, turning with a questioning look to Dom.

He shrugged. 'I don't really know too much about her. The longest I've ever seen her was at the Alpha ceremony last week.'

Alessia's eyes just about bulged from her head. 'What?! An Alpha ceremony? What happened to your Alpha?'

This time we looked at her like she was crazy.

'Surely you heard what happened?' I asked.

She arched a brow at me. 'Obviously not.'

I sighed. She had such an attitude. Since I was sure everyone else in the whole Shifter world probably knew what happened, I gave her a recap.

'No shit,' she said. Alessia looked at Dom, 'So your dad is the new Alpha now? And you've run off and left him there. That's ballsy.'

'Hey!' I cut in. 'He doesn't need that from you. You don't even know him.'

I looked at Dom, worried at the regretful look on his face. I knew this was already hard enough on him. I turned back and glared at Alessia.

She held her hands up in apology. 'Sorry. I didn't mean to stomp on any nerves. I'm gonna get out of here before I get all wrinkly and old-looking.'

When she swam back over to the edge, I moved closer to Dom and rested my hand on his arm. 'You okay?'

He just nodded and started swimming back as well. I decided to stay there and soak for a while. There was so much drama. Mine, Dom's and now Alessia's.

I floated on my back, inhaling through my nose and breathing out through my mouth. I soaked in the sound of the hot water slowly bubbling through the spring, enjoying the feel of the water running over me. It was bliss. And for a little while, I revelled in the sensation of thoughtless drifting.

Unfortunately it didn't last long. A shout from the passage to the main cavern from Alessia shook me out of my reverie.

'Dinner!'

This was soon followed by a nauseous feeling that told me she was in the middle of cooking meat.

Hope it's well done.

Maybe Dom will ask her to cook it through? On the other hand, maybe not, since he was trying not to give anything away about me. I sighed again and realised I'd been doing that a lot since Alessia had shown up. More company seemed to equate to more work. Hopefully she'd get a little less tiring as we went, though I supposed if I actually shared more about my life, I wouldn't need to worry so much.

I got slowly out of the hot spring, checked that no one was coming, then stripped down and dried off. I put a different layer of my clothes back on so I felt a little fresher. I left my wet clothes on some rocks near the hot spring to hopefully dry out a little away from the steam; it seemed like a better idea than putting them near the snow. Maybe.

I walked down the passage, feeling more nauseated with each step. Apparently being at the Academy had helped a bit, but since I'd been away for more than a week with no meat at all, the smell got to me almost as badly as it used to. Especially in the moist air. I walked around the corner and into the room.

'I'm sorry, I told her you didn't like the smell of meat cooking,' Dom called, looking uncomfortable about having said so.

'It's fine.' I gave him a smile, not wanting him to add any more guilt to his plate. 'I'll just sit near the entrance.'

He nodded, looking a little more glum than I would have liked, but I'd done what I could.

Alessia turned curious eyes to me. 'What, are you pregnant or something?'

I stopped in place and stared at her, completely dumbfounded. Dom let out a nervous laugh then told her I wasn't.

I shook my head, incredulous, and walked past to take a seat by the entrance. Dom brought me a couple of vegetables to eat that Alessia had cooked over the fire on sticks. They tasted nice enough. 'Thanks.'

She nodded back at me, then started serving up some food for herself and Dom. They sat over near the fire. I was a bit envious of their position by the heat while I was stuck near the frosty entrance to avoid the smell they'd saturated our cave with.

Despite Alessia's stupid question, we ate in a mostly companionable silence, the two of them occasionally making small talk. Once the food was done, we decided to get some sleep so we could leave first thing in the morning.

'I'll take first watch,' Alessia said, once we were sitting on our mats. 'I'm not so tired yet anyway.'

I didn't answer straightaway and thought about what could go wrong with that scenario. I obviously didn't completely trust her yet. We had maps and internal drawings she could steal. I'd apparently been silent too long because she spoke again.

'Look. I told you why I'm here. I'm not some dangerous criminal. Emmie sent me here to help you guys, I'm hardly gonna slit your throats in your sleep or something ridiculous like that. But hey, by all means, if you'd both like to take shifts all night, I'll just get some rest.'

Slit our throats in our sleep. Lovely. I'm so glad she mentioned that.

I looked at Dom. He seemed to think for a minute and then said, 'I'll take the second watch. Night.'

He laid down and within a few minutes had started snoring. I was still sitting up despite my tiredness after the travelling, the fight and the hot spring, plus getting some food into my stomach.

Something had been bothering me about Alessia and as I began to settle down I threw it out there. 'Other than whatever that punishment was from Emmie, why would you really stay and help? Surely you've got a bunch of friends and your family to hang out with from your Pack?'

She apparently decided that my question was genuine and not sarcastic because she answered me. 'Not really. I have my mum. I don't know my dad. And sure, I have a couple of friends but it's always the same stuff there. I begged Mum to let me go to the Academy, but she said I couldn't. Never would tell me why, either.'

Huh, interesting. Sounds a little like my life.

She continued. 'So when Emmie brought this up, I leapt at the chance to disappear and do something exciting. Even if it is insane. Which it is, by the way.'

I thought it over for a minute and decided maybe she was okay after all. 'That all makes sense. Well, hopefully it'll live up to your expectations. I'm gonna get some sleep. You'll wake Dom soon?'

She looked like she was reining in a smile. 'Sure thing. Night.'

'Night.'

I was woken by Dom lightly shaking my shoulder. From the cave entrance, I could see the morning was beginning to lighten, but it wasn't time for us to move along yet. I gave him a bleary smile and waved him off so he could get some more sleep.

I sat awake, thinking about Alessia and her life. It was like a mirror of my own; only one parent around, and that parent not wanting her to go off and join the Academy. I doubted the reasons were similar. I could actually understand her jumping at the chance to leave the Pack and have some sort of adventure, especially when she wouldn't really have any friends around except during Academy breaks.

From my spot near the cave entrance, I watched as the storm eased slightly, the snow falling lightly on the ground. It made almost no noise, and much less than the rising and falling breaths that Dom and Alessia made in their sleep.

When the first rays of sun pierced the cave opening, I decided to get up, shake myself out a little and stretch quietly before getting breakfast ready for everyone. Funnily enough, when I started unwrapping food, Dom woke up almost immediately. I grinned as I continued to prepare it.

Once I had it done, I waved Dom over, then woke Alessia so she could eat too. She grumbled at me a few times before I successfully managed to get her to move. 'Gee, you're lucky we weren't being attacked or anything. You'd have been killed, like, seven times already.'

She huffed at me. 'Bull. I'd have been just fine. But the only two I smell around here are you guys. Besides you, it's just steamy air, snow and food. Hardly a death sentence.'

I ignored the continued grumbles and sat to eat my food with Dom. After Alessia had packed up her stuff, she joined us. We didn't talk much at all throughout the meal. Once I was done, I got up and packed my things. Just before we went to leave, I remembered my stuff from the hot spring and went to grab it. Once I saw it, I felt a little sad about not being able to enjoy another swim. With one last longing glance at the bubbling water, I made my way out to catch up with the others.

DECISIONS

W E STOPPED IN A new cave each night, thankfully without any further attacks. Alessia seemed quite sure we weren't being followed, pointing out that no one with a brain would be heading so close to Crone Keep.

On the last evening before we reached the end of the mountains, further behind than I'd hoped, we had to spread out to find a cave. I took the middle path, Dom went down, and Alessia went further up.

I'd been walking for what seemed like hours when I finally found another cave. Cautiously I edged closer, sniffing the air to figure out if there was anyone inside. The heat gave it away before the smell this time. I'd just about reached the entrance when I felt the warmth; it wasn't steamy like the spring, but hot and dry like a fire. I stopped dead in my tracks, about to edge away. The last thing we needed right before Crone Keep was another fight, especially when we'd only just recovered from the last one.

I took a step back when I heard a voice. 'Wait, Elita. Don't go.'

My heart froze at the same instant as my feet.

'Please, don't be afraid. I want only to talk with you.'

The voice sounded young, maybe around my age. I didn't know whether to stay or run. To head into the warmth or flee into the cold. I knew if I ran into any trouble inside, the others would eventually come and find me, especially if I didn't make it to our agreed meeting point by sundown.

'Really, you are safe. I am alone and wish only to talk with you. It is important.'

It was ridiculous that someone would even know my name in the middle of nowhere on the mountain. Deciding to risk it, I walked inside.

My eyes adjusted quickly to the orange flames lighting the depths of the cavern, and I took in the teen girl in front of me. She had light blonde hair that came down to her waist and wore a simple gown of pale green that matched her eyes. I noticed that she remained still and quiet while I looked her over and assessed whether she was a threat or not.

Eerily, the moment I'd decided everything was okay, she smiled and then spoke. 'I am Cassandra.' When I nodded but said nothing, she continued. 'And you are Elita... White?'

What, she knows me but isn't sure of my last name? Weird.

I nodded at her. 'Yes. I'm Elita.'

In the silence that followed, I continued to study her. This time, I noticed her presence. It was... stifling. She seemed to take up a lot of space in the room, despite looking only a little older than me. I tilted my head, wondering what she was. Certainly not human from the scent, but not a Shifter either. A Sorceress perhaps?

213

She smiled again. 'Close.'

Freaky.

'I am a little more than just a Sorceress. Perhaps you might know who I am, if you think about it?'

I screwed up my face, trying to remember the lessons I'd taken with Miss Stone, when suddenly it hit me like a blow to the face. 'You're The Seer.'

Another smile.

'So, uh, why did you call me in here?'

'Excellent question. But first, please come and sit by the fire. Warm yourself from the cold. I have some food, if you'll accept it?'

I thought it over, then went and sat. She passed me some food—vegetables and bread, already warmed up, like she knew when I'd arrive. I smiled in thanks and started to eat. It was still hot, like she knew exactly when I'd be here *and* when I'd start eating.

I looked over my shoulder, beginning to wonder if Dom and Alessia were waiting at the meeting point already, and if they'd come looking soon.

'Your friends will find us just as soon as I am ready, don't worry. They are perfectly safe and not overly worried about you as yet.'

'What do you mean, when you are ready? What is it that you need to talk to me about? I mean, like, you're The Seer. The original Sorceress. Why do you want to talk to, well, a nobody?'

She gave me a warm smile; it lit up her eyes more than her previous placid and amused ones. 'I need to talk to you about your mission, and about the prophecy.'

My stomach turned to lead and thudded down. I'd been trying not to think about the prophecy, especially since my attempts at researching it had resulted in the attack, and death of our Alpha and other Pack members. The only good thing that had come from the whole ordeal was learning that my mum was actually alive.

'I don't really know anything about the prophecy, or even what it says.'

'Ah, well since I was the one who made the original prophecy, I can tell you what it said, if you would like?'

Do I really want to know about this prophecy? Well, knowing what it says can't hurt, right?

I nodded slowly. 'I'd like to hear it.'

I looked at The Seer and waited for her to tell me. She zoned out and stared into space, and then, without warning, her eyes turned from their light shade of green to completely white. It was like her irises disappeared. Without meaning to, I scooted away from her.

'On the eve of her eighteenth Winter Solstice, a wolf of White, born of a Sorceress, will come to bear her mark in the Valley of Cladden. Armed with Fang, Flame and Essence, she will purge the Crones of Old from this earth forevermore.'

I stared blankly. It made no sense. 'Why in Salvatore's name would I be the one in that prophecy? I'm no one. Surely there is someone else out there, an adult even—or you—who would have an easier job of purging the earth of the Crones?!'

She smiled again, looking quite amused, particularly when I'd cursed. 'I cannot answer your questions about that, for it will come to make sense to you in due course. However, there is something I must tell you. Despite the Crones trying to hunt you down at your Academy, having somehow managed to acquire information of your whereabouts, the prophecy still lies dormant.'

'So wait, does that mean that it won't happen? That I don't have to do that?'

I felt a rush of relief so extreme that I sagged where I sat. I hadn't realised how worried I'd been about a prophecy I hadn't even understood.

This time her smile turned sad. 'At this moment, yes. However, that is soon to change if you continue on your path.'

I sat up, dread pooling inside of me. 'What do you mean?'

Sorrowful eyes locked onto mine. 'If you continue with this mission, the Crones will discover who you are and, in so doing, the prophecy will be activated. They will try to hunt you down and destroy you, before you are able to destroy them.'

My heart stuttered, almost coming to a stop.

It's my mother or the prophecy? Save my mother and be hunted by the Crones, or leave her to die and stay safe?

Tears filled my eyes, so full I couldn't see The Seer clearly anymore. 'Why? How is that fair? Why would you do that?'

Her gaze dropped to the ground. 'I did not choose this for you, Elita. The Earth Mother has chosen. I did elect to intervene, to give you a warning, so that you may have a choice in what will come of your life, but that is all I can offer you: this choice.'

A choice that was a double-edged sword. One that could be wonderful for everyone and horrible for me, or another that could be good for me and leave everyone else with the problem of the Crones and my mum to die a prisoner.

Surely it wouldn't matter to anyone. No one even knows about the prophecy. But there's no way I could leave my mum there when I have a chance to save her. Is there? Argh!

I don't know how long passed while I tried to think through my options, but eventually The Seer spoke again. 'You do not need to decide right this moment. Your companions will be arriving very shortly, and I would suggest they may need some encouragement to enter the cave, just as you did. Though I daresay that would be best coming from you.'

My head reeled. What would I even say to them once they arrived? Dom knew, but Alessia didn't. I did know one thing for certain, though. Before this, I didn't realise I even had a choice, and despite it maybe being better if I'd never known, I knew I needed to say one more thing. 'Thank you. For giving me a choice instead of letting me blindly make it on my own.'

'You are welcome, Elita. I hope you choose wisely.'

I nodded, then turned to the cave entrance when I heard Dom and Alessia calling for me.

'In here, guys!' I yelled.

They came into the cave looking worried, but relief quickly washed over their features once they saw me. For Dom it was followed by concern. Alessia just looked pissed.

Before she could have a go at me, I spoke. 'Guys, this is Cassandra. The Seer.' I pointed behind me, but at the blank expression on their faces, I quickly turned and realised she had disappeared.

Alessia's look morphed into one that plainly said I was crazy. 'I think maybe all that time in the snow has gotten to your head. Though I'm not sure that's an excuse since you seem to have made yourself a fire and started eating food without us.' She walked over then sat and began eating. 'You could have at least waited at the meeting point for us to show up instead of leaving us to worry and find you.'

When Dom could finally get a word in, he voiced his concern. 'What happened with The Seer?'

I don't know that I'd ever felt as much appreciation for him as I did right at that moment. I was almost wondering if I had gone crazy and imagined the whole thing. I was feeling rather grateful that she'd left the food as a sign.

'She told me about the, uh, that thing we're looking for.'

I eyed the back of Alessia's head after I spoke, to make it clearer to Dom.

'Oh, uh, right. Anything helpful?'

I went to answer, but Alessia cut in. 'Oh, get over it you two, and just spit it out. What am I gonna do about whatever the secret is? It can't be that bad.'

I looked at Dom, wondering if I should just tell her. It would certainly be easier if I could just say what I needed to. After a minute of deliberating, he nodded and shrugged.

Okay, here goes nothing. Hopefully she won't lose it.

'So, a short version of events. My mother is a Sorceress who left me when I was three to try and protect me from a prophecy that I'm in. When she left, she was kidnapped by The Crones of Old and has been held captive since. When I learned about the prophecy, Dom and I started looking into it at school, even though we were told not to,' a flush rose to my cheeks. 'Because of that, a Crone and some of her Sorceresses broke into the Academy, looking for whoever was searching. They had my mum there with them, chained up. So now we are going to rescue her.' I looked at Dom. 'Does that cover it?'

He laughed. 'Yeah, in a nutshell.'

I nodded, satisfied, and turned back to Alessia. She looked like she'd gone into shock as she was processing. Though it didn't last long.

'You have got to be shitting me,' she said, fingers pushed into her forehead.

I shook my head. 'Nope, unfortunately not.'

She opened her mouth to speak again, but this time Dom cut her off.

'What about the prophecy? What did The Seer say?'

I slumped back down in my seat. This was the hard part. I knew the judgements would come soon, first from these two and then from whoever else found out.

I relayed it back to them word-for-word, each one somehow etched into my mind already. 'Then she told me that right now, the prophecy is dormant and I could avoid it and live my life because they've never seen me and don't know who I am. But she said the only way to stay safe like that is to abandon my mum. To not rescue her.'

I looked at both of them, desperation oozing out of me. I wanted someone to make the decision for me, but they both sat in silence. They didn't know what to do either, apparently. I sighed. 'Any thoughts?'

Alessia piped up with a half-hearted response. 'You'd be a hero.'

'I don't want to be a hero. I want my mum back and to live a normal life with my parents.'

Dom chimed in. 'Do you really have a choice? Will you leave your mum there?'

I slumped down further, my heart aching. 'No, I don't think so.'

'Well, then let's just continue on. I'll be there to help you. You won't be alone.'

Dom looked at Alessia expectantly and I laughed.

'I don't think Alessia is obliged to help me with this. It's insane and I'll be lucky if I don't end up dead before my next birthday, or even before the end of the week at this rate.'

To my surprise, Alessia looked like she was really considering it. I was shocked when she spoke again in a serious tone. 'If we make it out of here, I might stick around and help.' She smiled, almost looking triumphant and added. 'I'll probably even get to go to the Academy and see it!'

I laughed again. 'Well, that's one way to look at it. But, thank you. For sticking around. I know you don't need to.'

She shrugged. 'It's no big deal. I'm doing it more for me than you anyway. I like a challenge.'

My dread eased a little. Knowing they had my back made a real difference. I knew it would be dangerous and that I needed to figure out a lot of things before I faced the Crones. My biggest question was... why me? Why would some random hybrid Shifter-Sorceress be the one to do it when there were so many others with more experience? Even The Seer. Surely she could destroy them. She was here first, after all.

Once Dom and Alessia had finished eating, they quizzed me further about the whole situation. When I told them about the eyes, they were intrigued. I'd already decided I'd be happy not to see that particular gift again.

Once they'd asked all the questions they could think of, we set up shifts for standing guard. First me, then Dom, then Alessia.

I pulled out my mat and blanket then sat down on it to do my watch. Dom and Alessia curled up on their own gear. Alessia was asleep within a few minutes, which left me and Dom sitting awake. I thought he'd just try to close his eyes and sleep, but he wanted to talk.

'Are you sure about wanting to go, Elita? I know what I said before, about getting your mum, but you know she'd understand if you just went back home. I mean, from what you told me about the attack, it seemed like she was trying to protect you. And even before, she left so you could be hidden from the Crones, so they couldn't find you.'

The pit in my stomach, the one I'd been working so hard to fill up and cover over, opened again.

Could I really abandon my mum? When I'm so close. Even if it is what she wants.

'I think you were right the first time, Dom. I don't think I could leave her there. Not even if she wanted me to. Not now that I know she's alive. I want to know my mum, even if I don't get much time with her, you know?'

He was quiet for a moment, then answered. 'Yep, I get it. I really do. But I just wanted to bring it up, because I get that you want it, I just thought I should mention what she might want. Have you thought about your Dad? About how he'd feel about all of this? I'm sure both our dads are really worried.'

The pit in my stomach widened and my eyes filled with tears. Even though I was angry with Dad, I'd been trying to avoid thinking about him. I knew he'd be so devastated and worried about me.

I sniffed. 'Yeah. I've thought about him a bit. I know he'll be super worried. But I need to save my mum. I just don't think I'd be able to live with myself if I didn't. Even if it costs me my life.'

I just hope it doesn't cost yours or Alessia's.

TEST

W HEN DOM WOKE ME in the morning, I felt extra tired, like I'd walked further than all the other days put to-gether. But I knew that wasn't it. My emotions were just spent from all the events that had led to this moment. And there was still one more obstacle I needed to pass through before it was time to leave.

Once I finished my breakfast, I took a deep breath, let it out slowly and turned to Alessia, who was, of course, already staring at me after taking such a loud breath.

'I need to tell you something else.'

Her eyes widened; she looked incredulous. 'Another thing? Surely you guys are out of surprises.'

I gave her a wry grin and shook my head.

She huffed. 'Fine, out with it.'

'I've had my birthday already. And I can only partially Shift into a wolf.'

I held my breath, waiting for her reaction. When she laughed at me, I relaxed a little.

'Well, it doesn't seem that outrageous considering you're half and half. Though honestly, I don't see why you shouldn't be able to make the full change.'

I shrugged it off. But really, I was sure it was because I just didn't fit in anywhere. I knew I'd never be all Shifter, or all Sorceress. I was just some kind of a hybrid freak.

Why would I get to have the best of both worlds?

'Oh, well,' she said. 'Whatever. Have you practised fighting in your new form or doing anything else in it?'

'Well, I had a run with Dom in his Shifted form, and I kept up with him all right.'

'That's a bit of an understatement,' Dom interjected with a smile. 'I was running full out and was nearly dead when I got to the end. And she was barely puffed. And I cheated by taking a head start.'

I felt a flush of pride at the compliment, and went to thank him when Alessia cut in.

'Maybe you're just slow. Perhaps a little early morning race is in order before we leave.'

'Seriously?' I said. 'Won't that just be a waste of our energy?'

She scoffed. 'Please. If what Dom says is right, then I don't see why you need to worry at all. And I can take care of myself.'

She walked over to the cave entrance and out into the snow. She looked at the two paths and settled her gaze on the one leading higher through the mountains. 'Up it is.'

I heaved out a breath, sure that this was a waste of time. 'Fine. Let's make it quick.'

'Done. I saw a cave up there yesterday before I came back. First one there and back wins?' She looked at me expectantly. 'Well? Shift already.'

Pushy much? Yeesh.

So that I wouldn't get distracted watching the magic, I closed my eyes and focused on Shifting. Within a few moments I felt my senses heighten and could hear the deeper breathing of a wolf. I opened my eyes and saw a light-coloured wolf in front of me.

I noted the slight widening of her eyes when she saw me in my half-Shifted form, but before long, she'd turned and made her way to the entrance. Dom wished me luck as he trailed along behind me and let me know he'd wait here with our things.

I sprinted as fast as I could towards the top of the mountains. With my enhanced vision, I could see the best spots to step to keep my footing steady in the thick snow. I pushed myself as fast as I could go, feeling a slight burn as I reached the steepest section of the mountain path.

Alessia's sandy coat was about parallel to me as we ran. I could hear the pads of her paws pushing into the mush with each stride. I could hear her panting slightly as she increased her speed.

We were neck and neck; first me in front, then her. We stayed like this for most of the path, but towards the end she made a little ground. I pushed harder.

I could see the cave we were aiming for. I went as fast as I could, trying to make the entrance first.

Almost there. Come on!

My foot and her paw seemed to cross the threshold at the same time. I wheezed out a breath, really feeling the exertion compared to when I raced Dom, leading me to think he must have gone easy on him. I turned to see how Alessia was doing.

As I turned, she leapt at me. Shocked, I tried my best to move out of her way. She pursued, stalking forwards, herding me towards the back of the cave. I took a risk and glanced over my shoulder as I took a step. There was nowhere to go.

I kept my voice as even as I could. 'Alessia, what are you doing?'

She snarled at me. Stunned and not thinking, I took another step towards the rear of the cave. I didn't know what to do. I thought she was my friend, I didn't want to hurt her. This was insane.

She leapt at me, claws out. This time I dodged then came up from underneath and shoved her. I smelt the blood where I'd scratched her unintentionally.

What is going on? I need to get out of here.

I began to edge around to the side wall as quickly as I could, making my way towards the cave entrance.

She doubled back and blocked my way, snarling viciously.

I can't believe Dom and I trusted her.

This time she dove at me, teeth bared. Panicked, I put my hands up to deflect and pushed her harder. Her teeth grazed my hands, but my claws tore scratches across her face.

I didn't know whether to be sorry or not. I was so confused. There was blood dripping from her face onto the snow that had drifted inside, turning it a deep, dark red.

'Alessia, please stop. Don't do this.'

I held my hands out in front of me, waiting for her to attack again. I bent my knees as I pressed my feet into the ground, trying to maintain my balance and composure.

I breathed deeply, watching her carefully to see her next move. She looked at me with sharp eyes. Then all of a sudden she just sat, and gave me a ridiculous grin from her bleeding wolfy face.

Unbelievable.

I glared. 'You have got to be kidding me! Are you insane?'

The air around her shimmered, and she Shifted back into her human form. Little earthy sparks mixed in with the sandy colour of her fur for a moment until she stood in front of me, with the same grin on her bleeding face.

'Oh, relax,' she said. 'I needed to make sure you could fight in that form. Though it would have been more helpful if you'd had your weapons so we could see how well you hold them while you have your claws, which look pretty cool by the way.'

'You are seriously crazy. Why didn't you just suggest a fight back down in the other cave instead of running up here for no reason and then attacking me?'

'Well, firstly, it wasn't for no reason, I wanted to beat you. And secondly, there's no way Dom would have stood back and let me try to bite your head off.'

My eyes bulged. 'What, you would have actually taken a chunk?'

'Sure. If you were that sloppy, though I didn't think you would be. And hey, better to take a chunk out here and turn around and go home, rather than getting annihilated by the Crones or their Sorceresses when we get to Crone Keep. We need to be quick enough to destabilise them and attack before they have time to cast, or we'll be dead.'

I knew what she said made sense, but I was still pretty incredulous about what she'd done. 'Well, what about Dom? Are you gonna go attack him now too?'

She rolled her eyes. 'Of course not. He's a Beta's son, well Alpha's son now, and he's been Shifting for, like, a year or more. He'll be able to take care of himself. And obviously you can, too.' She smiled sardonically at me. 'You're welcome.'

What an idiot.

I stormed past her and out of the cave, Shifting as I walked. The coloured explosions only slowed me a little. She quickly caught up and fell into step beside me. I tried to go a bit faster but she picked up her pace, and since she was taller than me, the only thing I could do to get ahead was run. I wasn't going to give her the satisfaction.

When we walked back into the cave, Dom jumped up. 'What the heck were you two doing? I could hear growls from down here. Why are you both bleeding?!'

I scowled. 'Because Alessia attacked me to *see if I could take care of myself.*'

He turned to her and said, 'Huh, that was actually a pretty good idea.'

The look of surprise on Alessia's face mirrored the one I was sure was on mine. After a second, I snapped at him. 'What?! Are you kidding me? You're on her side?'

'Yeah, really?' she added. 'I thought you'd be cut about me trying to chomp up your girlfriend.'

Dom's face went pink. 'She's not my girlfriend. Seriously. And no, I'm glad she got to practise before we get to Crone Keep.'

I bit my tongue and, ignoring them both, put my pack on. I walked to the entrance and waited for them outside.

I heard Alessia snicker behind me. When they came outside, I started walking straight along the mountain path that eventually led down.

We reached the base of the mountain at sunset. We were fairly close to Crone Keep and could see its dark stone turrets occasionally through the trees. If we continued on, we'd reach it tonight or in the morning.

I had walked ahead of them, wanting to be alone and now waited for the pair of them to catch up. They reached me in less than a minute. I took a quiet breath out and turned to face them. I tried to keep my annoyance under control.

'Oh, come on, Elita,' said Dom. 'You know it was good practise!'

'Whatever. Can we just sort out the plan?'

'Sure,' said Alessia. 'What do we need to decide?'

She clearly didn't have any issue with what she had done.

229

'Well, are we splitting up to scout the area? Will we enter tonight, tomorrow during the day or tomorrow evening? If we camp, where will we do that, so there isn't a chance of us being found?'

As Alessia and Dom considered my questions for a minute, I looked around and waited. I knew we'd need to be alert in case the Crone Sorceresses had magical traps in place or patrolled further out than our information had shown.

Alessia answered first. 'I reckon we scout tonight, then find a spot a bit further back to camp out during the day, sleeping in shifts. What do you guys think?'

Dom quickly agreed with that plan, and I did so reluctantly as well. Not because it was a bad plan, but because I was still irritated about earlier and the fact that Dom was so quick to jump on her ideas again.

'Should we split up, or...?'

This time Dom answered. 'I think it would be a good idea to split up. Less chance we'll be distracted by the noises we make moving through. We have the advantage of better hearing, so if we're alone we should be able to hear them before they know we're around.'

I nodded. 'That makes sense. But how will we let each other know if something has gone wrong?'

Alessia shrugged. 'Scream.'

I stared at her, trying to gauge if she was serious or not.

'What?' she said. 'If one of them has one of us, the best chance we've got is if the other two hear and come to help before more

Sorceresses show up. We'll be dead if too many show up. This way, we still have a chance at surprise. It's not likely that our scream would be heard by anyone back in the Keep.'

'I suppose you're right,' I agreed. Then laughed as I thought the idea through. 'Do you have a good scream, Dom?'

When he laughed, his shoulders relaxed a little. 'Yeah, I'm sure I can manage a nice manly squeal for you ladies.'

I gave him a genuine smile as my feelings of annoyance faded away. 'Okay, cool. Well, let's spread out. Dom, you go to the right, Alessia to the left, and I'll go straight ahead. Make sure you don't go past the side of the Keep—we'll need to be on this side of it to get in. Alessia, the waterfall will be on your side actually. Do you want me to take that way instead?'

'I'm sweet. I'm sure I'll be just fine.'

'Okay. Let's do it.'

I weaved through the trees carefully. I paid attention to my surroundings, including the noise that my steps made and those of the animals around me as well as the slowly fading sounds of both Dom and Alessia as they scouted their areas.

I continued on until what must have been about midnight before I caught the first sign of anything different. Along the ground there were five stones laid in a particular setting, right in the middle of a clearing. There were no sounds, just the stones sitting in an evenly spaced circle.

Maybe they cast spells out here?

I walked into the circle and looked more carefully around it. There were faint lines connecting the stones.

Roughly in the shape of a star.

Don't panic. Don't panic.

I walked quickly back the way I came, retracing my steps. Right at a line between the stones, I smacked straight into some kind of invisible wall. I pushed against what I'd thought was nothing, but then I noticed an incandescent shimmery quality to the air between the stones, one that wasn't there before I'd walked in. I was trapped.

My heart started to race as panic set in. I didn't know what to do. Would this trap automatically alert someone, or was it one they checked on their patrol? Either way, I was screwed. I needed to do something. Frantically, I tried to disturb the lines of the pentagram in the dirt, but it just kept fixing itself. I tried to shove the stones instead.

They wouldn't budge.

Argh! What do I do!? Should I shout? Stay quiet and wait?

Right at that moment, I realised we hadn't made any plans for a follow-up meeting point. I didn't even know when or if they'd come looking.

TRAPPED

I took a deep breath, feeling ridiculous, and screamed. Not as loud as I could, but enough that Alessia and Dom should be able to hear me. I hoped that none of the Sorceresses showed up before they did.

I sat down as close as I could to one of the large rocks and listened. Time passed at a crawl. I was beginning to wonder if I should scream louder, in case they were too far away to hear me.

Right as I opened my mouth, I heard footsteps. Two sets, both running. I took in the scents around me, but neither were close enough to detect. One set of footsteps was coming from Dom's direction, but I started feeling queasy when I realised the second set were coming from the direction of the Keep, not from where Alessia should be.

I tried to focus on my breathing while I waited for the new-comers to get close enough to pick up their scents. Despite the frosty air, beads of sweat began to form on my temples. I drew lines along my hand as I stayed tucked against the rock closest to the Keep; trying to stay hidden.

Finally, they were close enough to smell. One was definitely Dom but the other scent was unfamiliar. Like a human but different. I had a flash of being back in the library during the attack. Magic. There was a Sorceress coming too.

I held my knees tucked into my chest, hoping that Dom would make it before the Sorceress. They were both close, but I knew Dom would be able to tell someone else was advancing. I thought I heard the sound of more footsteps but they receded before I could focus on them.

Dom burst through the tree line and spotted me. I frantically waved my hands at him to stop him from racing straight into the pentagram with me.

'Hide,' I hissed.

He nodded and ducked quickly back into the underbrush of the trees; hiding himself behind one of the thicker trunks and its surrounding greenery. The Sorceress's steps echoed loudly as she skidded to a halt at the edge of the clearing, her breath coming in short, loud bursts.

I kept my position and waited. She must have stopped to catch her breath when she realised no one was standing in the trap.

Maybe she'll just leave?

After a minute I heard the movement of snow-soaked leaves on the ground as she neared. Another step or two and she would be level with me. I turned my head to my left, so I could track her more easily.

I heard another faint set of footsteps in the distance, but they stopped again. Shifting my focus, I took a deep breath then stood and locked eyes with the Sorceress as she reached the rock.

She sneered at me. 'What have we got here? An itty-bitty human?'

I glared back at her but stayed silent.

'Nothing to say, little girl?'

I narrowed my eyes at her. If she wanted me, she'd have to open the pentagram. She walked around the clearing, pinning me with her gaze until she stood directly in front of me.

I watched carefully as she bent down to the rock. She drew some kind of symbol and the pentagram glowed a deep orange.

As soon as the light dimmed, and before she even took a step into the pentagram, I Shifted and ran to the side of the clearing from where Dom had originally arrived. I didn't want to lead her to Alessia, but wanted Dom to be able to follow.

I heard her curse, then start to pursue me. Her words were muffled by the thud of my footsteps on the slushy mountainside.

Probably casting some sort of spell.

I weaved between the trees to throw her off and focused beyond the sound of my own footsteps and on those of my pursuers. Aside from her comparatively sluggish movements, I could hear Dom and one other.

Hopefully that's Alessia.

I continued on my path, heading straight ahead rather than curving towards the Keep, trying desperately not to draw any more attention.

Once there was an adequate amount of distance between us, I found a tree with enough foliage to hide me and climbed it.

I watched and waited, listening and scenting the air. Using any advantage I had.

She was close.

The Sorceress burst through the small area below me without stopping or looking up. As she arrived directly underneath my branch, I leapt down on top of her and wrapped my right arm around her neck. I covered her mouth tight with my left hand. No spells.

She teetered back a few steps before regaining her balance. She rammed me back into a tree. Jarred but determined, I kept my hold, especially on her mouth.

Dom burst suddenly into the clearing, his eyes glued to me and the Sorceress. In the midst of my struggle, I registered his relief, but swiftly turned my attention back to the Sorceress. I pulled my arm tighter and tighter and she began to waver. Her footing became less steady and after another minute, I felt her slump as she collapsed.

I let go and jumped back, watching intently to make sure she stayed down. She was breathing, but not moving. Relieved, I staggered back, my hands resting on my knees as I caught my breath and looked at Dom. 'Sorry about the scream,' I huffed.

He eyed me with concern. 'No sweat. Just glad you're okay.'

At the sound of light footsteps we looked over to see Alessia appear from beside a large tree dusted in a smattering of snow.

She heaved a sigh of relief. 'Sorry. I was almost at the waterfall when I heard you, but didn't want to miss the opportunity to scope it out. Figured Dom would have your back.' She peered at the crumpled form of the Sorceress and looked back at me pointedly as she pulled some rope from her belt. 'Though it looks like you didn't need the help after all. What happened?'

She set to work tying the Sorceress to the nearest tree.

I felt a little squeamish at the idea of something finding her tied to a tree trunk. 'Don't you think something might eat her out here?'

She shook her head. 'She'll be right. I'm sure she'll just annihilate it with her killer glare or something.' After tying for a minute longer she paused and looked back at me. 'So, are you gonna tell me what happened?'

'Oh, right. I came across a clearing with a circle of rocks and walked into it to get past then realised there was—'

She laughed. 'You walked into a containment pentagram? Surely you should have known better?' She looked at Dom, eyebrows raised.

I turned to him as well, wondering if I should have.

'Nah,' he said. 'I didn't learn about them at the Academy until this year. Elita's only in First Year.'

Alessia snorted. 'I learned about them years ago and I don't even go to the Academy.'

I bristled. 'Yeah, but I didn't live with a Pack, just my dad. And as you can tell, he obviously wasn't too forthcoming on Sorceresses. I did plenty of training in fighting and whatever, but never learned much about them.' I shook my head dismissively. 'Oh well, lesson learned.' Wanting to move on, I added, 'Where will we go from here? And how will we stop her alerting the other Sorceresses?'

We all turned to look at her unconscious form on the ground. I pursed my lips. 'We're going to have to go in tonight, aren't we? Or take her with us?'

'Or we could just kill her,' Alessia suggested.

I shook my head.

Dom balked too. 'I'm not killing her in cold blood. She's unconscious.'

Alessia rolled her eyes. 'Fine. Whatever. We'll go tonight. We'd better get moving, though. We have a decent amount of ground to cover to get into the waterfall area of Crone Keep. And we need to swing back and grab our packs.'

I gave the Sorceress a final look. She appeared almost kind in her unconscious state. Her copper hair fell softly over half of her face and, relaxed as she was, she didn't appear as vicious as she had before.

I shook off the small amount of concern I had for the Sorceress who'd tried to attack me and followed Dom and Alessia away.

When we reached our packs, I opened mine and had a drink of water from my flask. Feeling slightly more refreshed, I put it away and pulled on my pack. I turned to the others and waited.

My stomach tightened with the realisation that I would soon be seeing my mum. After we managed to infiltrate the Keep and find her anyway. I tried to focus on my breathing to relax my stomach, but it didn't work as well as normal.

I must have looked as anxious as I felt because Dom came to stand by me and squeezed my shoulder lightly.

'Everything will be fine. Don't worry.'

Alessia finished her drink and stood abruptly. 'Let's get going. The longer we wait, the more likely that crazy witch will be running back to warn them we're coming.' She strode past the two of us, shaking her head.

Irritated at her dismissal of my worries, I reluctantly followed behind. Dom walked beside me until the trees were too thick to do anything but move in a single line.

We kept up a fast pace. This time we didn't stop or split up. Alessia maintained a consistent flow all the way across the forested mountainside.

It became mind numbing. Step, weave, step, step, step, weave. Moving in and out of the trees was simple in the quiet night air, with the moon making enough of an appearance that the path was easy to see.

I'd been able to hear the waterfall rushing for a long while before Alessia finally came to an abrupt halt. I was so lost in thought that I almost ran right into her. Dom did run into me causing us both to be jolted forward.

Alessia hit a rock with her shin and turned and cursed at us. Dom ducked his head and mumbled an apology.

'That's surprising. Your eyes are normally always glued on your girlfriend.'

'Oh, will you cut it out already?' I grumbled. 'We aren't to-gether.'

She flashed her teeth at me in a provocative grin. I rolled my eyes and looked past her to the waterfall, wondering if it would freeze over once the storms worsened.

My eyes were immediately drawn to Crone Keep. It loomed above us even from our rocky vantage point. The char-coal-coloured stone blended into the mountains around it, es-pecially with them both covered in snow. The turrets rose omi-nously around the Keep, drawing my eyes to all the places we could be watched from.

I tore my gaze away and paid attention to the stone gorge below us. All we needed to do was go down it, then make our way across the base and through the small path visible next to the waterfall.

Alessia stood ahead of us and pointed. 'Okay. So the best way to get down there is to use the path to the right of here. There are decent shadows by the rocks that should keep us hidden.'

'Great! Let's go,' I said and made to move around her.

'Hold up, Miss I-Have-A-Death-Wish. According to the intel a Sorceress patrols around the base of the gorge at least once every hour before heading into the forest for what I assume is the rest of their round. We'll have to wait for her to come by again before we enter.'

I sighed and resigned myself to the fact that my anxiety defi-nitely wasn't going to calm down until I could actually see my mum. Or more likely when we rescued her and got the hell out.

I found a tree and leaned against it while we waited.

None of us spoke but my feeling of wariness grew as I monitored our surroundings.

When the sky passed from a dark bluey-black to a slightly lighter shade of navy, I began to worry. If we didn't go soon we'd have to risk the daylight or wait for the next night and chance the missing Sorceress showing up.

Just as I was about to suggest we retreat for the evening, I heard it. Footsteps. Then I smelled the magic. I laid flat to the ground to peer over the edge of the gorge.

A Sorceress with long black hair and a blood-red cloak walked from beside the waterfall and into the open rock base of the gorge. She moved along attentively, focusing on anything that may have been out of place. I carefully wriggled back from the edge to avoid being seen.

As I laid my head to the side, I saw Dom and Alessia also pressed to the ground. Their heads faced the direction of the Sorceress. I turned mine to face the same way. I took in her scent, briefly wondering if the others smelled the magic the same as I did.

When she exited the gorge I froze, the urge to suddenly sneeze overwhelming me. I pushed my tongue into the roof of my mouth to stop the sensation, then breathed out a small sigh of relief when the feeling passed.

The Sorceress got further away, but still we waited. Not moving, breathing evenly.

The moment I could no longer hear her footsteps or smell the scent of magic, I inhaled a welcome breath of icy air and sat up. The others did the same.

I looked at them intently. 'Ready?'

They both nodded. I stood and pulled out my pack from behind the tree, knowing we'd need to leave them by the boats under the waterfall.

This time I led the way. I took each step with care but maintained enough speed to make sure we wouldn't take too long. I walked around boulders as tall as my head, and over rocks the size of my fists, careful not to disturb them.

I used my heightened senses to make sure the immediate area was clear. As we neared the waterfall, it became harder to hear. I could smell the magic but knew that was no longer as useful considering where we were.

I turned to look at the others, eyebrows raised. They nodded and I continued on.

We crept inside the cavern behind the waterfall and spotted two small boats tied to posts. I heaved a sigh of relief that the notes were right about them being there.

Around the water's edge there was just rocky ground; it was about a metre wide on every side. There were two passages that led from the cavern.

If the internal drawings were correct, we needed to take the passage to the left. I led the way around to the other side, trying my best to listen for any steps coming our way.

I peered into the passage but could only make out a dim light in the distance. I continued past the entrance and over to one of the boats. I pointed to it and then at my pack, indicating we should put them in.

I took mine off and sat it on the ground, then carefully stepped into the boat. Once I was in, Alessia passed me her pack, which I stowed under one of the three slatted seats. She passed me the other two, one by one, so I could do the same with them.

I moved back to the edge of the boat and Dom held out a hand to help me back to the rocky shore. I stepped out carefully and moved away from the boat. Right then, my head whipped to the passage on the right. Someone was coming, and I wondered if we'd set off some kind of magical alarm.

PRACTICAL

I SHOVED ALESSIA AND pointed to the passage on the left. I darted into the entrance behind her and Dom. I pushed myself against the wall next to them and waited, listening, as my heart hammered in my chest. There was more than one set of footsteps. There were at least five.

The other Sorceress must have found the one we tied up.

I knew now that we'd need to move faster to find my mum, though I was sure they'd be thinking that an attack was imminent rather than the reality: that three teens were breaking in to rescue a prisoner. Hopefully there wasn't more than one; I knew we wouldn't have time to rescue others and leaving anyone to the Crones was cruel.

Once the footsteps had disappeared behind the waterfall, I peered out. Seeing the room was now empty, I quickly went and checked the packs were well hidden in the boat.

I returned to an incredulous look from Alessia, presumably at going back out.

'What?' I whispered. 'If they get spotted, we're done for. They'll swarm the place trying to find us. At least from here we could have just fought our way out and escaped.'

She rolled her eyes. 'Oh, please, like you're gonna leave your mum here. Let's just go.'

I looked at Dom who was waiting patiently for us to finish our conversation. Once he realised we were, he gestured to the passage. 'Ready?'

I nodded sharply and Alessia did the same. He turned and started leading the way. The passage seemed to go on forever. The sound of the waterfall was muted through the thick stone walls of the Keep. I cringed at every small drip of condensation that hit the rocky ground. The air was so moist and dark that I could barely see. I shivered as I trailed my hand along the icy wall to keep on track.

Without warning, Dom stopped in front of us. I peered around him and discovered we'd reached a set of stairs. They were made of rock too and looked shiny with frost. Towards the top of the stairs I could see a soft glow of light.

'Come on, go.' Alessia urged.

Dom nodded, then started to climb the stairs. 'Careful, they're slippery.'

There was no rail to hold on to, so I kept a hand on the wall, this time for support on the slick, smooth steps.

As we neared the top, the rhythmic beat of boots on the stone announced more company. If anyone looked down here now, they'd see us. I ducked down with the others, into a low crouching position, close to the side of the wall that was darkened with shadows.

The footsteps came closer, then passed and moved in another direction. I sagged in relief and tried to calm my racing heart. We still had a while to go before we'd reach the prisoner section.

We waited another minute or two before moving. Dom continued to the top of the staircase and carefully peered around the corners. I waited anxiously. I knew there shouldn't be anyone there, because I couldn't hear them, but we were in a place of magic, so the feeling of apprehension stuck with me.

After a moment, he slipped out of the passage and moved to the left. I was ready to push Alessia up when she didn't immediately follow him.

I rounded the corner and saw the new passage for myself. It was wider and better lit from torches mounted on the walls. To the right, where the footsteps had come from, was a pair of passages that led in different directions. To the left was just one passage and a doorway.

When we heard someone coming from the corridor to the right, Dom led us towards the left side. He darted across the hall and opened the door, beckoning us in. With no time to spare, we followed behind him. I shut the door as softly as I could, muting the footfalls from outside.

My heart rate spiked as whoever it was came closer. I turned to look at the others, panicked.

I briefly looked around and realised we were in a meeting room. It was filled with wooden chairs and a stone slab table. Not many places to hide, but it would be enough if needed since the table was widest facing the door.

I ran, my feet touching the ground as lightly as I could, and joined the others sitting behind the table on the floor. Right after I crouched down, the door opened.

Silence.

My heart raced. It seemed so loud in my own ears that I was sure the Sorceress at the door would hear it.

The sound of someone else approaching the doorway sent the heat of panic flushing through my body despite the chill of the room, but then it was pulled shut.

A voice outside the door called out, 'All clear in this room. You come up with anything?'

'No,' another voice grumbled. 'Everywhere is empty. I'm sure if someone was coming in here, we'd have found them by now. I'm hungry and tired. Let's go and eat so I can sleep. This shift has been long enough already.'

I slid down from my crouch and sat on the floor, leaning heavily against the table.

'Well, that was a close call,' Dom said.

Alessia snorted. 'You reckon? We're lucky they don't have Shifter senses or we'd have been fighting our way out of that.'

I pulled my knees closer to my chest. 'That's true. Do you guys think we should wait here for a while? Until we're sure they're finished searching? Or you know, until we think they have.'

'I think so,' said Dom. 'Alessia?'

'Yep. Let's hang tight for a little while at least. We really can't risk waiting too long. I think most of them will be in bed or heading there soon. There are only a couple of hours until the sun comes up.'

I nodded and relaxed further against the cold, stone table. Waiting.

As each minute passed, I felt as though I was getting less and less oxygen. I needed to move.

'Okay, I can't wait any longer.' I jumped up. 'Let's go.'

Dom huffed out a breath. 'Awesome. That was killing me!'

Alessia shook her head and tutted at us as she stood up. Dom led the way to the door. I felt bad making him go first, but he knew the internal drawings better than Alessia and I did.

He put his ear to the tall, wooden door. Alessia scoffed and quickly turned it into a cough when Dom glared at her. I thought it was overkill too, but I was firmly on the side of better safe than sorry. Dom listened at the door for a moment longer, then cracked it open and peered through the gap.

He pushed the door wide and moved to the right, Alessia right behind him. We were back on track.

I followed them through the passages until we reached one with two doors on opposite sides. We needed to take the one on the left. Dom turned the handle. It wouldn't budge. As he shoved into it, I looked around frantically, shivering in the icy air and hoping no one was going to appear.

'What's wrong with the door?' Alessia hissed.

'It won't open, it feels blocked,' Dom said, his voice as strained as I felt.

'We're just going to have to go through the right one. I'm sure I saw they joined up somewhere, right?'

'Yep,' said Dom. 'But it will take us through the kitchens and eating quarters.'

Alessia's head whipped around. 'Shit. You're kidding me?'

Dom shook his head. 'But it's either that or we'll need to go back out to where the boats are and enter from the other way. We took this path because it avoided the main areas and we should have been able to make it without running into anyone.'

'Shit,' she repeated. 'Let's just do it. But keep the noise right down.'

I gave her a "duh" look, and then nodded to Dom. He took a deep breath and put his ear to the door. He gave Alessia a narrow look, but this time she didn't protest at all. He shook his head, then cracked the door open. He gestured that it was clear, then walked inside.

I followed closely behind him. I tried to leave enough distance between us to not crowd him, but not so much that it left us vulnerable. I felt Alessia close on my heels.

I was in unfamiliar territory. While I knew the places lined up, I didn't know the specifics of this area well enough and prayed to Salvatore that Dom did. He led us straight along the dreary, poorly lit passage. There weren't many sounds but the smell of magic was strong here.

Ahead of us I could see doors on both sides of the room and then a dead end. My chest tightened. I had no clue which way to go, but I assumed one was the kitchen and the other was the eating area.

As we neared the doors, we all stopped. The sound of voices travelled from the door on the right. We all moved to the wall, and put our backs against it. Waiting.

The voices didn't get louder, or quieter. They remained the same.

I waved to get Dom and Alessia's attention and pointed to the door on the left. We were running out of options. They both nodded. We continued along the corridor slowly, listening for any changes in the room.

As we neared the doors, the voices paused mid-conversation. For what seemed like the hundredth time since I'd found out about my mum, my chest constricted.

Will I ever get to see her?

Then, a new voice came from inside, questioning the others in an authoritative tone about why they were still up. After some continued grumbling, I heard chairs scrape back and suddenly they were coming in our direction.

My eyes widened and I shoved Dom, then ran across to the other door. I opened it quickly, putting pressure on the hinges to make sure it didn't creak. They both ran past me into the room. I pulled it shut.

We were in the kitchen. There were old iron pots hanging over fire pits that were blackened from use. Stone benches lined the room with piles of dirty dishes stacked on top. I scanned the room until I found what I really needed. Another door.

There!

I ran over but skidded to a halt as I saw Dom waving frantically at me.

'Stop! Wait!' Dom hissed quietly. 'We should take that one.'

He pointed to a door on the other side of the room. Panic-stricken at the choice, but fraught with the fear of getting caught I nodded and ran over to him and Alessia. We went through and found ourselves in another corridor. This one was dank and faded into darkness in both directions, though a set of stairs was just visible to the right.

'Which way?' Alessia whispered.

Dom was quiet for a moment, then pointed to the right. 'Up those stairs.'

'Okay. Let's go, before they come this way.'

We hurried to the end of the corridor. My pulse throbbing in my temple from all the near misses was making it harder to focus on the sounds around me. I hoped that Alessia and Dom were more together than I was.

The idea of being so close to my mum but never getting to see her was too much.

Dom tugged on my arm. I realised I'd stopped.

He smiled reassuringly at me. 'Come on. We're almost there. We can do this.'

He's right. We can totally do this.

'Thanks, Dom.'

'Anytime.'

The corridor ended in a set of stairs to the left. When we reached the top and made it onto the landing, I looked around. We had entered a large hall of some kind. This place looked a lot like the sketches of the landing area outside the prisoner holding cells.

I was sure one of these doors would lead to my mum, but which one? The whole area reeked of magic and we could hear muted voices from a few of the rooms. Determined to get to my mum now, I signalled to Dom and gestured across the room. 'Which way?' He pointed to the left.

'Which door?' I whispered, hopeful that he'd know the answer.

He gave me a tight smile but shook his head. 'I don't know. Just that it's through a door on the left. I think this is the area where they have their offices and meeting rooms.'

I sighed. This was going to be tough.

'It doesn't matter.' Alessia muttered. 'Just means we'll need to try a few. I vote we split up, and each listen in at a door, since there are three at that end, then meet back here and pick.'

It was the best option we had. 'Okay. Let's do it. Dom, the right. Alessia, the left. I'll take the one in the middle.'

I immediately turned and sprinted across the hall to my door and pressed my ear against it. An unnatural silence greeted me. I could see Dom doing the same. I heard a gasp at the same time as the sound of a door opening. I whipped my head to Alessia. It was her door.

She'd hesitated. No time to turn and run. Dom and I headed for her as the door opened wide. The features of the young, golden-haired Sorceress were full of shock when she saw Alessia in front of her. She opened her mouth, ready to cast or call for help, then hesitated as she noticed Dom and I running towards her. Alessia took her chance and punched the Sorceress straight in the face.

She fell like a ton of rocks. Alessia managed to catch her before she hit the ground. 'Grab her feet.'

Dom shot forward and grabbed them. They carried her back into the room she'd come from. I quickly followed behind and shut the door.

The room appeared to be an office. I raced around the desk to pull out a chair. They dumped her in it, taking little care with the action, her head snapping back, then forwards with the momentum.

The room was lined with shelves that held files and books, ranging from small volumes to large tomes. I briefly wondered if there was magic in them that I could learn. The thought didn't last long. The Sorceress was stirring.

I looked at Alessia and Dom and wondered what we should do. If she shouted, we were in trouble. Alessia pulled out one of the potions she had. She grabbed a cloth from her belt and tipped a little of the potion onto it, then held it over the Sorceress's mouth.

Her head immediately flopped down against her chest when Alessia released it. Dom kept hold of her while Alessia and I looked around for something to tie her up with. Nothing.

'We don't have any more time. Let's just lay her behind the desk and hope no one comes looking for her. Dom, help me move her.'

They picked up her limp form and laid her on the ground. Alessia made sure to tuck up her knees and asked me to stand near the door to check if I could see her. I shook my head.

'Good. Turn off the light.'

I walked over to the little light that sat in the corner and turned the small valve off. The flame went out immediately and we were left in the dark. I heard the others move back to the door at the same time as I did.

We listened and when a minute of nothing passed, I spoke. 'Dom, what did you hear at your door?'

'It just sounded like someone was writing with a quill. I heard a faint scratching sound. Easier to tell in class with lots of them going, but I think it's the same sound. You?'

'Dead silence. Like, not natural, if you know what I mean?'

'Well, that sounds like our room,' said Alessia. 'Now, we just need to know if it's locked. I'm assuming, since you couldn't hear a thing, that there's a silence charm on the room. If we can get inside and shut the door no one will hear anything that goes on in there. I'm sure there will be at least one Sorceress guarding the prisoners.'

'Do you think there'll be more than one person being held captive? Do we let them go as well?' I asked

She tossed up her hands. 'How would I bloody know? Let's just get your mum and go. If she says one of them needs saving, we'll worry about it then.'

Seems practical.

'Sounds like a plan,' Dom said.

I put my ear to the door and, hearing nothing, opened it. I looked around, relieved my senses were working well. No one was in the hall. The others followed me out and over to what we hoped were the prisoner holding cells.

I looked at both of them in turn; this was it. At their nods I turned back to the door.

I took a deep, steadying breath, exhaled and opened the door.

PERIL

I RUSHED INSIDE. THERE was a small desk just inside the door to the left. A Sorceress sat there. Everything seemed to move in slow motion as she spotted me and jumped from her chair. I vaguely noticed it fall to the ground in her haste, the iron arms clanging loudly.

So much for stealth.

I ran straight for her. Concerned about drawing more attention, I kept my sword sheathed and decided to use my bare hands. She pulled a knife from her belt and brought it down in an arc, aiming for my neck. I dodged to my right and immediately threw a punch, feeling satisfied as it connected to the left side of her face with a crunch. She staggered back. She was no experienced fighter, as each advance she made was foreshadowed by obvious movements; eyes looking, knees bending, the direction of her feet.

Before the Sorceress had a chance to come at me again, Alessia threw a vial at her feet. She dropped to the stone floor with a dull thud and didn't so much as twitch. I turned to Alessia, eyebrows raised.

'Is she dead?'

'No,' came a warm voice from one of the cells. 'Just unconscious. I'd know that aroma anywhere; essence of mandragora mixed with hemlock root.'

My head whipped around. There were three cells lining the walls. The bars along the front shimmered with tones of white and crimson.

My gaze darted to Dom, as hope flared in my chest.

Mum?

I walked along the cells, looking in each until I got to the end. Inside was the woman I'd seen at the Academy. She was sitting on the ground, with her legs crossed beneath a worn dress. Her light hair was pulled back by a thin, ragged cord. Her amber eyes locked with mine, a smile lighting her face.

'Elita?' Her voice was hopeful.

'Mum?'

My knees crashed into the floor and I sat back on my heels. My vision blurred from the tears that sprang up in my eyes. I couldn't believe it.

I hastily wiped them away, wanting to look at her properly now that I had the chance. She was standing on the other side of the bars, smiling at me.

'It's me.' Her lips curved up gently.

'Sorry to cut into the reunion,' said Alessia, although she sounded anything but. 'We need to get a move on if we're going to make it out of here without too much trouble.'

My mum turned to Alessia, and I caught an odd look flicker through her eyes for a split second. But when she spoke, she simply agreed. She looked back at me with a soft gaze. 'You really shouldn't have come, Elita. It means the world to me that you are here. I thought I would never see you again. But you shouldn't have risked yourself.' She looked at my friends. 'None of you should have. You should all leave now. There is no way to open the cells without the Crones finding out.'

'We're not leaving you!'

'Not a chance,' said Dom, speaking for the first time. 'We travelled a long way and had too many close calls.' He looked at me and smiled grimly before turning back to my mum. 'We've made too many hard decisions to leave without you.'

'The prophecy?' my mum whispered, her voice cracking.

I stood up straighter, determined to show her my strength. 'Yeah, the prophecy. I met The Seer on the way here.'

She nodded, crestfallen. 'I tried so hard to keep it from you. But we can talk later. If you won't leave without me, we need to get moving now. Better to alert them between watches, rather than at the end of one when another is already coming. That will be soon.

She pointed to the end of the room. 'You can open the gate with the lever on that wall, but as soon as you do an alert will sound to the Sorceress who set the spell over the bars. Those that are within the Keep will come, then more will follow.' Her eyes became pleading. 'Are you sure you won't just leave without me?'

I shook my head. 'There's no going back now and I won't leave you here.'

She nodded, her expression was sad, but I could see a clear glimmer of hope. I focused on that.

'Okay. Do you know the best way out of here?' she asked. 'They covered my head when they brought me back here again.'

'Yep,' Dom said, as he walked back to the door. 'We know the way, but we'll have to be quick because our original entry was blocked. We'll probably meet more Sorceresses using the alternate route, but it can't be avoided. Elita, come and join me at the door in case anyone arrives straightaway.'

I took a moment longer to stare into my mum's eyes before I dragged myself towards the door. I couldn't believe I'd found her. It was almost unbearable to tear myself away and not be there to embrace her immediately when the cell door opened.

Alessia stood at the wall by the lever with her eyes on my mum, waiting. 'Ready?'

My mum moved as close as she could get to the cell door without touching the shimmering bars, then nodded. When Alessia looked at me, I pulled my short sword and gave her a nod as well. Dom tilted his head in agreement.

'Okay. Here we go,' she said, then yanked the lever on the wall.

The minute the bars raised, my mum came out and ran towards the door. Dom flung it wide.

The first Sorceress appeared as we entered the wide hall. A vial flew past my head and smashed at her feet. She dropped to the floor and we kept moving. I was almost at the stairs when the sound of feet rose from the level below.

I knew getting caught in the hall would be bad, so I charged straight down. As two Sorceresses ran towards me, I moved closer to the left of the stairwell, sweeping my sword in a tight arc. The sharp blade sliced through skin as though it was butter. I followed through, rotating my blade and connecting the pommel with the Sorceress's temple. She dropped to the ground, unconscious. Dom and Alessia had made quick work of the other one. My mum followed from the rear, her eyes roving the space behind us.

We made it into the kitchen before another two were upon us. This time, before they made it around the stone bench, I heard my mum cast a spell. I couldn't see anything out of the ordinary, but when I looked back, the Sorceresses were shrouded in a spark-filled haze of orange and red. They dropped to the floor, mouths wide in pain.

We made it out into the corridor between the kitchen and the eating hall. I sprinted across and pulled the eating hall door closed as I heard the kitchen door snap shut behind me. My mum whispered some words at each door and they briefly glowed blue before fading back to normal. I turned and looked straight ahead at the passage we needed to go down and my heart stopped dead.

A Crone. Right at the top of the stairs leading to our escape. Her wraith-like form floated above the ground. A feral snarl contorted her face.

I was rooted to the spot. Footsteps sounded inside the kitchen and the rattle of the handle signalled that more Sorceresses were trying to get to us. We were trapped.

I tried to convince my feet to move, but they wouldn't. The thought of losing my mother, of losing my friends, had me stuck. My own life seemed of little consequence.

Somewhere in my mind, I registered the fact that we needed to hurry. To make a move. To get out of here. But the Crone with black pits for eyes, and a mouth so red it looked as though she'd taken a drink from a cup of blood, was keeping me locked in place.

My mum shoved in front of me, and as she bumped into my shoulder, it shook me out of my deep well of fear. 'You should get out of our way, Dracaena.'

'Is that so?' Her deep, hollow voice conveyed complete disdain and hatred.

Mum wasted no time. She began to summon her power. This time I saw it rise like a flame to her hand. As it sped towards the Crone, she was already conjuring more.

In the midst of my haze, I'd missed Alessia and Dom Shifting and engaging in a fight. Their weapons had been discarded right beneath my feet in an attempt to keep them safe.

Without further delay, I Shifted. My claws and teeth lengthened, my vision and hearing sharpened, and I focused on those around me.

Dom and Alessia were holding one Sorceress back each, who had entered through the now-broken kitchen door. Before I could assess which of them to help, another Sorceress broke through the other door. She lunged right for me. No longer hesitant, I dodged to my left and swiped at her face. My claws left a ragged tear that instantly welled with blood.

She hissed and faltered in her attack. It was all I needed. I lunged forward with the short sword in my left hand. She managed to move out of the way, but I pursued her. I attacked with sword and claw, aiming for any piece of her I could get to. Each time she opened her mouth to cast, I swiped at her head.

She backed herself into a corner, and I briefly flashed back to the day in the mountain cave with Dad. My sword met little resistance as it punctured her chest. As I ripped the blade out, I felt it snag a bone. I yanked and it came completely free. Her eyes faded as my sword left her body and she collapsed to the floor. I stood for a moment, horrified at what I'd done. At the life I'd ripped away.

I shook my head violently to refocus then turned back to see my mum still throwing her magical fire at the Crone. The balls of black and blood-red that flew back from the Crone's hands looked deadly. My heart constricted. I moved to help her, but another Sorceress crossed my path.

This one had a face devoid of emotion. She was so pale, I wondered if she was devoid of life too. The moment of wonder cost me. I felt a scorching heat on my left arm a moment later.

Panicked, I dropped my sword and patted my arm while simultaneously ducking from the next ball of fire. Pain forgotten,

I dove straight for her midsection. Her head gave a sickening, yet satisfying, crunch as she hit the stone floor. She didn't move.

I turned to look at the fight. Alessia and Dom were holding their own, with only a few gashes and burn marks between them, but my mum was losing ground and looking wearier by the minute. I scanned the area frantically for inspiration and spotted the weapon belts on the ground back in the centre of the hallway.

I crawled to the middle of the corridor, staying low to avoid attention. I glanced in my mum's direction and caught the glare of the Crone. She threw a ball of black magic right at me. Fear choked me, but loosened its hold as the ball hit a clear shield in front of me. I looked in wonder at my mum, sure that she was responsible.

I could only see the side of her face, but her expression was tight. She was going to run out of energy soon and we'd be out of time. I scuttled the rest of the way to the weapons belts and huffed a small sigh of victory as I pulled out the last vial of potion.

I looked behind me, saw that Dom and Alessia were getting the upper hand in their fights and didn't need me, then jumped up and ran to my mum.

The Crone's eyes flashed with so much hostility that I faltered before I could stop myself. I shivered, then moved close to my mum's ear to whisper my plan.

She gave a tiny shake of her head then muttered, 'It won't work for long.'

We didn't need much time, but needed her to lower the shield so I could throw the vial. We had to wait until the right moment.

I looked across to Dom and my stomach turned over. He had torn out the throat of one of the Sorceresses. Her blood was flooding the floor and her body gave a spasm before it fell limp. He charged over to help Alessia.

In no time, they'd taken her down and were moving back towards us. I saw Alessia begin to shimmer as she Shifted back into human form. Her arms were blackened and her skin was torn on one thigh. There was only a small amount of blood, so I assumed it was not too bad. She picked up the belts I'd discarded after collecting the potion, and joined us quickly, Dom trailing closely behind.

I turned back to my mum, who was still trading rapid balls of magic with the Crone.

'Now, Mum!' I whispered in her ear.

I raised my arm to throw, but as I released the potion, the Crone also released her own attack of dark magic; a black glowing ball of death.

I froze in place as the Crone's ball flew towards me. A rough shove came from my side. I hit the floor as the sound of the vial smashing reached my ears. Almost immediately afterward the heavy weight of a wolf fell on top of me.

'Dom!' I screamed.

He was lifted from me. I pulled myself up quickly, frantic. He'd Shifted back to his human form and was limp between Mum and Alessia.

'He's alive. For now,' my mum said, her voice worn. 'We need to leave.'

My despair for Dom flooded me, but I nodded and got moving. I led the way past the Crone; she was starting to stir. Mum and Alessia followed behind me carrying Dom. We weren't moving fast enough.

When we reached a set of stairs my mum uttered some words of power and I heard Dom groan. I was so relieved I felt tears well up in my eyes. I blinked them away and quickly checked on him.

I nearly fell down. Dom was awake and groggy but I could see his skin was turning black, a streak of it was snaking out above his collar line. My eyes flicked to my mum.

Alessia cut in before she could speak. 'Just keep going. They're already coming. Dom, we need you to help us move you or we won't make it out of here.'

As we pressed on, I could hear the added shuffle of his footsteps between my mum and Alessia. He was definitely moving slower than normal, but he was helping.

Is he going to make it? Will we get out of here? Are we all going to die? Please don't let us die. Please don't let Dom die.

Around and around the thoughts continued as I forced my brain to remember the path out of the Keep.

When we reached the top of the final stairs leading to the cavern with the boat, I felt a relief so intense that I had to command my knees not to buckle.

I flew down the stairs and stumbled along the slick passage so I could get the boat untied. When I reached the passage exit a force smashed into me. I hit the wall, hard. My vision wobbled. I pulled myself up and looked ahead.

There was a Sorceress and she was casting again. I yanked a throwing knife from each side of my belt. I threw the one in my left hand immediately. It interrupted her words but didn't connect with her body. With the second one I aimed, it hit true—right through the throat.

She clutched her throat as she dropped to the ground, gurgling on her own blood. I looked around wildly. There were no more attackers, but I could hear Mum, Alessia and Dom coming behind me, thank Salvatore.

Ignoring the wave of dizziness that came over me, I ran to the boat and started to untie it. Alessia climbed in, then yelled at me with a strained voice. 'Help Dom in.'

I put my arm around him so he could step over the edge and lower himself in. He sagged down into a sitting position on the floor of the boat, laying an arm across one of the bench seats and resting his head atop it.

What have I done?

'Elita.' My mum looked back at the stairs from beside me. It sounded as though the whole Keep were starting to descend on us. 'Quickly. In the boat.'

Her tight, worried smile told me everything I needed to know. It wasn't happening.

'No, Mum. Get in first or we both stay here and die.' It was both of us leaving or both of us staying. I wasn't losing her again.

I watched as frustration marred her face. I glared.

Whatever. Just get in the damn boat.

She huffed and quickly climbed in. I jumped in behind her. Our feet had barely hit the floor of the boat before Alessia shoved us away from the bank.

As we neared the waterfall a dozen Sorceresses piled into the cavern. They paused and joined hands, as they started a chant. My chest constricted as mum muttered her own words furiously beside me. When they'd built to a crescendo, with their power wavering in front of them, the unthinkable happened.

The Crone, in her wraith-like form, and practically sizzling with magic, flew right through the Sorceresses at the bottom of the stairs. Fury consumed her face. In her blind anger, she'd destroyed the spell of her own Sorceresses.

My relief was short lived because a giant ball of crackling magic rested in her palms that she held in the direction of our boat. Alessia's hand reached for mine and squeezed. We glanced at each other. The first scared expression I'd ever seen on her covered her face and I wondered if she could actually see the magic.

She didn't want to die. Neither did I. I gave her a short squeeze back and prepared for the blast.

My heart raced, and I squeezed tighter. I braced myself.

The crackling black ball crashed into an invisible wall that surrounded us. The black began to seep over us, surrounding the wall, searching for a way in. My mum stumbled and I yanked my hand away to support her and stop her from falling back.

At that exact moment, our boat went under the waterfall. The water smashed into the invisible shield then flowed in thick rivulets around us to rejoin the water beneath. By the time we reached the other side, the Crone's magic had dissipated. My mum sagged down into her seat.

I didn't know what to do. The Crone and her Sorceresses would pursue us and there was nothing I could do from the boat.

As I looked at my friends and family, I didn't know who to reach for first. I wanted to hug my mum, to check on Dom, to give Alessia's hand another squeeze.

I chose Dom. I looked at the black expanding across his skin. I pulled up his shirt. The black mark originated from his heart and had spread from there. Lost in thoughts of despair, I laid my hand on the mark, and prayed I'd feel a heartbeat in his deathly still body.

TIME

T HERE IT WAS. A single beat. A pause. Then another.

Tears streamed down my face. The black continued to inch its way across his body before my eyes.

My mum spoke gently, 'Make sure he stays upright. It will slow the spread a little, until we can get him some help.'

I nodded, numb. Alessia came to my side and helped me gently pull him into a position that looked a little more comfortable and upright, but his head flopped back to his arm on the seat. I pulled my jacket from my pack and curled it up under his head, so the position wasn't so unnatural.

At the sound of muttering, I turned to look at my mum and saw her hands were raised again. She had resumed casting. I wondered what else she was doing when the boat started to pick up speed.

I looked to the shore behind us and saw the Crone and her Sorceresses, and vaguely made out the confusion on their faces. Except for the Crone. The anger pulsing from her was palpable.

When it was clear they could no longer see us and weren't in pursuit, I sagged in relief onto the floor of the boat. I turned my focus back on Dom and let my feelings free.

When my mum came to me and squeezed my hand, the emotions overwhelmed me. The idea that I had traded Dom's life for my mum's was like rubbing salt in a wound.

Tearing my eyes from Dom, I looked at my mum with all the hope I could manage and spoke between sobs. 'Can you do anything? Can you help him?'

Her look gave me the answer I needed, but she spoke anyway. 'I'm sorry, sweetheart. I can't heal him. The closest Pack along this river is the Cladden Pack. We should take him there, to see if their Medicine Woman can help.'

Alessia interjected. 'Would a Medicine Woman even be able to help a curse like that? It is a curse, right?'

My mum nodded. 'Yes, it's a curse. I don't know if she will be able to help, but it's worth a try. They know the most about how to aid Shifters.'

Alessia pinned her with a stare. 'How do you know that?'

My mum shrugged. 'I used to be a liaison between the Shifters and the Ladies of Light. It was my job to know and understand the customs and practices.'

'That's how you met Dad?' I asked quietly, trying to keep from dwelling on Dom's still form.

She gave me a warm smile. 'Yes. That's how I met him.' She paused for a moment, seeming unsure. 'How is he?'

'I haven't seen him since I left for the Academy but, besides being upset once I found out about you being a Sorceress, he was good.'

She nodded, the worry plain on her face. I didn't have the emotional space to stress about Dad with Dom the way he was. I leaned my head gently against Dom's shoulder and took his hand in mine.

I lifted the bottom of his shirt and saw that the black was continuing to spread, mostly further down, but not as far up. I hoped it would stay away from his head long enough for us to get him some help.

'What do we do if the Medicine Woman can't—' My voice broke.

Both Alessia and my mum reached for me; my mum placed a hand on my knee and Alessia squeezed my shoulder. I sat unseeing as despair spiralled through me.

'If she can't help, we'll take him to the Ladies of Light. I'm sure they can do something.'

I nodded, feeling a small amount of comfort, then rested my head against Dom's shoulder, feeling numb.

I jerked awake when a hand touched my arm. I'd almost reached for a weapon before I realised who it was. My mum and Alessia both looked at me, their expressions were tight and worried.

My stomach felt like a boulder had smashed into it. My gaze darted to Dom. He was even paler than before and his chest, up to the base of his neck, was almost completely covered in black now.

My mum's voice distracted me from being sucked back into my emotions. 'We're about to reach the point where we'll need to stop the boat. From there it'll be on foot. To be honest, they won't take kindly to me, so I suggest you two go without me. Also,' she hesitated, looking at Dom, 'I think it's best that you both go and get the Medicine Woman to come back here. I don't think he'd make the trip, and the time it would take you to get him there would be too much to spare if she can't help.'

'How do we get there?' asked Alessia.

'When I stop the boat, you just need to get out and run straight in the direction I tell you. Either you'll find them, or they'll find you.'

Alessia nodded and looked at me. 'What about Elita's, uh, Shifted form. We don't really have time to explain it all.'

Mum thought for a moment. 'Just Shift to run there but Shift back right before you get to the Pack. You'll know from the scent, of course, when you are getting close. The Medicine Woman won't care so much, at least not until later.'

I nodded. It all made sense, but... My gaze flickered back to Dom. I felt as though a ball of acid was trying to burn a hole through me. My mum took my hand again.

'I'll keep him safe, Elita. I promise. No one will see us unless I want them to. Truly.' She looked up. 'We're almost there. Are you both ready?'

My eyes didn't leave Dom's limp form as I answered quietly. 'Ready.'

Alessia pulled her jacket tighter against the cold. 'Me too.'

We came to a marker that only my mum could see, because she stopped the boat next to the bank in a precise place, and pointed due North.

'Run. As fast as you can. Stop for nothing you don't have to. Go!'

There was no time for goodbyes, but I took a second to hug my mother tightly; partly in case something happened, and partly because I just needed to. Then we jumped from the boat, Shifted, and ran.

I didn't take in the sights or smells of the unfamiliar place, just focused on putting one foot in front of the other as quickly as I could. This time it wasn't for fun, not for a race, but because of my friend. To save his life.

Alessia and I kept pace, and I was glad. We needed to arrive together. She knew more about Packs than I did, and we couldn't waste any time finding who we needed.

We'd been running for longer than I'd hoped when the scent of Shifters became so thick it was like a smack in the face; like walking into the Academy for the first time.

Alessia slowed to a stop and I followed suit. Not only had we reached the Pack, but it looked as though they were coming to us. As soon as I spotted them, I Shifted to my human form, hoping desperately that they hadn't noticed such a subtle change from that distance.

A black wolf Shifted into a tall, rough-looking man in front of us. Beside him, a grey wolf stood still. The wolf was only slightly less intimidating than the giant man.

Sensing that this was the Pack's Alpha from his presence, Alessia and I bowed our hands then looked back at him, trying to catch our breaths. After tilting his head to survey us, he gave us a slight nod.

'What brings you to the Cladden Pack, cubs?' His voice had a deep, booming sound to it.

I felt Alessia bristle at being called a cub and cut in to talk before she could. 'We need help. Our friend has been hit by a curse from a Crone. He isn't doing well. Can your Medicine Woman come and take a look at him? Please?'

'What were you cubs doing anywhere near a Crone?'

Alessia butted in this time. 'We really don't have time. If we don't hurry,' she looked at me, uncertainty clouding her features, 'he probably won't make it.'

I darted my gaze to the Alpha, worried he might take Alessia's comment as an insult, but needing him to accept what she'd said.

He was quiet a moment longer, but when he spoke next, it wasn't to us, it was to the wolf by his side. I took a moment to study his grey companion. On closer inspection, the wolf seemed a little frail.

It huffed out a breath in the cold air, then Shifted. In its place was a short, old woman. 'Of course I'll help, Thaddeus. Show me the way, girls. I'll run in my wolf form.' She smiled kindly, then added, 'I don't run quite as quick on two legs anymore.'

Tears welled in my eyes at the easy offer of help. 'Thank you. We came from back that way.'

The woman nodded, but before she could Shift again, Thaddeus spoke. Concern was clear on his face. 'Mother. Wait. I will send someone with you.'

She tutted at him. 'Do what you will, son. I won't wait. They can meet me there.'

I looked quickly back at the Alpha. He opened his mouth to speak but thought better of it and shook his head.

'I wish you well, cubs. I must return to the Pack.'

'Thank you. You have no idea how much this means,' I said.

He nodded, then Shifted back into his wolf form and left immediately.

The old woman gestured back the way we'd come. 'Well, let's go.'

Without another word, she Shifted and took off in that direction. I met Alessia's eyes for a moment and then we both Shifted. As we were standing so close to one another, the earthy tones of my Shift mixed with the lighter colours of hers; I felt like I was seeing double and shook my head to clear my vision.

We sprinted off, trying to catch up with the old woman. She was pretty quick. As we gained on her, she slowed slightly and turned to look at us. Her step faltered for a moment when she caught sight of me, her eyes widening.

My relief was almost overwhelming when she turned her head back and kept running, without stopping to question me.

Tiredness pulled at me as we made the last of the journey. I was exhausted from all the emotions that were running my life on top of the physical fights and travelling.

In what seemed like much less time than it had on the way there, I caught sight of the boat floating in the water. I sped up, determined to reach it quickly so I could check on Dom. When I arrived a few moments before the others I jumped straight into the boat, Shifting as I sat.

The blackness had reached part way up his neck and I could see it running out over his hands as well. I was so focused on checking his condition, that I hardly noticed the boat move as the Medicine Woman climbed in.

'Sorceress,' she said in greeting to my mother. Then to me, 'What an interesting Shifting ability you have girl. I should like to hear more about it some time.'

I nodded, my eyes on Dom. The woman's hand reached out and she waved it over his face, then added her other hand which she waved along the rest of him. She touched a black part of his skin and pushed into it. Her face crumpled deeply with concentration.

After a few more minutes of prodding, poking and muttering to herself, she looked up at me. Her face was grave. 'I am afraid there is nothing I can do for your friend.'

'Nothing?! What do I do then? How do I help him?'

She looked at me for a moment, her eyes sharp, then turned to my mum. 'You must take him to the Ladies of Light, which I am sure you would know. You will need to move quickly. I assume you have a spell you can cast to slow down what is happening to the boy, but it is evident he is running out of time.'

I looked up at my mum, sure that the questions running through my head would be clear on my face.

Her brow furrowed. 'I may be able to do something more until we get there. I don't know if he will make the journey if we do not move swiftly.'

I nodded. 'Which way do we go? Should we try to find a way to carry him on land, or will the boat be better?'

She thought for a moment, before deciding that the boat would be the best option. Once we'd agreed on that, the Medicine Woman jumped back to the bank with a lightness and grace I hadn't thought she'd still possess. She turned to me. 'I bid you farewell and wish you luck with your friend. I do hope you will visit soon, so that I might learn more about your peculiar circumstances.'

I looked at her with a strained smile. 'I'll do my best to come back. Thank you for trying to help my friend.'

She nodded then turned away.

Once my mum had the boat moving, I sat back beside Dom, determined to keep him company during the trip. I was sure that my closeness would somehow keep him alive.

I felt the reassuring touches of my mum and Alessia at different times during our journey. I assumed to try to comfort me.

It felt like forever before Alessia called out that she could see the castle ahead. Hope flared inside me at the realisation that we were close to help.

As we reached the small boat ramp opposite the castle grounds, I tore my eyes from Dom's form and glanced up. My mouth dropped open. It really was a castle. I craned my neck up to look at the full height of it. The white stones were even and huge, and it had four large turrets around the top. There were many windows with their small wooden covers flung open to let in the light and air. A large wooden drawbridge lowered over a moat that surrounded its base.

What I couldn't see was any sign of life. I turned to look at my mum. 'Where are all the Sorceresses?'

'Oh, don't worry. They're in there. In fact, I'd say we'll have company very shortly if we don't get moving.'

I nodded, staring at Dom. Then I turned to Alessia. 'Do you want to secure the boat?'

She gave me a tight smile, then leapt out of the boat and onto the little dock. While she tied one of her intricate knots, I turned to my mum with concern. 'Will they be happy to see you?'

She was quiet for a moment before answering. 'I'm not sure. I doubt they were very happy when I went on an assignment to liaise with the Shifters thirteen years ago and never came back. I'd say they used a lot of resources trying to find me.'

I hesitated, scared of what the answer would be. 'But will they help us? Help Dom?'

She gave me another kind, reassuring smile that made me feel warm and loved. 'I'm positive they will help him if they can.'

The last part of her sentence cut through me like a knife. *If* was a problem for me. I'd make them if I had to. Somehow.

'Come on, Elita. Give me a hand to get him out,' Alessia said, interrupting my thoughts.

I turned back to Dom, trying to ignore the widening pit in my stomach.

What if they can't save him?

I bent down and lifted his arm over my shoulder, then slid mine around his back. I hoisted him up with a grunt. Alessia grabbed him under the arms and I moved to grab his ankles. Together we managed to pull him onto the dock and lay him down gently.

'Our packs?' I asked.

'Just leave them,' Alessia suggested.

'No, bring them if you can,' my mum said. 'I doubt you will leave via the river from here. More likely you will leave on horseback. We have some horses here accustomed to Shifters, should the need arise.' Then as an afterthought she added, 'Well we used to anyway. I doubt that much has changed.'

I climbed back down, grabbed Alessia's pack out and chucked it to her, then I picked mine up and pulled it on. I handed Dom's to my mum. I wondered if she'd refuse for some reason, but she took it without a word and slung it over her shoulder.

She looked as though she'd lost a lot of weight and seemed small in her baggy dress, especially holding Dom's large pack. I met her amber gaze briefly with my own and gave her the best smile I could offer. It hardly touched my eyes.

I climbed back out to join Alessia, then surveyed Dom. I was wondering exactly how we were going to get him all the way over to the castle, when I heard the fast approach of company.

There were four of them on foot, each in a different coloured cloak: blue, white, orange and brown. They approached us at an unnerving speed, and I took a step back nervously.

When they were almost upon us, my mum stepped out from behind us, and stood firmly in front. Unsure of their intentions, I reached to my belt and placed my hand on a sword.

PLEA

THE SORCERESSES HESITATED IN shock as recognition sunk in. Excitement lit their features as they continued towards us.

'Margot?' screamed the one in the orange cloak.

My mum wavered. 'Estelle?'

The Sorceress grinned, her white teeth glinting in the sunlight. When they reached us, Estelle crashed into my mum, giving her a fiercely tight hug. 'I can't believe you're alive. I thought...'

My mum hugged her back then turned to the others and embraced them too, although the hug she gave to the Sorceress in the brown cloak seemed less warm than the others. Questions started coming from all of them before she pointed to us.

'We will have time to talk later, I am sure. But for now, these children need help.'

Estelle's pale face creased into a light frown under her black hair. She turned back to my mum, looking confused. 'Shifters? Cubs? What business do you have with them? Why have you brought them to us?'

My mum stepped away and her voice seemed colder. 'The young man has been hit with a Crone's curse. They need magical aid, or do you no longer care for others?'

Estelle recoiled as if she'd been slapped. The others shifted a little, more wary than before. The look on Estelle's face transformed into one of hurt and apology.

'Of course we will help, or at least take them to seek aid from the Ladies. You know as well as I do that they will choose whether to bestow their gifts or not.'

My mum nodded. 'Do you have horses we could use?'

At that, the Sorceress in the white cloak whispered into the wind. I heard a light whistle and then nothing. I looked around, curious. Nothing happened but my mum was watching the castle, so I turned my gaze to it as well.

My patience was wearing thin. I knelt down and checked on Dom again and let out a strangled breath when I discovered he had gotten worse; the black had crept up the veins into his face.

Suddenly, the sound of hooves materialised. I looked back towards the castle and saw horses coming. A herd of pure white Validos were travelling at an incredible speed towards us. I realised, in a moment of wonder, that the white-cloaked Sorceress had called for the horses on the wind.

They gradually came to a halt before us, dust from the path blowing up in their wake. I covered my eyes with my forearm for a few moments until it settled.

I peered up at Alessia, who was already looking at me. 'Help me get him up?'

She bent down but was interrupted by a silky voice. 'Allow me to help.'

I lifted my eyes and was curious when I realised it was the Sorceress in the white cloak. She held out both hands, and seemed to concentrate with great intensity on Dom. After a moment, the air around him thickened and became tangible and he was lifted from the ground. He seemed to gently levitate, first at a hover, and then up to waist height as if he was being carried. My eyes were glued to the solid white air that was moving around his body.

I focused my hearing on the Sorceress, but I heard nothing. Every bit of magic I'd seen to this point had involved a Sorceress casting out loud. But not this.

Woah! I wonder if I will be able to do that?

I instantly felt guilty for thinking about magic when Dom was so close to death. I watched him extra carefully, determined to make up for my lapse, as he moved steadily closer to one of the horses. Estelle and the Sorceress in the blue cloak moved over to either side of the horse, and as Dom floated over the top, they grabbed him and moved him into position. The closer he got to the saddle, the more the air and glow dissipated.

I turned my wide eyes back to the Sorceress in the white cloak. Before I could say anything, Alessia cut in. 'Well, that was bloody brilliant.'

The Sorceress laughed, a delighted ring to the tone. 'Why, thank you, young cub.'

When she gave a little curtsy to Alessia, I had to hold back a grin. It was a small relief to know that I could still do that. Then I remembered Dom and my lips turned down as panic settled back in.

I hadn't heard her approach, but suddenly my mum was there beside me. Her arm went around my shoulders and she squeezed me tightly. 'Come, sweetheart. We'll be there in no time at all.'

I nodded and moved to a horse. The Sorceress in the blue cloak stood nearby as I got up, ready to help me if I needed it, but I didn't. 'Thank you,' I said and offered a tight smile.

She looked me in the eye and smiled back; the blue in them moved and I became a little dizzy.

'Hali,' my mum called. 'Enough.'

Her gentle smile turned mischievous and she winked at me, then turned away to mount her own horse. I looked across at my mum, confused. She just shook her head.

Estelle took charge. She clicked her heels into her horse softly, and took off, leading the way. I watched in awe as Dom remained on his horse as we rode, not moving so much as an inch from the position he was being held in.

Within a few minutes we were nearing the drawbridge into the castle, but we didn't seem to be slowing, if anything we were gaining speed. I held onto my horse, willing it to slow down.

I looked around wildly at the Sorceresses. None of them seemed at all concerned with the fact that we were about to ride directly into the moat surrounding the castle.

My gaze swung to my left, to Alessia. Her skin was pale and clammy. She met my eyes and there was dread plain on her face.

Estelle was just about to go in. I began to yell out to my mum, when she shouted at me. 'Hold on to your horse!'

Without further warning, Estelle's horse went over.

But she didn't go down, she stayed flat. Each of the horses followed suit. My heart felt like it had abandoned my chest all together. When my horse took one step over the edge it appeared again, racing like a hummingbird's in flight.

My mouth dropped open. Each hoof that touched down, hit a translucent path that sparked with golden light on impact. I quickly glanced at Alessia and saw her slumped in relief on her horse.

I was so distracted that I hadn't thought about the giant drawbridge that was blocking our path. Before I had a chance to panic, I passed right through it.

So, this is what magic is really like!

Once we were through the spell, the Validos continued more slowly along a stone path. We entered a giant courtyard. In the centre was a large fountain where water burst from the top, but by the time it reached the bottom it was nothing but a light, effervescent mist. Beneath the fountain lay a vibrant flower bed filled with an assortment of different coloured roses and greenery.

The smell was breathtaking. It was green, fresh and sweet. I gave a long inhale through my nose, trying to absorb the aroma before we moved past.

My eyes flicked back in front of me and a giant castle wall loomed. The stone was plain except for the intricate floral patterns carved into a small section of them, one of roses. I briefly wondered if there was a special link between Sorceresses and roses, but then we came to a halt and the thought vanished, replaced by dread about what was to come.

I watched the others slide down from their horses and did the same, landing firmly on my feet. I straightened up and moved over to Dom and his horse.

I turned to the Sorceress in the white cloak expectantly. This expectation was interrupted by the opening of the stone doors. It was as if one minute they were just door-shaped carvings in the wall, and the next they became real doors that could be opened.

In the doorway stood a Sorceress, who looked maybe five years older than me. She had cascading orange hair that came down to her waist and wore a dress of deep blue and silver. She looked like royalty.

Her face was wise and gentle as she looked out at our group. When her eyes hit me, Alessia and Dom, they widened a little. When they reached my mum, they bulged in shock.

She lost all decorum after that. Her shocked gasp travelled over to us and, after half a moment's hesitation, she simply ran straight to my mum. She embraced her and the strangest thing happened, it was as though my mum became enveloped in a shimmering bubble for a few seconds, then suddenly it disappeared.

The Sorceress had tears trickling delicately down her face. 'Margot? Is it really you? Oh, how I have missed you.'

'It is me, Isla.' My mum looked homesick, but happy at the same time. She embraced Isla again.

'I dearly wish to know what has happened, but I feel a sense of urgency from our young friends?' Her sentence finished on a high, wondering note, clearly showing her interest.

When her eyes met mine, I stepped forward and bowed my head. I knew Shifters had no need to bow here, but she seemed to be respected by those around her and I knew we were here to ask for help, which I was sure she could refuse.

'We come to seek aid for my friend. He was hit by a Crone curse. I...' I paused and looked up to him, still on the horse, and my throat squeezed tight. 'I don't know how long he has left.'

She considered me for a moment then looked briefly to my mum again, surprise lighting her features. Her gentle face became subtly more stern. I wondered if she knew, and if she'd still help us if she did.

'Please?' I begged, dropping to my knees.

Alessia stepped to my side, her hand tight on my shoulder. I didn't look away from the Sorceress in front of me, but I hoped Alessia wasn't glaring at her.

The Sorceress's eyes blurred for a moment, as though she was thinking about something else, and then came back into focus. She turned to the white-cloaked Sorceress and told her to bring Dom.

I sagged to the ground, heaving a sigh of relief. After a moment Alessia bent down to help me to my feet.

'Come on, Elita. Let's stick close to Dom. Okay?'

I nodded and pulled her into a tight hug. She froze for a moment before giving me a quick squeeze back. She clasped my hand and pulled me towards the castle doors behind Dom, who was now floating along in the air.

The inside of the castle was opulent, there were gems layered in detailed patterns around the cavernous room and where the light hit them through an open window, coloured patterns were cast over everyone.

When we reached a door towards the back of the large room, the Sorceress in the white cloak pulled Dom slowly upward to a standing position. I rushed forward, panicked, but she kept him balanced. When his feet were almost to the floor, I got a better look at his face.

The black veins were reaching up and over his cheeks. I cut my gaze to Isla and saw that her face had become worried. Her vision blurred once more for a few moments before she re-focused on us.

'We need to move with haste. The infirmary, Fei. As quickly as you can with care. Everyone, follow along.'

Fei dropped her white cloak to the ground, revealing a white gown with simple swirling patterns on it. She stepped ahead, and floated Dom behind her; it looked as though he was standing on his own, but his head drooped forward.

She began to walk quickly through the door. The way he levitated rather than walked was surreal, and when I thought about how close he was to dying, I simply felt nauseous.

I followed them with Alessia by my side and heard everyone else trailing along behind us. I paid little attention to which way we walked, instead focusing, with rising dread, on the thickening of the black veins that disappeared into Dom's hairline.

When we reached a white door, it was opened by someone from inside. Fei led the way in. My small sliver of relief at reaching what seemed to be the infirmary was short-lived when she laid Dom on the white bedding; the black was so stark in contrast.

It had almost reached his eyes.

I knelt beside him and grabbed his hand. It was cold.

My heart kicked into an erratic frenzy. I turned to the door and saw we'd been joined by two more Sorceresses. One with black hair and a red dress that trailed along the floor behind her and one with blonde hair and worry creasing her soft features. Their regality matched that of Isla.

The Ladies of Light.

The recognition was reassuring. Surely they could help.

When the blonde-haired one laid eyes on Dom she moved swiftly to the bed. The other two followed her. 'We may be too late, but let us try, sisters,' she whispered in a calm, rhythmic voice. 'Step back, young one.'

I moved away from Dom and over to Alessia's side. My mum joined us and placed a comforting hand on my shoulder.

The Ladies of Light encircled him and lifted up their hands with their palms out to each other. A bubble of white light formed around Dom, obscuring him from view.

I tried to step forward, but my mum squeezed my shoulder, reminding me to stay back.

Whiteness flashed in the eyes of the Ladies of Light and then through the bubble surrounding Dom.

One flash. Two. Then a third.

The bubble went black then disappeared.

Dom didn't move.

DID YOU ENJOY ELITA'S STORY?

Please consider leaving a review on your favourite platforms to help share the word to other readers.

NEED TO KNOW WHAT HAPPENS NEXT?

Visit https://linktr.ee/slauthor03 to join Shay's reader group on Facebook, connect on social media, or sign up to her website. You will get the latest updates by connecting on these platforms.

MEET THE AUTHOR

SHAY LAURENT

Shay is a fantasy author who lives in south-western Sydney with her partner, three young princesses, and two pretty kitties. Aside from getting all the cuddles, her life mostly involves psychology, writing, and photography—not necessarily in that order.

Long before Shay started writing, she fell in love with all things fantasy. She thrives on escaping into the magic and mayhem of other authors, and spinning the tales that run wild in her mind in her own books.

If you sign up to Shay's newsletter at www.shaylaurent.com you can get a free exclusive digital copy of her 48,000-word adult urban fantasy novella *Haunted By Legacy*.

Acknowledgements

T HANK YOU FIRSTLY TO my parents. You have both supported me since childhood to pursue my dreams and offered me words of encouragement whenever I needed them along the way.

To my husband, Aaron, for believing in me. Thank you also for your understanding and patience on all the nights I went to bed late and for putting the girls to bed so I could finish just one more writing sprint.

Sam, there aren't enough words to thank you properly for all the help you have given me on this journey. I truly appreciate all the hours you've put into supporting me and creating this book; encouraging me, giving your opinions, answering and asking questions, helping me to find the best solutions. Without a doubt, *Wolf of Choice* wouldn't be here without you!

Thanks to Rachel and Emma for reading my book and giving me the tools to make the story even better! Thanks also to my writing group for your thoughts and feedback on my chapters. Each and every comment is appreciated. Special thanks to Jodie for answering my late-night horse questions!

Dionne, thank you for taking the time to answer my questions about the publishing process. Without your insights this journey wouldn't have been so smooth!